TOXICS

ISABEL BURT

Kelly

Hope you enjoy it!

Isabel T.

SilverWood

Published in 2013

SilverWood Books
30 Queen Charlotte Street, Bristol, BS1 4HJ
www.silverwoodbooks.co.uk

ISBN 978-1-78132-186-7 (paperback)
ISBN 978-1-78132-187-4 (ebook)

British Library Cataloguing in Publication Data
A CIP catalogue record for this book is available from
the British Library

Set in Sabon by SilverWood Books

For E.I.B.

Contents

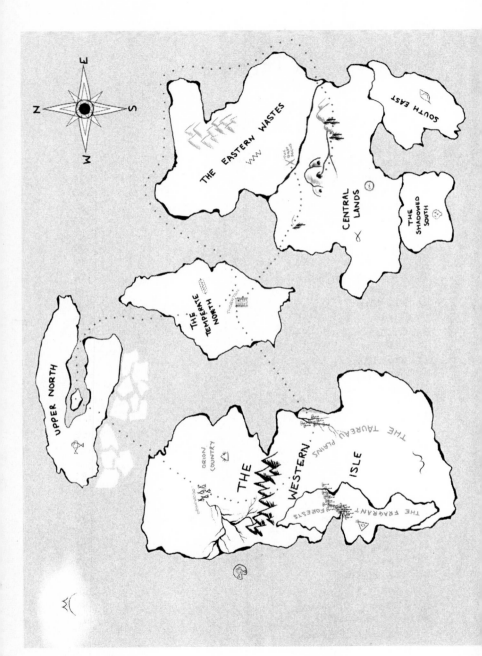

1

The Old World

The mist lay across the tops of the hills. Its curves clung to the land, vast shadows and shapes in the half-light. As Felicity watched, it slid silently into the hollow of the dell in which she crouched. It spoke to her, and its voice was distant, a bare breath of sound.

'Felicity,' it whispered.

Felicity shivered as beads of moisture crept up her bare arms. They spread to her neck and onto her cheeks. She was enveloped by the cool vapour, and in its shroud, the mist-voice spoke again. 'Follow me,' it said, and she found herself standing and following the moving, swirling fog along the bottom of the valley. Her feet slipped on the unseen path, and she tripped on a rock concealed in the haze, falling forwards.

The mist stopped. It rose up, a towering edifice threatening to tumble over her as she regathered her thoughts. Terrified, she closed her eyes, hoping it would disappear. *Where am I? How did I get here?* she thought with confusion.

Memories flashed across her mind, and she focused on them to avoid the terror of this creeping, speaking fog. She had been at her mother's school reunion...there were some old wooden doors...darkness. Sitting down. What had she sat on? She knew the answer to this held an importance, but she struggled to think. Perhaps she was dreaming, she thought now. Perhaps if she bit the inside of her cheeks, she would wake up. She bit hard.

'Ow!' That hurt. She opened her eyes. The gloomy ground was still there. She lifted her head. The creepy mist was still there. She looked behind her.

'Oh my God,' she muttered. For behind her was an army of moving shadows. They spread out in the dusky light. Her heart was pumping fast now. She took some very deep breaths and, without turning, pushed her voice into the gloom. 'I am Felicity Isabel Penfold,' she said firmly, trying to stand as she spoke out into the rapidly darkening light.

'Welcome, Felicity Isabel Penfold,' said a voice close behind her. She jumped and slowly turned. Her mind gabbled. *I will not be scared. This is just a horrible dream, and soon I shall awaken and find my way back to the dusty staircase and the old women outside.*

'No, Felicity Isabel Penfold, you won't,' said the voice, as she finally faced it. The fog cleared as if by command to allow Felicity and the voice to see each other.

Felicity was looking at a youngish man. But there was something quite different about him. She peered at him. Eyes, almond-shaped and hazel brown. Her inspection continued down his face. Largish nose and wide, smiling mouth. Smiling, she realised and quickly returned to his eyes. They were crinkled up at the outer corners.

'How do you know my name?' she asked. 'And further-more, why are you laughing at me?'

'You just told me your name,' he replied, 'and I don't know if it's normal in your world to stare so rudely at some-one, but in my world we are more respectful. I was smiling at your bad manners. I think they are funny,' he explained politely, but still half-smiling.

'Well!' said Felicity, quite loudly. She could feel the blood rushing up to fill her face and neck with colour. She was glad of the fading light. And then his words clarified in her mind. 'Our world,' he had said.

'Where am I?' she asked. The voice of Alice, her best friend (most days), came into her head. 'Jesus, Felicity, what are you up to now?!' How she wished Al were here. She realised her voice had sounded odd. She had an awful feeling that on top of being found on her hands and knees, she quite possibly was about to cry in front of this strange, handsome creature. And as swiftly as that passed through her mind, she realised he had heard her thoughts, that he could actually read her mind.

'You are confused and tired.' He spoke gently. 'I apologise for not introducing myself, but you are an amazing creature, and I was simply fascinated by your rudeness,' he explained, and in so doing, he bowed low to Felicity. 'Reubenfourthousandth at your service.'

Felicity did not understand anything, but she felt she could trust this strangely old-fashioned young man. *If that is what he is.*

I am not exactly as you think, his voice broke into her mind, *but we are more similar than you know.*

'I don't care what you are,' Felicity replied aloud, 'but please just tell me how to get home. I think there has been some mistake.'

'Felicity Isabel Penfold, we have been waiting for you for a very long time. You cannot return home until you fulfil your destiny. Our destiny. The entwined destiny of both our worlds.' His eyes looked deep into hers. *Follow me,* she heard him say in her thoughts. *Don't be scared. Follow me, and all will be as it should.* Reuben held out his hand. It was large and slightly square. It was a strong hand. Felicity took it and looked up at his face, but he was looking behind him now. Staring intently at something in the mist.

'Let's move,' he said to Felicity, and just as the swirling mist had opened for her to meet Reuben, so too did it clear a path for Reuben to push forwards. Reuben squeezed Felicity's hand for reassurance and began to walk.

Felicity looked behind her, somehow hoping to see Al scurrying up behind. She had dragged her friend to the reunion. But now Al and Mum were far, far behind. Or wherever, she thought. Mum said she had courage. Al called her crazy. This Reuben boy seemed to think she was someone important. Well, she thought, nothing to do but follow right now. Somehow she would sort this mess out. She always did.

11

2

Sib

Reuben set a fast pace, and Felicity was happy to keep close to him. She had no desire to see the shapes behind them come any closer. The trouble was, she kept tripping up. *Flipping mist*, she thought to herself, as she trod on something sharp.

'The mist is our friend, Felicity Isabel Penfold,' Reuben said softly as if not to offend the opaque cloud. 'It protects us from our enemies in sight and sound and thought.'

'I wish you wouldn't keep eavesdropping on my thoughts, Reuben – um – fourthousandth,' said Felicity. 'I think it's a bit prying, actually.'

'I do apologise, Felicity Isabel Penfold,' replied Reuben. 'An open mind invites a conversation in our world. I must help you learn how to close your thoughts when you wish for privacy. You see, here, all sees, all hears, all understands. All life is one, and all is balanced.' He sighed then, and Felicity wondered why. But more interestingly, she noticed that as Reuben spoke he seemed to grow, somehow. Felicity couldn't quite have said what happened. He just seemed bigger. She was all at once very tired.

'Open your heart, and share the strength of the mist, of the grass, of the life around you,' commanded Reuben, and before she could answer, she felt energy flowing back into her. She could have walked forever. Crossed mountains and forded rivers. Trekked until she reached the end of this strange, alive world.

'Wow! What was that?' she asked, but there was no response. 'Ouch,' she muttered as her toe stubbed against his hard heel. Reuben had stopped suddenly, and Felicity found herself holding her breath. There was something coming towards them. She could see the mist swirling into different patterns in the half-light. Reuben stepped out in front of her, and his voice held firm in the nebulous air.

'I am Reubenfourthousandth. Who might you be, approacher unknown?'

'I am Sibilinsixteenthousandth, and I wish to join you. My friends the Aquatics tell me of your great quest, and it is my most fervent desire to help you succeed,' said the murky shape.

'A Sibilin?!' Felicity heard Reuben exclaim, and now she was aware of whispering and murmuring coming from the distorted forms behind her.

'Hush,' he said to them. 'Sibilinsixteenthousandth is welcome and most needed.' *But why is he here?* he wondered to himself.

Felicity decided to sort out this name business. 'Reuben, your names are rather long. Can I use something easier to remember?'

Reuben and Sib both turned to stare at her, and she trembled. But she stood straight and held her breath.

'What would you suggest, Felicity Isabel Penfold the first?' replied Reuben, looking amused.

'Well, perhaps I could call you Reuben, and Sibilinsixteenthousandth – um – Sib?' she said.

Reuben chewed delicately at the side of his index finger as he considered.

'Of course,' he said at last. 'You are our guest, and we shall show our welcome by adopting your names.'

'And you can call me Felicity,' Felicity said. 'Just Felicity!' she added, a little breathless. Could they see how terrified she was? Mum said she never showed her feelings, but in this strange place, she felt transparent. As if they could all see right into her heart, not only her mind.

The mist cleared a little, and Felicity noticed Sib had crept closer. Felicity stared at him. *What on earth is he?*

she thought. He looked like a cross between a lizard and a snake. His skin was scaly, and his legs quite short, but he seemed to manage very well on them. His neck was long so Felicity had not realised how low to the ground his body was. He was bigger than the largest crocodile in the world that she had seen on TV once. He was smiling as he watched her assess him, and she flushed.

'We halt for the night,' commanded Reuben, interrupting the moment. 'And then we will talk,' he said quietly to Sib.

Felicity felt cold and wondered how they would find food and shelter in this strange, misty land. It was getting dark, and she wasn't keen to spend the night close to the unidentifiable assortment of moving shapes behind them. *What are they?* She shivered.

'Felicity, our world is very simple,' said Reuben, interrupting her fearful thoughts. She frowned, a tiny crease appearing above her blonde eyebrows. Her stomach rumbled loudly.

'Pardon me,' she said.

'Our world is very simple,' repeated Reuben, wondering why this exotic creature was looking so cross. 'If you have a question, then ask me with your thoughts. Words are there if needed, but often silence is enough. Communication flows freely between consenting creatures. The "shapes" you fear are simply a gathering of curious creatures. They have tagged along as I travelled from the Western Isle. They are good company, and you have nothing to fear from them.'

'Creatures?' asked Felicity.

'Beast and plant live in symbiotic harmony here, Felicity. All life has purpose, and plants have their voice, too. Is this not so in your world?'

'Well, we understand the huge importance of plants in the maintenance of our ecosystems,' she replied, thinking of Mr Harrelson's last Geography lesson, 'but I wouldn't say plants are allowed to speak.' She hoped this was not disrespectful to the odd things that were gathering around.

Felicity glanced at them and became transfixed by those closest to her; they were tiny wisps of colourful leaf balls that spun around in a random but ordered fashion. Rolling along the ground or flying up into the air, their movements seemed to have purpose.

'What are they?' she asked, but it was Sib who replied, 'They are Colour Changers,' he said, 'my enharmonic species. These are quite small, but they can cluster together if needed. Have you not them in your land, strange one?'

'Um, no,' she replied. Reuben had slipped away to organise the camp, and they were alone. Sib was staring at her as if asking a question, but without words. It was impossible to ignore his intense gaze any longer.

'What?!' said Felicity loudly. She wished Reuben would reappear. She felt uncomfortable with this lizardy thing.

'I move well with my short legs, do I?' He laughed softly, as he repeated her private thoughts. 'Sibilin retract their legs and skim the ground very fast in ripples when they have to, stranger,' he said. 'Like speech, my legs are there when I need them.'

Felicity was confused. Then she remembered. They could hear her thoughts if she let them drift freely. *For goodness' sake*, she thought, but she said, 'I apologise, Sib, and please call me Felicity. My name is Felicity Penfold.' Her voice cracked as she said her surname, and she knew she was starting to cry, but she didn't really care.

Sib moved a little away. He seemed uninterested in continuing their conversation. Reuben was scurrying about in the distance. Felicity could stand up no longer. She bumped down onto the mossy ground and sank until her cheek touched the spongy surface. She closed her eyes. *Just for a minute*, she thought.

Warm hands covered her in a brackenish sort of blanket, and as she fell asleep, she recognised Reuben's voice as the last thing she heard. 'Felicity is exhausted, Sibilin. She has travelled further than we can understand, and we must let her sleep. She has been so long-awaited...' but Felicity heard no more that night.

*

The green stars twinkled above as the ragtaggle group of travellers rested. Reuben and Sib built a crackling fire from the ferny bush that grew profusely on this part of the land, and some of the Colour Changers moved amongst the small group, distributing earth balls of crunchy sweetness that had been upturned in the loose soil.

Reuben eased back against his folded jacket. He watched Sib's face carefully. The Sibilin had half-lowered his eyelids, making it impossible to see the expression in his eyes. Reuben looked away. He drew in a deep breath and let the air leave his body slowly, carrying the tension of the day with it. Felicity stirred in her sleep, and his eyes turned to this beautiful stranger.

He guarded his thoughts and then allowed himself to think in a way that he had not since leaving Orion Country. What did the Orion leaders think of him to have entrusted him with this quest with hardly any real knowledge of the shape of things to come. His only course was to hold fast to his beliefs, which were unshakeable, that the Old World traditions were formed for pure, good reasons. That any imbalance could be rectified with a sharing of hearts and minds. Why did the Toxics not understand all life here was part of them also, that they belonged and were inherent to this world? He had grown up knowing that the Toxics were different. But he had believed them happy to be so. Then as an adolescent, he had learnt they were restless and even bitter. That he should avoid them when out with his friends. And now, it seemed, the whole world wanted him, Reuben, to form this quest party and persuade the Toxics to desist from their angry, destructive path. *But what exactly are the Toxics planning?*

If only he had a little more information. His elders had relied on his character. They knew he was obedient and strong. He would accept without question the great honour

16

of his mission. Now he was on the other side of the world, with an exotic stranger who it would take time for him to fully understand, and a Sibilin who he must trust and yet who put a shadow in his mind. The elders had said that 'all would become clear...trust the world, and it will show you its path...' and finally the only practical information, which even so, left much to his own resourcefulness, 'find the stranger in the east, and the others will find you.'

He sighed loudly, and Sib's eyelids flicked up, revealing their large, yellow irises.

'Sibilin,' Reuben said, tired of his anxieties, 'now I would know – why have you come? Why would you join me?'

'I heard that a young Orion was travelling the lands on a great quest,' began Sib in his whining voice. 'The Aquatics hold my deepest respect, and they suggested, even advised, that I should seek you in order to offer my services – they seem to feel I may have a part to play. Can you tell me, Reuben-fourthousandth, where you go? What is your mission?'

'I know only something of this story, Sib,' replied Reuben. He ate an earth ball slowly as he spoke, chewing carefully as if to draw out every last ounce of pleasure and energy from this crunchy treat. 'Yes, I was to travel far to the east, where a stranger would meet me. This has come to pass, as you see. There is an affinity between this stranger, Felicity, and myself, yet the balance is not full. There will be others. Key members. The Orion leaders who awarded me the honour of leading this quest would not tell me more. My ignorance is my protection. However, I am told those essential to the quest will find me.

'Our task is to prevent the Toxics in their mission of destruction. They threaten our world. The full story of the quest is unknown. Perhaps even to my Orion elders. There is likely to be danger, of course. Yet I trust still the harmony of our world to lead us safely to our final destiny. If you feel you are meant to be here, and if you wish to face the challenges ahead with courage, then you are welcome, Sibilinsixteenthousandth,' said Reuben, with a big smile. 'Your kind can be misunderstood, but I will have you. The Sibilin keep themselves separate, like the Toxics. With you by my side, we can restore an atmosphere of trust. We will bring light to the darkness of this beautiful, intelligent world that I so love and believe in.' And as he said those words, he felt the full lifeforce of the world flow through his veins and heal his anxieties. He knew he would do anything – anything at all, to save his beloved Old World.

Sib looked across at this beautiful Orion male as his impassioned words called out in the dark night, his features irradiated by the flickering fire. Something unexpected stirred. Sib had no illusions; loyalty was not a Sibilin trait. He came out of curiosity, rather than obedience to the Aquatics. But this Orion was truly captivating. Yet it was with a feeling of unease he found himself saying, 'Then let the quest party be three.'

3

Felicity

Felicity dreamt. Of home and of her family. Her father was holding her up to the sky. His fingers dug into her sides, and she was giggling breathlessly. Her mother was scolding him, 'Put her down, Jack. She is scared.' But she wasn't. She loved flying in the sky. Her father smelt of lemons and spice as he hugged her, laughing, before setting her on the ground. The day he had left for good, she had climbed into his wardrobe. The empty hangers clanked as she crawled inside and sat on the hard, wooden floor. The empty space smelt of lemons and spice.

Her mother seemed to cry all day. Mainly in her bedroom. Her beautiful face twisted into ugly grief as her heart broke, her great love gone. The house felt cold, empty. Felicity tried to explain the feeling to Al one day.

'It's as if the roof has been ripped off. Mum has gone mad, and Freya just goes out every night with her friends.'

'Your mum isn't mad, Flissy,' Al had replied as they sat on the splintery swing seat in Felicity's garden.

The cats were fighting again. Felicity's sister, Freya, had a cat. Princess Mew had had kittens, and Felicity had asked to keep the tiny, black runt of the litter. He was so small and defenceless. However, within a year his length equalled the neighbour's collie, and his entrance through a window was announced with a large, heavy thud. He had grown into a black panther – and his tiny mother hated him. Their growling and spitting became so noisy Felicity and Al went inside.

'Can't you simply rehome him, Flissy?' said Al. The fighting was awful.

'No, he belongs here!' said Felicity.

Al looked at her friend's face and said no more. Her own parents were terribly boring. They didn't talk much, and they certainly never had loud, exciting fights like Flissy's used to. Once when Al had stayed over, Flissy's parents were shouting so loud it had woken her up. It was amazing. She could hear crockery being smashed. In the morning there was no evidence downstairs, and Flissy had not mentioned it, but Al knew she had woken too.

They lay on Flissy's bed on their backs. They did a few sit-ups, then ate a bag of Haribos and watched silly videos of cats being weird online.

'When are you going to see your father?' asked Al.

'Never,' replied Felicity.

A loud crack broke into Felicity's dreams. The fire was fat and hot with spitting logs. She opened her eyes and looked straight into the crinkled tiny hedgehog eyes of a Colour Changer who was offering her a drink. The cup was wooden, and the outside surface scratchy with bark. Felicity took it gratefully. She sipped the sweet amber drink reminiscent of honey and lemon and sighed. She had no choice. She needed Reuben until she could find a way of returning home. She leant back, sipping the delicious drink, and let her eyes close.

Her thoughts returned to her last memory of home. Back to that day at her mother's reunion. The key to getting home had to be remembering what had happened before landing on the damp, mossy floor of this world. She went through it again, step by step. She had found the wooden entrance door to the old school, and leaving Al with her mother outside for a minute, she had stepped into the musty hall. Floorboards worn from a thousand girls' feet stretched out into the darkness beyond. Her mother had once told her that the twisted matron had sent 'bad girls' off in the middle of the night with a green saucer and an old knife to scrape up black smears of prehistoric gum. She had looked down with vague interest to see if she could identify these nuggets of penance.

Then a sound had made her peer into the dark depths at the back of the hall. Was the floor trembling a little? Or was it her? She glanced back to the rectangle of light. She felt rebellious. Angry. She was cross with her mother for what had happened. So what if she was trespassing. She took a small step into the gloom.

At the back of the hall, there was a staircase. The sound had come from there. But she had to go further into the darkness. She took a huge breath and walked straight across the dividing space. The floorboards creaked as she passed over them. The staircase sat at the back of the hall like a huge squatting toad. Its treads branched to the left and to the right, fat arms outstretched to embrace the wood mountaineer. Felicity stepped onto the first step. The dust filled her nose, and she sneezed.

'Bless you,' said a voice. The hairs on Felicity's arms lifted. She let out her breath very, very slowly and peered intently up and down the soaring staircase. There was no one there. Who spoke? Did the staircase speak? Was she going mad like her mother? She sat down, her legs trembling a little. At her back was something small and hard. It dug in. Then her head started to spin. It felt horrible. She remembered thinking she must be ill. That she should get back outside. The little hard lump still poked into her spine, and the throbbing in her head was unbearable. She was in the dark, surrounded by dark, with a battering and roaring in her ears like an old ship sinking in a storm. When she could bear the noise no more, she was flung, shipwrecked, into the eerie silence that followed.

'So that is how you came to me, Felicity Isabel Penfold,' said Reuben with a big grin. His voice snapped her out of her reverie, and she opened her eyes. No school hall here. Just an exotic, handsome boy-creature, a slinking lizard, and a very large fire.

'Do you mind?' she said. But really she wasn't sure she

21

did mind. She felt she could trust this boy. However, she wasn't going to let him keep taking advantage of her. 'I would like some privacy in my own head occasionally,' she added, flicking her curly hair back from her neck.

Reuben stared at her blonde curls as they nestled back onto her shoulder. Then he sat back and said, 'Well, you must learn to close your thoughts from me. Think only of the thought as if looking at a page. Allow no side thoughts to creep in. With them, enter the minds of others.'

'I will try,' Felicity said. She looked at him. He truly believed she was some sort of saviour. Obviously he was wrong, but she quite liked him. *Perhaps if I help, he will show me the way back home, but still...*

'Reuben, why am I here?' she asked. She sat up straight and faced Reuben. 'Actually, I have to tell you – I think this is a big mistake. I am just a girl. Just a girl who wandered off and wishes she hadn't. I do not belong here. I don't have any special powers apart from being able to wiggle my ears and crack my fingers.' She could hear her voice in the night air. It sounded pathetic.

'You are here for the quest, Felicity. My quest is to save our ailing world,' said Reuben. 'Nothing more, nothing less. I was sent to the far east to find a stranger who would help me. You are she, Felicity. You are she,' he repeated, looking directly into her eyes.

Felicity felt that strange energy flow back into her. She heard her breathing calm and still. Reuben's eyes glowed in the campfire. Felicity felt very warm. *Maybe. Home is weird now. Cold and strange.* She sighed. *Why not?*

'Maybe,' she said aloud, 'but I am not staying long'. She swept her glance to all within hearing. 'You may as well all understand that whatever force brought me here – fine! I will do the job, the thing, the heroine ending, but then I'm going home.'

4

Gus

The sun shone clear as Felicity woke to a beautiful new world. The mists had dispersed, and there was a feeling of anticipation and excitement. The bedraggled band of followers gathered together their few belongings and prepared to travel. Reuben told Felicity they were heading northwest. The followers seemed determined to stay with Reuben. *They're like band groupies*, thought Felicity as she sat hugging her knees and watching them. She was nestled into the bracken that had kept her warm through the night.

There were more Orion like Reuben, but whilst they appeared to be human, they had long, furry black-and-white striped tails that they moved gracefully behind them. *Like a cat*. The Orion certainly moved with a grace and beauty that did not appear to have been endowed upon some of the other creatures.

There were no other Sibilin. She peeped at Sib as he moved about the camp. He could move extremely fast, and Felicity saw the other creatures keep a wary eye on him. His huge scaly head turned towards her. Felicity shuddered and looked away.

Peering into the spiky bushes, she was fascinated by what she saw. There was a group of tall plants – almost trees. Their heads were a collection of grooved, broad leaves that glimmered and shimmered in the early sunshine, vast geisha fans of the brightest green. Their outstretched branches hovered, dangling aerial roots elegantly like long golden sleeves. Felicity was transfixed. There was a regality about these plants. She noticed the other plants and beasts made way for them wherever they quietly moved.

'They are the Greens,' said Reuben, making Felicity jump. 'It is their kind who makes the roots that store all knowledge.'

'How do they move?' she asked.

'On fat root balls that spin slowly.'

Like castors, thought Felicity, *how clever.*

'Reuben, if you think I am meant to be here, then you must have some idea of what on earth I am supposed to do? I can walk a fair distance, thanks to the Welsh hills. I hate spiders and all bugs, and I don't like being wet, so I really do think you might have the wrong person. Was it my friend Al you were after? She is taller than me and runs really fast. She loves nature programmes. She would fit right in here.' Felicity took a breath. She was panting.

'Felicity, Felicity, you are the one. I felt it the moment I saw you on your hands and knees,' said Reuben, laughing. 'Your friend Al would be most welcome, but it is you who has been chosen by my world. Do you not feel the connection?'

Felicity looked up at the vast sky and across the camp, as if seeking a sign. She inhaled the air. She felt nothing.

'I'm sorry, Reuben. I feel nothing,' she replied. 'Although...' She felt a tiny tremor pass through her as she gazed at this proud young man. A tiny surge of energy and with it came a memory. A buried memory of a dream. His face in the dream.

'Well, the Aquatics will help us,' said Reuben. He was keen to move. Felicity would see – she was the one. She had to be. 'The Aquatics commune with the Oceanids at all times,' he continued. 'Their knowledge is secure. Your part will be revealed in time. Have confidence, dearest Felicity.' Taking her by surprise, he put his arms around her and held her for a moment. He was warm, and his jacket smelt of spice and earth. She stayed still. *Okay. This is a bit weird. But it's good.* She inhaled discreetly, hoping to capture his scent. He patted her on the back as he released her. He started to walk ahead, but Felicity caught up with him.

'Reuben, why is your world broken? Last night you said your world was broken. If you need my help, I have to understand what is happening here?'

Reuben took her hand and walked with her. 'Listen,' he said. 'We have little time, but I will try to explain. We have many creatures and plants on our world, and as we travel, you will meet or hear of them all. However, there is one kind who feel neglected, and over time they have become bitter. They seek to destroy our world, the world they feel has betrayed them. Exactly how and when is not entirely known. But the wisest and oldest of our species have begun to react to protect and defend our world. I am chosen to lead this quest. Its aim is to counteract the destructive forces of the Toxics.'

'Toxics?' repeated Felicity, and strangely, the name felt bitter on her tongue. As if this mystical world was trying to tell her something. 'What do we do to stop them, then?' she asked practically. 'What are they doing? Killing people? Well, beasts and plants?'

'Their plan is not known yet. We know they wish the traditions and laws of the Old World to end. We know they have turned black with bitterness and resentment. We do not know precisely what they intend. But Sib tells me they are gathering force in the Shadowed South. The Aquatics advise we head northwest. We must find the other members of the quest, or hope they find us soon.'

'Who are these Aquatics?' asked Felicity.

'They are plants who give us information as we travel. They work with the Oceanids, large sea creatures and the oldest of the beasts. It is the Oceanids, together with the elder Greens, who formed the idea of the quest. They felt it was time to protect the world.'

Felicity's eyes rolled upwards in an expression of despair. So many new kinds. So much information. She would keep it simple. One, stay with Reuben. She liked and trusted him.

And he was rather gorgeous, after all. Two, stay away from these black, vile Toxics. Three, try to memorise all these creatures and plants so Reuben did not think her stupid. Four, help if she could, although it was not her fight (even if she had dreamt of Reuben once). Five, work out how to get back to the place she had landed and see if she could find a way back to that staircase.

A Colour Changer flurried past, passing out earth balls. Felicity took one and rolled it between her palms. Biting into the juicy ball, she was pleasantly relieved to find it tasted rather nice. Like a pomegranate but more filling. Reuben watched her.

'Eat at least two, Felicity. We may not stop today. The journey to the Temperate North is far, and we have much land to cross.' As he spoke his golden eyes travelled slowly over her, assessing her strength. She seemed a little slender, like his enharmonics, the Fragrants, but there was stamina in her frame. Felicity began to blush as Reuben stared at her. His eyes jumped up to her face as he sensed her unease. He smiled to reassure her.

'You are stronger than you look!' he said, still smiling.

'Hockey pitches are cold in January,' she replied cryptically, as she stood up straight, brushing off the leaves and dust. 'I will manage.'

Reuben tipped his head to the side. She said some odd things, this Felicity, but she was in his world now, and he trusted it.

'With the power of our earth, yes,' he replied. 'If you–' but Reuben broke off as they both heard roaring and shouting on the perimeter of the camp. He spun round to face the intruders and was surprised to see two Lupata. *They are a long way from home*, he thought. They padded into the clearing, and between them walked a Toxic.

Felicity's eyes widened as these huge creatures came right up to Reuben. They were huge. A wolf built like a Shetland pony. Their heads hung heavily on broad shoulders, and their jaws thrust forward from deep, intelligent brows. The one closest to her flared its nostrils at her strange scent, and Felicity actually felt herself tremble. *I can't believe I am standing here. Why don't I just run?* She slowly edged out of the line of sight of the smelly, hairy duo. Reuben, however, seemed quite calm. His gaze was steady and only on the Toxic. The deep grey Lupata nearest Reuben spoke. He seemed to be the leader, as the white one turned its head and listened to his words.

'We found him wandering at the foot of the hills,' he said. His voice was predictably full and growling, but Felicity understood perfectly. In fact, now she came to think of it, she understood everyone perfectly. *Oh, the joy of perfect harmony*, she thought.

'Name yourself, Toxic,' commanded Reuben, and Felicity saw how tall and strong he suddenly appeared. He had drawn himself up, shoulders square and head raised, as he spoke. The ground had slightly risen where he stood, as if in readiness for the meeting. The band of followers had backed away, and all movement ceased as Reuben addressed the Toxic.

Felicity peered past Reuben. The Toxic was standing in the full sunlight. It was the height of a very tall man. *Is it a plant?* she wondered. It was grey-green, and long spikes stuck out of its limblike appendages. It had two legs and three arm branches, with its head simply a fatter version, more bulbous. *Yuk!* The involuntary thought popped into her head. It was disgusting. It tipped its head sideways and looked straight at her with its large black left eye. She met its glance. Its eye was deep, dark fathoms of pain. It spoke to her of sadness and loss and loneliness. Felicity felt a tear trickling down her cheek.

'I am Reubenfourthousandth,' Reuben said to the thing.

'I am Toxictoxicth,' it replied.

What a lovely voice, thought Felicity, surprised. She heard a few sniggers from the bushes around her.

'Silence,' called out Reuben. 'We are all of the Old World,

and in that world there has never been a place for disrespect and small thoughts.'

The Toxic seemed to relax at Reuben's words. Felicity took a better look at him and decided his eyes were a lovely shape, as long as you avoided meeting them, even if the rest of him resembled a particularly repulsive giant cactus.

Reuben spoke quietly to the two Lupata, and Felicity let out her breath with relief as they backed away and sat down. One of them started rootling in the ground, and she saw him unearth a lump. *So that's where the earth balls come from,* she realised. He crunched it greedily, and a large drool of saliva hung down from his pink and black gums.

'Why have you risked yourself to come to our quest?' Reuben asked the Toxic.

Why isn't he scared of him? Felicity wondered. *He has just said he is a Toxic.* But Reuben seemed comfortable with letting the Lupata leave their prisoner stand free. She sat down, reassured by Reuben's attitude. It was his world. He must know what he was doing. The thing wasn't black – perhaps that meant something.

'I have heard mutterings of this quest for many months now,' the Toxic was saying in his melodious voice.

Felicity started gently scratching at the ground with a stick, to see if she could find another juicy earth ball, whilst she listened.

'The Old World is dying, and my kind are to blame. They cause imbalance to the essential harmonies with their anger. Chaos is erupting throughout the south. The power of communication is becoming limited, and with this, the energy of our Old World that flows seamlessly between us all and our land is being weakened. As we all know, life's flow depends on an open mind and an open heart. All can see and understand. Words are only a part of the flow. The Toxics breed fear and mistrust, and the flows of communication are being stunted. The plants and beasts can no longer connect with the land from whence they come. They grow weak, and the truly malicious Toxics have formed a small army that grows fast. They encourage insularity and spread their malicious intents as they begin to traverse the world, hundredd by hundredd. These new Toxics recruit wherever they go. They say it is time to act.'

'What do they want so badly?' asked Reuben.

'A new world in which we Toxics can belong.'

'You live amongst us already.'

'Yes, but you know our story,' continued the creature, who Felicity had decided to call Gus. She wasn't really sure why. Perhaps it was his big, black eyes. They reminded her of a big gorilla she had once fallen in love with at a zoo. Gus. Her mother had been forced to buy her a hard plastic replica, which had stayed in her bed for the next four years, chilling her cheek in a satisfying way. Gus the Toxic was talking fast now. Sib had reappeared, and he sat a little distance away, listening.

'Your story is the story of all of us, Toxic,' said Reuben, interrupting the flow of speech. 'Do not be afraid,' he said to the followers and gestured to Felicity to come closer. 'This Toxic is clearly not blackened with bitterness yet. He comes in peace. Let us all remind ourselves of the sad history of his kind. Of the birth of the Toxics and the beginning of the downfall of the Old World.' He sat down gracefully, and Gus folded himself neatly together and continued. Felicity gave up grubbing for food and focused on the story.

'It is said that in the old ages all life lived in great harmony and balance with the Great Spirit. It created pure goodness and joy, which seeped out into all other worlds. Sometimes an Orion travelled to those worlds to share our message of love and joy. The Great Spirit was proud of his wonderful creation, which was doing so well. His pride was his undoing. He took his eyes away for a moment, and the Toxics were born.

'A male Fragrant fell in love with a female Orion beast. It is foretold, "When two enharmonics join, a special force is created, but to reproduce is against the great one. It cannot be."

'But they did. They found the tiny part of themselves that matched, and they reproduced. The thing that came from them was ugly, strange, and they separated in shame, telling no one. They left it to its own fate, in the natural way of things.

'But it survived. It had the powers of both species and the love of none. It reached maturity, watching, learning, yearning.

'The first one reproduced itself out of utter loneliness. Subsequent Toxics learned to do the same, but it was a miserable, pathetic affair.

'The descendants scattered throughout the lands, unwanted even by their own kind. The plants and the beasts saw these sad creatures that lived in the shadows of their world, and they ignored them, misfits of ugliness in an otherwise perfect, beautiful world. They were misunderstood and sometimes reviled. Over the years they became angry and bitter. Bitterness turned to wickedness, and revenge became their cry. Their only hope was the Great Spirit of the Old World, who had comforted them from the beginning. But why did he not intervene? Life has its own destiny, they were told. It is rumoured he planted a Root deep in another world, in order that at the right time, the two worlds would entwine and somehow heal each other. This was his design, and it would come to pass as all things do, they said. But the years passed and nothing changed.'

The story moved something in Felicity's heart. The more she heard of this sad, proud world, the more she was beginning to understand. Maybe this was not her world, she thought, but how very real and tragic it all felt.

'We thank you for reminding us, Gus,' said Reuben. There were a few mutters of confusion as Reuben gave the Toxic Felicity's name.

'How did you –' exclaimed Felicity, and then she realised. 'Oh, of course!'

'It is a very fine name,' said Gus, and he fixed his big, black eyes on Felicity. Felicity thought his funny, spiky face was trying to smile, although she couldn't be sure.

'Why have you come to find me?' Reuben asked the Toxic.

'I was living with the Greens, in their homelands – the South East, but visiting the darker parts of the Shadowed South frequently. I feel different from my kind. I see no sense in resentment and bitterness. I don't feel ugly. I am happy to be different. Intrigued. I have felt lonely, but I face the Great Spirit, and I feel joy. I face the sun and the wind and the night moons as I travel across the glorious lands, and I feel hope. I must join your quest. I can understand the new Toxics' strange language. I see their fury and black hearts, yet I feel tiny slivers of light trying to penetrate the darkest recesses. My place is with you. I think I can help. I consulted the Aquatics. They told me to seek the quest.'

'Did they give you any further information on the Toxics' plans?' asked Reuben. His shoulders were slumped, and Felicity felt her fingers twitching to touch him. To lay a small hand on his shoulders upon which so much was resting. *Thank you, dear Felicity,* came his voice into her head. Felicity felt a warm sliding in her stomach. *You are very important to me,* whispered his voice in her head. *I need you, Felicity. Listen and learn.*

So Felicity listened. As the sun climbed high in the sky, the rumbling voice of Gus spoke of all he knew of the Toxics' plans. The Aquatics had discovered a plot to find the Roots of the Old World and, furthermore, to reveal the place of the ancient Root that held the knowledge and secrets of the beginning of the world.

'No one apart from the Taureau are allowed into the Sacred Caves which contain the Roots,' said Reuben.

'Yes, but the leader of the army, who has named himself Arrass, is reputed to have found a way,' said Gus.

Reuben was silent. In the pause, Felicity could hear a tiny bird singing high in a bush and an echoing reply from another. The sun was warm, and she felt thirsty. She was just wondering how to ask for some of that wonderful honey drink when Gus spoke again.

'Furthermore, Reuben, he means to destroy it all. The ancient Root first and then all of them. He declares all knowledge will be burnt and hacked until the caves are empty.'

The roar and outrage of the beasts and plants filled the air. They cried in pain and terror. Felicity looked about her. She felt odd. She saw herself from above. A small human surrounded by a horde of screaming, turbulent creatures and plants. Is this how the first explorers felt on landing? She wished Al could be here with her. But the noise of the outraged plants and beasts overcame her, and as she stopped thinking and listened to the sound, the Old World gave up its strength to her. She felt unified with these wonderful, strange beings. She realised she knew what they were. She felt their love and their pain. There were plants and beasts of all the world in this quest, although she had yet to learn their names. There were Greens, Thorns, Fragrants and Colour Changers, Taureau, Lupata, Orion, and of course, one Sibilin. *There are more in the oceans and the skies*, the land whispered, and she felt honoured that it opened its heart to her. She looked up and saw vast flying shapes soaring high. She was filled with wonder and joy. *What a truly incredible place.* But for now she filled her lungs with the pure air and found herself joining their cry, 'Life is joy,' 'Joy is love, 'Love heals all.'

5

Travelling North

As the troupe finally moved off, Gus and Reuben were deep in conversation, and Felicity found herself walking alongside Sib. It was hard to keep up with his scuffling steps; she had to run at a steady jog to match his pace. They left later than Reuben would have liked; the sun had reached its apex and was now slowly dropping. The chilly mists were beginning to build up as it lost its warmth, and Felicity saw they were heading for a range of hills that looked overgrown with dark green trees. *This really does remind me of Wales*, she thought. But Wales was just a name in her head. She thought of family holidays. Her sister Freya. *No doubt torturing someone right this moment*, came the unbidden thought.

'Ouch!' she said as a huge thorn embedded itself in her calf.

'In our world, dark thoughts will darken our hearts, and the plants respond with dark actions,' said Sib.

'Planting its days' growth in my leg is not dark, it's just spiteful,' replied Felicity, licking and spitting on the small puncture wound in her leg.

'That must be washed at the next free-flowing stream,' said Sib, and then he began humming an irritating little tune.

'Sib, sib, sib, sib, sib,' he began to sing his name to the melody.

Oh, God, that's awful, thought Felicity, and she interrupted him, 'What is it with your long, long names?'

'Well, our names declare not just our identity, but our gravitas,' said Sib. 'Our gravitas being the weight of our inherited generational age.'

'Um, but why is this inherited generational age important?' said Felicity. She knew Al accused her of being arrogant, but she had never seen the need to pretend to be stupid, like some people. Her mother called it 'a fine brain', and she relied on it. She was certainly using it on this uninvited adventure. Sib was droning on in his slightly nasal voice. Perhaps it was the tiny nostrils, she thought, unkindly.

'Because those creatures and plants that have lived upon this earth the longest are due the greatest respect, of course,' Sib said, surprised Felicity didn't grasp this point. 'Our names are followed by generations. Hence Reuben fourthousandth is four thousand generations of Orion. Lifespan is irrelevant as we consider life continuous, so as it ends, it begins in another life form. We do not declare our personal years upon the earth – simply our species' generational age. We can see by visual evidence whether we are in the company of young, middle or old lives. All is simple, you see.'

'Not really,' said Felicity, now totally confused and very glad Al wasn't here to witness her stupidity. She was becoming rather hungry, too. *Am I the only one who ever feels hungry?*

No, we do, too, but we breathe deeply and let the life source flow into our bodies to sustain us until food can be found, replied Sib silently.

'That is just so disconcerting,' said Felicity.

'What?'

'The way you enter my mind when I am not even expecting it. It feels wrong.'

'I apologise,' said Sib, looking pleased.

'Apology accepted.'

'So a beast or plant who has a long life expectancy will have a smaller generational number – fewer generations of his kind will have walked upon the earth.'

'Oh, I see,' she said untruthfully.

'Apart from the Oceanids and their enharmonics, the Aquatics are said to have been here from the very beginning, and the Taureau claim the lowest generational titles as they live to extremely old ages,' continued Sib. 'But it is an age-old discussion.'

I suppose if the world is so well balanced, they wouldn't have much else to argue about – Felicity focused hard on her thoughts this time so Sib couldn't read them. She really wished she had never asked, but Sib didn't seem someone you should interrupt.

'It can get a little confusing, actually, so we tend to ignore our generational titles and only use them in formal situations.' Sib kept talking. 'For peace and harmony, it is generally acknowledged that the Oceanids and the Aquatics, followed closely by the Taureau, have the longest lifespans and therefore the lower generational numbers, so they claim the higher gravitas and have the strongest voices in a Banyan. Except for the Greens and the Strata, of course.'

Felicity's head was spinning. Even Sib looked a little confused with all this. She needed lunch and a drink and other things, which she felt awkward about requesting. Luckily Reuben and Gus had lapsed into silence, so she said to Sib in a loud voice, 'Thank you, Sib, that is so interesting. I can't take any more in just now, though, as I am so hungry I could die.'

'Felicity, Felicity,' said Reuben, who had heard her, 'don't say such a silly thing – we are all hungry, but you must call to the earth and to the air and to the water, and you will be nourished. We cannot stop until we reach the cover of the forests of the hill. Close your eyes and breathe deeply, Felicity. See the earth and all its treasures. See the cool, flowing waters of our rivers and of our oceans, and feel the open, vast spaces of our skies. This can sustain you. There is no need for hunger whilst we travel.'

Felicity squinted her eyes at Reuben as the lowering sun was shining full at her and she wanted to see his expression. *That sounds like Freya*, she thought, frowning, *when she is talking absolute rubbish to wind me up.* Reuben looked quite serious, but she found herself giggling. The giggles turned to breathy gasps of laughter, and she came to a halt on the dusty track they followed. She bent over and laughed until her stomach ached. She couldn't stop. The whole troupe halted and watched.

'Aaaagh, haaaaaah, haaaaah.' She gasped for air.

Reuben came close and put his hand on her back. 'Felicity, it's all good,' he said. 'You are being so strong. Come, we will rest briefly and nourish ourselves,' he said to the fascinated followers.

'No, no, don't stop for me,' said Felicity as her breath slowly returned.

Reuben stood for a moment as if in indecision; then he said, 'We stop. Five moments. Two earth balls each to be distributed. Then we move to the forest for dusk.' The Colour Changers were back, distributing the earth balls. Felicity watched the spinning leaf-balls, their beautiful colours of autumn catching the light as they flipped about.

'Their enharmonics are the Sibilin,' said Reuben, who had come to sit by her.

'Yes, Sib told me,' she replied.

Reuben raised one of his neat eyebrows.

'Balance is so important here, isn't it?' said Felicity as she sipped the delicious drink he passed her.

'Yes, of course, what is life without balance, Felicity?' He looked straight at her with this answer. Her tummy squirmed a little, and she felt herself blush. His eyes crinkled up at the corners as his beautiful smile appeared. She handed him back the bark cup, and as he took it, he briefly held her hand with both of his.

'Felicity, trust me. We must trust each other. I have confidence you will find your strengths as our journey unfolds. And I trust my world to safely return you to where you are meant to be, at the end.'

But where is that? Felicity thought as the memories of her empty home trickled ice through her heart. Reuben squeezed her hand. She closed her eyes and felt a small tear seep out as she did. She opened them and took a big, calming breath. He was smiling such a kind smile. He warmed her heart. She felt happy. Useful. She smiled back, and Reuben seemed to understand. She would not question this whole thing anymore. She would go with this crazy Old World's plans. Properly. It might be fun.

'Gus tells me the Aquatics have communed with their enharmonics, the Oceanids. They have ancient knowledge and are chief defenders of the Old World. The Strata also. Because of the Strata, the Oceanids were long aware of the growing threat. But it is not their way to act in haste.'

Felicity's head was shouting at her. *What do they look like, these Aquatics and Oceanids? What are the Strata, now? And what on earth is an enharmonic?*

Reuben gently touched her cheek with the back of his warm hand. 'Later, Felicity, I promise,' he said and strode off, strapping the cups to his woven belt and breaking into a gentle trot to get to the front of the troupe and Gus.

Felicity didn't feel like talking for a while. They walked for most of the afternoon. The land's barren contours slowly changed as the dip and swell of the ground became lightly cloaked in soft greenery. With the larger ferns and small thickets came a damp, clinging air. Felicity wished she had put on her coat the day of the school reunion. Perhaps her mother had a point, sometimes. She decided to speak to her. *Maybe she can hear.* She was beginning to realise anything was possible. Quietly she murmured her imaginary conversation.

'Mum, I am tramping through a wild land with an assortment of mildly scary creatures, and yet I am fine. Apparently I am a key member in a quest to save this Old World. Yes, you heard me. There is a very handsome boy – an Orion. Yes, he speaks nicely, Mum. We are about to enter a very dark forest, and it's all rather damp. I wish I had my coat. The fog here is thick at night. No, it's okay; Reuben will look after me...' She found herself smiling and then noticed a Green looking down at her and was silent again.

There was a shout from up ahead, and the Green rolled off fast, his branch arms brushing the floor like a wide broom. Felicity's stomach rumbled loudly. She hoped there might be something different to eat in the forest. For in front of her there rose a verdant hill. Almost a mountain, she thought, as they gathered at its foot. Felicity looked behind her across the open moorlike landscape they had crossed this afternoon. She was glad they would have more protection tonight. Gus was clearly different from his species, but Felicity imagined those long vicious spikes on an unfriendly Toxic, and she shivered.

'Felicity, you are cold. Here, take this.' Reuben dropped back and passed her a soft, woollen wrap. Its weave was close, yet it moved like silk, and it was an indefinable colour, a sort of rain-washed palette of summer. It was stunning. *And warm*. Reuben smiled at her pleasure.

'My people weave them,' he said proudly. 'Forgive me for leaving you alone so much today. Tonight we will talk and eat forest peas. They will warm you up.'

'Good,' said Felicity and then followed him.

*

The huge fire blazed as the troupe settled for the evening. They had not travelled far into the forest; the mists and the darkness had descended with speed, obscuring all. Felicity watched the flames as they curled and crackled. *Chestnuts and marshmallows*, she thought hungrily. The enormous Lupata added logs with their huge mouths. Felicity watched them warily. Gus noticed her interest.

'The Lupata live in the frozen north of the Eastern Wastes, and they are a cautious breed,' he said, his mellow voice blending with the smouldering fire. 'They are strong and courageous. To earn a Lupata's trust is to earn a friend for life. Their loyalty is only matched by the Taureau. Their tempers can be quick, and we treat them with respect.

'We will arrive in the Temperate North at the time of

the Lupata matings. It is the time of year when all Lupata approaching maturity seek their enharmonic Thorn in order to trigger their maturity, which then enables them to find their Lupata mate. It is a very vigorous time. The young Lupata have a long, hard trek to the Temperate North. Once there, they have to find the energy to breach the Thorn defences. With the enharmonic bondings completed, they must then spar for their mates. It is a time of honour and joy. Often mature pairs with the strength will make the long journey to watch the rituals of their kind.'

'It sounds rather exciting,' said Felicity. She wished they might be there now. She hoped the Temperate North was not too far away. She lay down on the warm, ferny floor and gathered her wrap around her. Reuben glanced across at her, and Gus lolloped away, giving him room to lie next to her. He held out a large, wooden bowl, which contained a mound of small peas. They were brown and scaly. After a quick check to see how others were eating them, she took a small handful, tipped back her head and trickled them into her mouth. They were salty and spicy, and as she crunched and swallowed them, she felt a pleasant burning in her stomach. They were truly delicious. She took some more.

'They are good, aren't they?' said Reuben, with a big grin. 'It is a treat to have these on our journey. Each region has its own specialities, but these forest peas are greatly treasured.'

'I don't feel cold anymore,' said Felicity.

'No, they will warm you up better than the fire or my wrap,' he replied, helping himself to a huge handful. He tipped back his head, and Felicity dared to ask, 'Where is your tail? I see the other Orion with us have the most stunning black-and-white furry tails, but you don't seem to have one.'

Reuben looked at Felicity and said nothing. She swallowed. He breathed in deeply and then spoke, his words escaping softly. Felicity was mesmerised by the shape of his full lips as they moved. 'I was not born with a tail. My mother assured me this was for a good reason, as are all things, and the meaning would one day come to light.'

'It has not been easy for you?' said Felicity.

'No, and yet like all things, this difficulty has given me more than it has taken. Perhaps that is why I was chosen to lead the quest.'

'Perhaps,' said Felicity. She put her small hand on his arm, and he felt her warmth flow through him. They sat quietly, crunching forest peas and not needing to speak. Felicity yawned.

'Sleep now. We travel through the narrow pass of the hill tomorrow. It is arduous, and you need rest,' said Reuben.

Felicity lay down and tried not to think of home. Tomorrow she would ask Reuben about the Aquatics, who seemed to hold their destiny. Satiated from the forest peas, exhaustion finally claimed her. The last thing she heard was the thrashing of the treetops high up the hill as the wind picked up and played with their soft, leafy roofs.

6

Georges

The sun was barely peeping over the summit of the dark hill as Reuben called everyone to awake. Beasts and plants rose and took food. More forest peas, discovered Felicity. It seemed they simply ate one food from each area in which they travelled. They didn't seem to carry much at all, just a few coverings and containers. She watched carefully but couldn't see any evidence of secreted food. Or weapons, thankfully. It made travelling so easy, and there was absolute trust that the land would provide each day. Felicity thought of her world as it was now. Food travelling backwards and forwards across its surface aimlessly; mountains of waste rotting in stinking heaps; people starving in countries affected by climate or wars. She sat up. *How I wish we had remembered some of this simplicity.*

Reuben approached and held out his hand to help her rise. 'I hear some of your thoughts, Felicity,' he said. 'You must accept that even in your world there is a plan. I feel your sadness and despair. But life is joy, and all will balance somewhere, for those concerned. Maybe not in your world, but in another world that you have yet to discover. Never despair. It is extinguished energy.'

Felicity took his hand and slowly let the breath go she had subconsciously been holding. As she exhaled, she felt the despair leave. *There is always hope*, she thought, *and beauty, even if it takes a little time to find it.* She thought of the wonderful givers of her world. Those who gave all their time and lives to helping the plants, the beasts, the people.

'Yes, there is balance,' she replied, 'but in my world, it is sometimes hard to find. I envy you your beautiful world, Reuben.'

Reuben offered her some of the cool, green liquid they had washed the spicy peas down with last night, and she sipped a little before asking, 'Reuben, what are the Aquatics?' The drink chilled her stomach as she drank some more. It tasted so refreshing; she felt it cleanse her from the inside. A little burp bubbled up, and she struggled to keep it down, panicking that Reuben would hear. But he was brushing out the last traces of the fire whilst he spoke. 'We have a very long day, Felicity. I will let Sib tell you about the Aquatics. He will enjoy sharing his knowledge with you.'

As they began to climb the dense forest path, Reuben called Sib to walk by Felicity.

'Well, Felicity, where do I start?' said Sib. He sounded a little irritated, and Felicity wondered why. He spoke quickly. 'The Aquatics grow at the edges of all our waters. Their main growth is in the warm western lagoons and lakes, close to the oceans where their enharmonics, the Oceanids, live. But their tuberous shoots spread out across the whole world in a vast mat. Their hollow tubers sift the water in which they float, and as all that happens leaves its traces upon the earth by nightfall, so, too, they gather information along with their nutrients. Our world is full of water: oceans and rivers, cascading waterfalls and streams, tiny rivulets – into each and all the Aquatics have their tendrils. They are the interconnecting web of communication of our lands.'

At that instant, a loud rumbling reached their ears. Sib stopped scuffling, and Felicity instinctively crouched down. They were deep in the forest, and the noise was deafening. The ground shook. Felicity looked about her. The left bank was still covered in dense vegetation. No escape there. To the right were glistening green banks. It seemed to be a bulge of rock covered in water that only allowed this slimy plant to grow.

Reuben was shouting instructions up ahead as the vibrations intensified. Felicity looked at Sib. Scaly head stretched to the length of his muscled neck, his nostrils flared as he tried to catch a scent. The two Lupata had gone to the front of the trail. They stood upright, heads raised and teeth bared, ready to defend. The tall Greens stood either side of the troupe, branches linked, a daisy chain of protection. The other plants and beasts huddled hopelessly in the centre. Felicity and Sib brought up the rear. Gus had quietly moved into position about a hundred feet back. *How on earth did he manage that?*

She quickly looked forwards again as Reuben shouted to the terrified group, 'Stand still, and wait for my instructions!' His voice sounded strong and confident in the shady pass.

Felicity saw him stride forwards towards the terrible noise. The two Lupata shadowed him closely. Another two creatures Felicity did not recognise moved forwards to take up their defensive positions. Reuben rounded a bend, and she saw him no more. The rumbling and thudding ceased about two minutes later. The ground stopped juddering. There was silence. Only a bird singing high in the trees was audible. Gus coughed gently behind them. He had quietly approached. Felicity looked directly into his big black eyes. They seemed calm. Her shoulders dropped a little.

'Have a drink, Felicity,' he said gently. He held out a container. It was beautiful. Woven coloured leaves covered in some sort of shiny glaze. Felicity took a sip. It was not the amber liquid of her first night, nor the cool, green drink of the forest. It was sweet and yet spicy. She took a little more.

'Thank you,' she said.

She heard some muttering from up ahead and peered at the spot where Reuben had disappeared. He reappeared smiling, and just after him arrived the most incredible creature. It was huge. It seemed to block out the sky as it rounded the bend. It took a few moments to take in its scale.

'A Taureau!' exclaimed Sib, beside her.

The Taureau walked slowly, yet Felicity could now hear the thud as its feet touched the ground.

'It looks like an overfed bull,' she said.

'A bull?' said Gus. 'What is a bull?'

'No, hang on,' she said, rudely ignoring Gus in her fascination. 'No, it's too hairy...too massive...it's like one of those pictures in history books of woolly mammoths, only bigger. So much bigger,' she said, inadvertently stepping back into one of Gus' spines.

'Ow,' she said, rubbing the back of her arm.

Sib smiled.

'Friends and followers,' said Reuben. 'We have a Taureau joining us. He will make his own introduction, of course.'

'Good afternoon, dear quest troupe and followers,' began the Taureau; his booming voice caused the poor Colour Changers to fly up into the air involuntarily. 'I most humbly apologise if my haste alarmed you. I understand from Reubenfourthousandth that I caused a little shake on the forest floor. For that, accept my sincerest apologies. I was keen to find you before dusk,' he said. The fur on his neck formed a fat, luxuriant cuff. His body was a deep, red-brown, dense, tangled mat. What a glorious colour – like a winter fox, thought Felicity. His head was so big it made Reuben standing beside him look like a child, and the Lupata who had seemed so large stood like tiny collie dogs at his heels.

'Now that is an aged Taureau,' said Gus.

'How old do you estimate, Toxic?' said Sib. Felicity realised it was probably the first time she had heard anyone other than Reuben talk to Gus.

'I should think he is the largest part of a whole genera-tion,' replied Gus, assessing the Taureau. Felicity chewed her bottom lip but stood firm. When she was really small, she had watched a herd of bulls snorting and roaring as they ran past her in the street, in southern Spain. She had told Al, once, and Al had snorted with delight at yet another inappropriate thing her parents had taken her to. But actually she couldn't remember being scared, or scarred, just overwhelmed by the colour and the roars of the crowd lining the pavements. She studied this magnificent beast as the images returned. *What would Al call him*, she wondered.

'Georges with an "s",' she pronounced with satisfaction.

'I beg your pardon, Felicity?' said Gus.

'I shall call him Georges,' she said. 'He reminds me of an old Frenchman. All words and gusto. I rather like him,' she added.

'That is interesting. The male Taureau prides himself on his attraction for females,' said Sib, smirking. 'Although this one, whilst being the largest I have ever witnessed, is also the ugliest I have ever seen.'

Felicity looked at Sib. His scaly eyes were wrinkled in delight as he shuffled from one fat, short leg to the other. Gus and Sib joined Reuben, who beckoned them all forwards, and Felicity reluctantly followed.

'Felicity, Gus, and Sib, I present to you, Taureautwo-thousandthfivehundredandtwenty-fourth,' he said.

The Taureau dipped his head in greeting. This was not a fast act. First he moved one leg in front of the other, then he shook his huge head and ever so slowly lowered it towards the earth until only the dark woolly jungle right between his ears was facing them. He snorted with the effort, and a group of Colour Changers were blown high into the sky. Everyone laughed, and the Taureau straightened up. He looked straight at Felicity. His eyes were a deep green and a little cloudy, but the expression in them was not. Felicity felt herself blush.

'It is an honour to meet such a fine young creature,' he said gallantly.

'I am happy to meet you, sir,' she replied. 'May I call you a more simple name?'

He bowed his head in agreement.

'Then I shall call you Georges,' she said.

'Felicity joins our quest from–'

'–afar,' finished Georges, still scrutinising Felicity.

Reuben hesitated, but as the Taureau said no more, he continued, 'And she finds our nomenclature difficult.' He looked up through the trees at the paling sky. 'The hour grows late, and we must reach the waters by nightfall. We shall all call you Georges, henceforth, with your permission, Taureautwothousandthfivehundredandtwenty-fourth. Now let us walk and talk.'

Everyone seemed eager to move off. This day had been long and exciting. Felicity wondered what food they would eat at the next camp.

*

They trekked hard and fast, and Felicity's legs were aching when at last they cleared the forest. In front, the landscape opened into a vast, grey plain. But in the distance Felicity saw a sparkle and smiled.

'Yes, Felicity, we reach the waters at last,' said Reuben, appearing as he always did without her noticing. She had missed him today. He wasn't very good at keeping his word to stay by her side. His mouth lifted in a mischievous grin, and she felt a bit strange. She shivered.

I miss your company, too, said his voice into her head, and then he continued aloud, 'but this trail throws new challenges each day.'

'Why is he here?' asked Felicity.

As if he was inside her head even when she wasn't aware of her thoughts, he replied, 'Georges was travelling before seeking a new mate, as his lifelong partner was lost many years ago. He says the rumours he hears are very worrying.'

'Has he heard of danger, then?' Felicity asked. She was still not sure how she felt about this mountain of a beast, in spite of his twinkly eyes, but if there was close danger she was glad to have him, too.

'No, don't be scared. We should be far from any Toxics, for now. No, his natural desire to preserve the Old World, which is inherent in a Taureau, simply prompted him to divert his journey to join us for a time, I think. He hasn't mentioned danger. His knowledge and strength are an unexpected gift. I hope to persuade him to stay with us as long as possible, in spite of the Taurelles.' Reuben's mouth lifted at one corner.

'Could you tell me more of Georges' kind?' asked Felicity, enjoying his company and determined to keep him by her side a little longer.

'Well, the Taureau are respected for their strength, their stamina, their stoicism, and they can carry wisdom. They, and not the Lupata, are chosen to guard the Sacred Caves because their strength, endurance and stability outweighs the fiery nature of the Lupata.'

Felicity was tired. Every question was answered with another mystery. What were the Sacred Caves, exactly? Why did they need guarding? Felicity sighed. It was hard not to think of home at times like this. How long would she have to be in this world? Would she ever be allowed home? A chill crept up her spine. She actually felt the hairs on her arms lift.

She glanced at Reuben, who was marching beside her. His profile was strong against the darkening sky. The bump on his nose fascinated her. She realised she was smiling. *I am terrified one minute and dreaming of kissing his nose the next.* The thought came unbidden to her mind. *Oh no, he is smiling now. Could he hear my thoughts? Did I conceal them?* Flustered, she strode forwards to catch up with Gus, who was trundling ahead of them.

As they crossed the slightly boggy plain, darkness fell. There was not much conversation. The Lupata led the group. Georges walked at the side of Reuben. The noise of his feet striking the ground was deadened in this boggy landscape, but the squelching was sufficiently loud. The thick fogs of before had not descended, but a clinging mist was rising from the earth. *Oh, this endless marching,* thought Felicity. Georges decided to sing to cheer her up.

He could feel her misery and wanted her to admire his deep, wonderful voice.

'La, la-la, la-laaaah, little Felicity la, la-la, la-laaaaaaaaaaaah,' he sang in a deep boom.

Felicity surreptitiously stuck her fingers in her ears. *He wouldn't see in the gloom*, she thought, not wanting to offend this proud old beast. His song lasted until they reached the water's edge.

Reuben and Georges organised the camp. Sib and Gus worked together to begin a fire from the driftwood on the beach. The Lupata scavenged for sand shoots, and the Colour Changers flew about distributing them. Felicity clutched her handful and bit into one. It was chewy and tasted a little like liquorice. It was dark grey and not attractive, but it was the best thing she had ever eaten, at that moment. Everyone sat or lay or leaned or piled up and chewed their sticks. The Lupata swallowed them whole. The Greens licked them delicately. She and Reuben chewed them slowly. Georges ate his entire supply in one mouthful and went in search of more. Felicity didn't like to ask how the leafy Colour Changers ate. But of course, Reuben was there in her head.

'They only require liquid,' he explained. 'It supplies them with all they need. When you are satisfied, Felicity, please sleep. You have done so well. Your kind are stronger than they look,' he said and reached out to touch her with a pat of reassurance, but found himself gently stroking her hair.

Felicity was quite pleased with her hair. It was a grubby blonde colour, but it was thick and grew fast. Its curl was enough to annoy her and enough to make her mother smile when she brushed it. It reached just above her waist and bounced when she walked. Reuben had been watching it with fascination for the last two days. The Orion hair was long and strong also. But it was dead straight. He tied his back with a woven cord. Reuben stroked her curls for a moment longer, and Felicity allowed it. She lay down with a sigh. Reuben felt Sib staring at him. He returned the gaze, his eyes steady and clear of expression. Sib looked away. Then Reuben left Felicity and strode amongst the weary travellers, ensuring everyone was settled. When he returned to Felicity, she was almost asleep.

'Sleep well, little Felicity,' he murmured as he finally lay down himself. His face was serious. 'For tomorrow we cross the seas to the Temperate North, and there I am not sure what to expect,' he murmured. Watching the flames gently flicker, his thoughts took him to his home. To Orion Country and the Orion women. He was ready to find his enharmonic, he knew. He felt the need within him. It was time to become mature.

7

Oceanids

As dawn broke, a huge torrent of water drenched the camp. Felicity leapt up with a scream. The others woke, gasping, and ran in all directions. They were soaked. The fire remains had splashed sideways, covering those too slow to move in black, soggy charcoal. Felicity looked for Reuben. He was standing on the shoreline, calmly talking to a whale, or something close to it. Its eye was as large as Felicity's head. This giant mammal's spume had saturated them, she realised. *They clearly don't do small in this world,* she thought, furiously squeezing out her soggy cape and shaking her sodden hair; the water droplets landed on her cheek, reeking of salty, smelly fish.

'Oh, gross!' Felicity said as she slushed through the sodden sand.

Reuben held his hand behind him to signal her to stop approaching whilst he continued his conversation with the creature.

Gus came up beside Felicity. 'A mighty Oceanid!' he exclaimed.

The mammoth's eye swivelled and bored into him. He felt himself thoroughly searched. As it returned its glare to Reuben, Felicity could see Gus' spines trembling. She wasn't sure how to touch him, with those long spikes, so she leant across and looked deep into his eyes. They were the same pools of sorrow as the first time she saw him. Dark and lonely. She felt the horror of isolation flowing through her like an icy draft.

Reuben had finished communicating with the Oceanid,

and he dropped back to Felicity and Gus.

'Right,' he said. 'Lupata board first, then all other followers, and key troupe members please bring up the rear. Georges, would you board last so Oceanidonethousandthfivehundred can redistribute our weight. You probably weigh more or less our equivalent.'

'What!' exclaimed Felicity. 'We are mounting that thing!'

The Oceanid's eye swivelled fast and pierced her with its black nothingness. She felt her mind being trawled. Images of the Welsh hills and waterfalls she so loved, the golden stone villages of her birth, beloved people, planes, bridges, her dog, and steeples...all flashed through her involuntarily as it flicked and picked her images. She fought to blank them. *How dare it?* But it was like a fist grabbing hold of her. Then it stopped. A voice came into her head, much like the voice of the mist the day she had bumped into this Old World. *My deepest apology for the intrusion, young stunted one, but time is short, and knowledge is essential.* Felicity's face reddened with anger, but she kept her eyes down and followed the others.

Georges was huffing at Reuben's comment. 'I weigh no more than a little feather,' he said. His neck was arched, and he tossed his huge head, snorting vociferously. The poor Colour Changers were being blown all over the place. Reuben raised his hands in apology.

'Your fine physique must attract the Taurelles in droves,' he said, with a most serious countenance.' A rampaging Taureau, and furthermore by far the largest anyone in this company had ever witnessed, was the last thing he needed this morning. The wind was picking up, and the Oceanid would only grace them with her offer of transport for so long. It was beneath the dignity of Oceanids to act as cargo-carriers, but the quest's importance broke all recognised rules. Reuben knew she must be acting on the orders of the Ancients, the elders of her kind. But she could still change her mind. They must board, and board right now.

The tall Greens stood in the shallow waves, craning across those unable to swim and climb up the warm banks of the creature. The encrusted sea-life melded to the mammal's blue-grey sides gave Felicity a hold, and she heaved herself up skilfully, glad for once of school gym with Miss Tucker. Georges made his grand entrance into the waves. He was unceremoniously lifted by a column of the largest Greens, their branches creaking with the strain of this vast beast's weight.

The mighty Oceanid set her course. She arched her smooth, warm back, and they all nestled in the dip. *Like ducklings on a mother's back*, thought Felicity, with a smile. She sat down to avoid falling and looked back at the land they were leaving very fast behind. The Oceanid slid smoothly and extremely efficiently through the dark green waters. Felicity sighed, and Reuben moved close to her.

Everyone was silent as they left the land and the first step of the journey behind. Reuben thought of his task. The Oceanid had informed him they must go north to find the next member. He was relieved. They were only three! He had to foil an army of bitter, enraged Toxics. He wondered how. The Orion elders had confidence he could achieve this. He looked up to the sky. *Help me*, but only the sea birds' cries returned.

The Lupata had informed Reuben they would leave once ashore. He had Georges for longer, of course, but he still wished they could stay. He chewed the side of his finger as he assessed the situation so far. Well, he had successfully travelled east and had picked up Felicity, who had clearly been sent by another world to help. He saw from her thoughts that she felt lost. He saw she had no information about the quest – not so different from him, really. But he could teach her about the Old World; she had already learnt so much. In her mind he read intelligence and great strength – and their connection was strong. He felt it like a rope of steel – they would work well together. She was small, of course, but he had seen tiny Orion defeat larger in childhood scuffles. The strength on the inside counted for far more – this he knew.

His plan, then, would be to travel fast, take on members that presented themselves, if they felt true to the quest, and then in the absence of any signs, he would return home to consult the Orion elders. It was like jumping into the void and simply trusting that the path of the quest would appear, like an invisible safety net. He would not falter. He trusted this Old World to help him. He had grown up with its mystical signs and hidden powers. However, it would be wise to seek and speak with the Aquatics to try to discover a clearer outline of what might be. The rebel Toxics were sadly misguided, and he knew it must stop. He shook his head, as if to resettle its weight for a moment.

Felicity saw the movement and wondered where his big mind was wandering. She looked at him discreetly. He really was so...well, gorgeous! His dark hair was whipping about as the wind loosened it from the cord, and his olive, downy skin glowed in the flashes of sunshine. She found herself staring at the slight bump on the bridge of his nose. She wanted to touch it, to stroke her finger down it. She leant back on the warm beast and stared up at the skies. *So like our beautiful earth and sky*, she thought sleepily. But if she turned her head, the weird and wonderful collection of lives reclining and standing in this dugonic dell were a shocking reminder of where she was not.

The swell of the sea got larger, and Felicity started to feel queasy. She was surprised to find she did not feel cold. She watched the others to take her mind off the uncomfortable feeling. Georges was sidling carefully up to her. The sun was eclipsed as he eased himself in front of her. The Oceanid let out a groan of irritation as the movement of his massive bulk necessitated she reposition herself quickly.

Georges lowered his head, and Felicity tried not to cringe away. His face was not a pretty sight. His furry coat almost covered his eyes, tiny lights in a cavern of fur. His nose was encrusted with limpets or something like them, and his lips were caked with substances Felicity was not keen to analyse. *I suppose if you live for thousands of years, you pick up a few warts along the way,* she thought, trying to remember to block those thoughts, so as not to offend him. She had noticed as they moved further west that she could hear the murmuring of minds if she tried to tune in. Like a radio picking up a far-off station. It felt wrong to listen in to someone else's thoughts. But it was fun, she acknowledged, with a little guilt. She looked at Georges, hoping he had not read her assessment of his beauty. His eyes seemed calm. And something else as he sniffed her scent.

'Gross,' she muttered.

Georges looked at her and spoke. 'So, sweet-smelling young one,' he said in his gravelly, rumbling voice, 'what make you of this quest?'

'Um, I am honoured to be invited along?' said Felicity, uncertain of protocol with such an aged personage.

'The Old World has been shifting slowly on its axis,' said Georges. 'For many years, we Taureau have sensed these changes. So slowly they have insidiously crept in, and now, like and avalanche of boulders in my beautiful country, these unhappy Toxics try to tip our whole balance with their misery and their complaining.' His voice increased in volume as his anger rose, and Felicity looked desperately for Reuben. But it was Gus who came to her rescue.

'Forgive me, aged sire, for joining your talk, but being of their kind, I feel moved to help explain,' he said.

Georges kept his head facing Felicity. He did not move, nor acknowledge Gus had spoken. There was an awkward silence. Then Georges raised his massive shoulders, inhaling the longest breath. Felicity began counting. She reached forty before Georges began to let it go. He lifted his head to the sky and let the long stream of air gush out. Felicity was relieved. She had thought she was about to join the fate of the Colour Changers and be blown up into the air or, worse, into the deep, black water beneath them.

'This quest hopes to rectify the imbalance caused by your kind,' Georges said, finally turning his face towards Gus. 'It hopes to restore our world to its former harmony and beauty. The oldest, of whom I am proud to claim a part, must listen to the young ones. The younger generations own the world. It is their turn to fight for it and to shape it. Reuben the Orion is well chosen, but...' Georges faltered and fell silent at this point.

He slowly turned his head to Gus and said, 'If you want so much to be a part of this world, then first you had better take the time to listen to it and to learn. I have travelled and listened through the passing of the years. I have seen injustice from the old beasts and plants to the Toxics. I have also seen bitterness and closed hearts from you, the Toxics. Now all I hear is anger. We who have been allowed to rest many, many centuries on this world learn that all happens as it should. There is a reason for your birth, and there is a reason for your survival. This should have been resolved by now. But the imbalances increased as the bitterness and closed minds fed them. It is too late for unaided harmony. It is time this quest discovers the answers. Somewhere is a healing water to quench the fires of anger. Somewhere is the answer to put out the fury and cries of the new rebel Toxics that threaten not only themselves but the world they claim a right to inherit. Reuben shows courage in an Orion I have not witnessed in many hundreds of years, and the optimism of his youth is essential. If you are here, Toxic, then I, Georges, will accept the way of the world. It is a time of change. We must make sure this change is the right one. Let us work together. I will join this quest; will you work with me?'

The ancient Taureau and gentle Toxic faced each other, and the sea winds abated. The water swell dropped to a calm ripple. The Oceanid paused in her journey. All the passengers were listening. Georges' voice had travelled far, and high in the sky Felicity saw those shapes again. *What are they?*

Finally Gus bowed his odd, long head to Georges. Reuben watched with pleasure. He had so hoped Georges would stay. *Seeing a Toxic prepared to fight for the quest against his own kind must have done it,* he thought, unaware he had also impressed Georges with his courage. He put an arm around Felicity's shoulders. The Oceanid broke the moment with another pouring of water that saturated them all. There was laughter, and then someone shouted, 'Land! I see land!' They had arrived safely at the Temperate North.

8

Pippi

The Oceanid rolled sideways as she reached shallow water, and everyone slid clumsily into the sea. Felicity gasped for air as the rocking water repeatedly sucked her under its icy depths. She heard Reuben in her head, *Relax, Felicity. Relax and you will rise.* And she did, popping to the surface just in time to refill her aching lungs. The plants and beasts attained the shore in a variety of ways, and by the time Felicity stood trembling on the sand, the Oceanid had totally disappeared. Submerged like a silent submarine.

'Charming,' said Felicity, wringing out the scarf Reuben had lent her. She had been drying out nicely on the breezy crossing, and now all was soaked again.

'It is not usual for an Oceanid to take passengers,' said Sib, scuffling up to her. 'We are lucky she did not change her mind mid-ocean and leave us in the sea.' He looked pleased at this thought.

Felicity glanced at his tiny wrinkled eyes and wondered. But the thought of those dark, humpy depths simply made her very glad, at this moment, to be standing on firm, if slightly sinking ground. Reuben was shouting instructions to the assembled, soggy crew, and they began to move off. They had travelled all day on the water, and night was falling. Felicity had no idea how far they had come. *The air here smells different – like England*, she thought. It was grey and quite cold.

They climbed the dunes, and Felicity saw a landscape similar to home, but with villages of huge thorny hedges instead of houses. She shivered. The light was poor, and

Reuben was keen to get them all into the shelter of those Thorns. As they reached the edges of a village, Felicity heard snarling and yelping, and excited cries.

The two Lupata moved in front of them and said to Reuben, 'We leave you here, Reubenfourthousandth. We will listen for news of your quest. Have faith, young one.' And then they were gone, loping off, heads raised to find the source of the shouts.

'They don't mess around with lengthy good-byes,' muttered Felicity to herself. She was still cross from being deposited in a frothing sea, and she was hungry. Her mother was pleased she had a 'healthy appetite', and had taught her to go outside and work off some energy after meals rather than go hungry. Freya ate like a bird, but she didn't move much, either. Al claimed Felicity had two stomachs. Right now they both were complaining for food, she thought. She blew out her cheeks to dispel the hunger tension.

This terrain was so creepily like home and yet not. She had decided to enjoy this adventure, and she did trust Reuben to help her return home, but, in this countryside, with the smell of nutty leaves crushing under her feet – home felt a very, very long way away. As they trudged on through the dark, leafy lanes, she let the tears fall unchecked. She heard her mother's voice, 'Sometimes it's good to cry, darling.' She could smell her mother's soft fragrance, and the tears came faster. Sobs started to make her shoulders shake.

Without warning, a huge, furry warmth collided into her from a side alley, knocking her to the ground. A rough tongue licked her face, and a furry nose nuzzled under her chin, crunching her teeth together in a painful clack. Reuben ran back and helped her up, elbowing the young Lupata aside. But she wouldn't leave Felicity. She snarled gently at Reuben and stood between them, facing Reuben.

'It seems you have a protector, Felicity,' said Reuben, standing dead still.

The Lupata spoke. Her voice was not at all like the pair

who had left. It was clear and pure. *Like the chime of a golden bell*, thought Felicity. 'BACK OFF!' growled the pure, clear voice. Well, perhaps there was a hint of steel, Felicity conceded to herself.

'Steady, Lupata unnamed,' said Reuben quietly, and as she heard his voice, the Lupata relaxed a little. Her raised hackles slowly settled, and she introduced herself.

'I am Lupatafourthousandthandforty-four,' she said.

'I am Reubenfourthousandth,' replied Reuben with a smile. 'We share a generational age, Lupatafourthousandthandforty-four.'

'Oh, for goodness' sake, this is ridiculous,' interrupted Felicity. She turned to the young Lupata. 'I am not from your world, as you see. And I cannot manage your names. Would you mind terribly if I gave you a slightly shorter name?' she said, quickly wiping her eyes. But as she finished the sentence, she realised what she had just done. The Lupata had appeared as a beautiful, furry friend to her, but looking straight at her now, Felicity remembered she was actually a triple-sized wolf. It was hard to see her completely clearly in the gloom, but Felicity could see a large row of teeth as the Lupata replied, 'Young strange one, you may find an easier name for me if that helps you.'

Felicity looked at the outline of her defender. Why did she feel so close to this creature? It was a mystery, yet Felicity was beginning to see that all in this world fitted like pieces in a jigsaw.

The Lupata entered her mind. *Felicity, he calls you*, said the gentle voice in her head.

Felicity looked at the shining eyes of the female and enjoyed the silent conversation. *Do others hear us?* she asked.

If we want them to, replied the Lupata.

I had a beloved dog in my world. She was my best friend until she was too old to share her life with mine anymore. Would you be offended if I gave you her name?

What was her name?

Felicity knew the Lupata understood, and it filled the ache for home.

'Pippi,' she said aloud. She looked at the size of her new friend and wondered if the name was ridiculous. But Pippi had been two hundred percent loyal, three hundred percent brave, and her spirit was as big as this Lupata.

You are a good soul, Felicity of the strange world. I see your friend in your mind. Not so different from us, in many ways. I am honoured to accept her name.

Felicity felt a warm glow. Perhaps old Pippi could see them, she thought. She felt perhaps she really could. She smiled at what her dear dog would have done, faced with this namesake. Growled and faced her, she was absolutely sure, even though she would not have reached above the kneecap of this Lupata.

Reuben broke into their silent conversation. He spoke aloud, for the benefit of all. 'Tomorrow we will go to the great green city and find the arena, where the annual Lupata mating ceremonies have just begun. We have passed north to avoid the Toxics, who we are not yet ready to meet. Tomorrow I will consult with the Aquatics. I have fulfilled the first task, which was to find the stranger in the east.' He smiled at Felicity. 'Sib, Gus and now Georges honour us by joining the quest.' And here he bowed to each in turn before continuing, 'The Orion elders foretold that key members would seek and find me, and all is happening as foretold. We can enjoy a moment with the Lupata in their renowned and spectacular contests.'

It was Pippi who led the way to their campsite for the night. It was deep in the heart of this herbaceous settlement. Felicity was relieved the snarling and growling had settled down. The night was peaceful, and there were many, many stars above. Yet Felicity could still see the odd shape high in the sky. Pippi and Georges organised a fire. Gus was helping give out food, and Sib was involved in a deep conversation with a Green. Felicity grabbed her chance to ask Reuben at last about the sky shapes.

'They are the Strata,' he replied. 'They are the only living things of our world about which we know little. It is told they have been here as long as the first Green, who planted the first knowledge Root. They were the diplomats and the peacekeepers. Any breaches of harmony or balance would be resolved by them, if requested. They are the only living things with no enharmonic.'

Except the Toxics, thought Felicity.

'They remain solitary, detached, and therefore non-judgemental in all things. Until the birth of the Toxics, they were considered omnipotent as a solution to any troubles.'

'I thought you said the Old World was perfectly balanced and all understood all, and there was only joy and harmony,' said Felicity.

Reuben accepted some drink from Gus and took a sip. 'Well, yes. But life is a continuous flow and ebb, Felicity,' he explained, 'like the tides of our oceans and seas. Joy and peace rise and fall to a greater or lesser extent. You see we have strong creatures. The Lupata need to spar to hone their skills of aggression and defence. The Taureau seek the self-challenge of the greatest strengths, with the best earning the prized position of cave guardian. Every new young Green seeks knowledge, with the hopes to grow to a Stipple Green, the elite of the Greens. We Orion pride ourselves on wisdom and grace.

'Territories have to be defended, in order that the young can grow safely. Plants can become tempted to outgrow their lands or take on characteristics of another plant. Even in a world of peace and joy, life has a way of causing mischief occasionally. That is the spirit that keeps it thriving. Squabbles are resolved within a Banyan, within each community, but if peace cannot be found, then the Strata are called in to calmly and dispassionately restore balance.'

'What do they look like?' said Felicity. Sometimes these long explanations of this intricate world could be a little exhausting. And she was still absolutely ravenous. But the Strata were tantalisingly mysterious.

'Well, their wingspan is equal to the length of an Oceanid,' said Reuben. 'They are very muscular. They have feathers, not fur.'

Makes sense, she thought.

'Their eyesight is, of course, superb, as they fly at such great heights. Their heads are large, and their feet small. Their beauty is in their colours; they fly all the colours of the skyarc. Reds, yellows, blues, greens. Violets, crimsons, vibrant orange. And their feathers reflect the light. They are truly beautiful,' he said in a slightly hushed voice.

'Will they help us on this quest?' Felicity asked.

The others had gathered round the now blazing fireside, and it was Sib who answered her. 'The Aquatics that I spoke to suggested we will need their help,' he said, enjoying the power of his knowledge. Pippi had edged a little closer to Felicity as Sib and Gus had joined them.

Georges, as the senior authority on the old ways, added, 'When the time comes to enlist the Strata, we will know. They will present themselves – do not fear.'

Two of the tall Greens handed round some lumpy, grey balls. They looked revolting.

'What are these?' asked Felicity.

Pippi answered, 'They are the main food of the Temperate North, Felicity. Stod balls. Try one. They taste better than they look!'

Felicity bit into one. It tasted earthy and a little like a dumpling. It was easier to swallow once she got used to its lumpy texture. Everyone seemed very hungry. Perhaps it was the climate or the sea air of the journey. The stod balls diminished very fast. Georges ate tons, and there were a few grumbles of complaint.

'How do you expect me to find my little Taurelle?' he said to the complainers. 'I must keep up my legendary strength.'

Sitting just in front of him, Felicity heard a familiar noise emanate from behind her and thought she smelt something rather unpleasant, but decided it best not to mention it. As the fire burnt down to embers, the troupe fell silent. Pippi had stationed herself firmly beside Felicity, and Reuben had to gently lie down on the other side. Felicity loved to watch his face in the firelight. It was becoming a familiar and comforting sight as she went to sleep each night. She heard Pippi grumble. She wondered why Pippi had come. *I will ask her in the morning*, she thought sleepily.

*

The morning began with a fine drizzle of rain that seeped in between all the cracks and crevices of clothing Felicity had on. There was no need to dampen the embers of the fire this day. It was hard to get up, but with Georges snorting and Pippi growling, everyone was rounded up, and the march to the capital of the Temperate North began. Reuben told them to step out. Felicity decided to question Pippi on what was clearly going to be another gruelling trek.

'Are you here to join in the ceremonies?' she asked.

Pippi shielded Felicity from the now driving rain as she replied, 'Last year I participated, but my mate was killed on the journey back to the frozen wastes of our land. I have not borne cubs, and so I return. I achieved maturity here last year. I fought and gained my mate's respect, and then he was gone. I have had to make the arduous journey back. Luckily I am strong. I very much want cubs, and the danger was no matter.'

It didn't really explain why she had set herself as some sort of protector, thought Felicity, but she couldn't think how to approach this without sounding rude. So she said, 'Tell me about your land,' and snuggled in behind the Lupata's shoulder. *She smells of wet dog*, thought Felicity. Pungent but wonderfully familiar.

'We have mountains of thick forest and plains that ice over in the cold seasons. The forests become carpeted with snow, and we make deep burrows in the loose soil where we shelter our young. A little further south, the caves begin. They are our playgrounds in the warmer months. Deep caverns of varying rocks, swirling shapes of magic interspersed with rivers and tributaries where the Aquatics visit us with news of the world and our friends.'

'Your world is so similar to mine, and yet so different,' replied Felicity.

'What is your homeland like, Felicity?' asked Pippi.

This was the first time someone had thought to ask Felicity about home. Even Reuben was so intent on his precious quest. It was strange that no one had been curious. Perhaps it was the feeling of completeness that this world had had for so long that curiosity had waned over the centuries. Felicity was silent, and Pippi patiently waited. The sound of thumping and slithering, sliding and crunching as the small army travelled was all that could be heard. Felicity found that now someone had asked her, she didn't want to talk about home. She concentrated on the feeling of her damp jeans sticking to her legs as she walked. She glanced quickly up at Pippi's huge head. Perhaps if she left it long enough, Pippi would forget the question.

No, I won't, said an amused voice in her head. *But no matter. Another time.*

9

The Aquatics

They had been walking most of the morning, and Felicity was flagging. Fortunately at that moment Reuben called a halt.

'We stop here for an hour or so. I must talk with the Aquatics,' he said. 'Felicity!' he called out, not seeing her at first. 'Follow me,' he commanded.

'Lovely,' murmured Felicity. 'Just as I was going to collapse.' She sighed, and Pippi licked her as she passed.

'Felicity, take a breath and use the energy of the land as I taught you,' said Reuben, seeing how tired she was.

Felicity looked around. There were no wide, open spaces or exotic landscapes. Just thick, thorny hedges, mulchy paths and plenty of rain. How on earth was this squabby place supposed to energise her? Reuben stopped and held her hand. He breathed deeply, with his eyes closed. Then slowly, with his warm hand holding hers, she felt a balmy, soothing energy fill her up. From her tingling toes, up through her calves, across her lower back and round to her tummy, it just rolled on and on. She found herself breathing a deep, deep breath as the lovely feeling travelled up through her chest, over her shoulders, and then down her arms to her fingertips. Reuben opened his eyes and looked at her. Their hazel brown depths flickered and shone.

'Good?' he said, smiling.

'Mmmm, yes,' she replied, smiling back at him so that he noticed the little dimple in her left cheek. She blushed as his gaze stayed on her face.

'Come on,' he said suddenly, breaking the spell.

They walked through dark green paths until Felicity was utterly disorientated. Was there no open space in this stuffy land? Then finally, they entered a clearing. The thick hedges had ended abruptly, and they stood in a small meadow, with a brook softly babbling at the far side. The rain had stopped, and a pale sun was shining onto the wet grass. Reuben let go of her hand and squatted down, peering into the stream. He swished the water as if he was trying to see something more clearly. Then he lay right down and turned his ear towards the water.

'What are you doing?' Felicity said, trying not to giggle.

'Ssssh!' he replied.

Felicity was silent. The water gurgled and spat a little. Reuben lay very quietly. Felicity flopped down on the soggy grass, trying to put the corner of the cape under her bottom. In the quiet of the moment her ears picked up a strange sound, a new noise. It was like a soft wind travelling down a tunnel. 'What's that noise?' Her voice was loud in this peaceful place.

'SSSSSSH!' said Reuben, frowning with concentration. He sat up but continued to stare intently into the bubbling flow. As Felicity accustomed herself to the strange noise, she realised it had pattern and rhythm. It was a chorus of sibilant whispers rising and falling like an orchestra of wind, and as she tuned her ear to its sounds, she heard its music. The Aquatics were singing. Singing to Reuben; their rubbery tendrils gently rising and falling in time with the crescendo and diminuendo of sound.

'*Do not linger, linger in the north.*
The Toxics build, gather more and more.
Hurry, brave Reuben, hurry on your way.
Go to the matings; go this very day.
There they'll find you, those who seek the quest.
Tarry not; fast be on your way.
Come back home, Reuben, come back to the west.
You'll need full maturity to fulfil this quest.

Stay alert…stay alert…stay alert…' and then all Felicity could hear was the whispering sound again.

'Wait!' said Reuben. 'Please wait. I have questions,' and he swirled the water around with his hand. But the tendrils had stopped rising and falling, and they slowly retracted down deep back into the watercourse. Reuben dropped his head.

Felicity sat still. She chewed her bottom lip. It felt cold. She looked up. Big grey clouds scudded above them. Her damp hair whipped her cheek. She shivered. Reuben continued to sit absolutely still. Felicity struggled to her feet, stiff with immobility. She walked down the small slope towards Reuben, but hesitated as she came close. *He looks sad*, she thought.

'Sit by me, Felicity. Sit and be.' Reuben spoke softly.

Felicity knelt down and laid her hand tenderly on his arm. She couldn't help it. She knew she was beginning to care very much about this kind, brave, young Orion. Reuben's shoulders lifted as he took a huge breath and then slowly, slowly let it out. Felicity could smell his warm, musky scent. They were so close she could see the beads of damp moisture clinging to a lock of hair that flicked his temple in the breeze. She closed her eyes.

Then he spoke. She was not sure whether his voice was in her head or in her ears. *Felicity, dear Felicity, I have so much to tell you about me and my world. This quest demands much from me. But you must know, young Felicity, how my heart is eased to have you come and share my path. Once we leave the Temperate North, which we must very soon, I will tell you of my people. I long to share with you. My time is close. My enharmonic calls me to soul-bond and let us both reach our maturity. You will know more of me, Felicity, once she triggers my maturity.*

'I promise you, dear Felicity,' he was whispering now, 'I will find a way,' and Felicity felt his warm breath on her face. She couldn't breathe. *What does he mean?* But nothing mattered. Her mind was simply full of his voice, of his smell, of his almond-shaped eyes. He smiled and then gently backed away. *He knows*, she thought, *how I feel*.

A flock of birds broke the silence as they flapped up from a bush, disturbed by someone. Reuben grabbed her hand, and they ran to the nearest hedge.

'Reuben, Felicity!' growled Pippi's familiar voice as she burst into the clearing. 'The day passes.' She leapt to stand between them. Kneeling down, she offered Felicity her back.

'A ride?' said Felicity.

'Yes, Pippi is right. We have delayed too long,' said Reuben.

Felicity climbed up carefully, using Pippi's bent front leg to help her mount. 'Wow!' she said and then grabbed the coarse fur as Pippi bounded away.

10

Scratt

The matings had commenced. They arrived at the town, Thornton, in the late afternoon. In front of them were the Derngates. Felicity peered up at the tall wooden structures. They were magnificent. Gnarled and knotted, they could have grown there naturally, but the tightly woven strands knitting them together revealed their construction. Today they were flung wide in honour of the contests, and the small band of quest followers passed through. Georges followed, needing the entire gap for himself.

The roars of excitement from the crowd were the first thing to reach Felicity's ears. But as they reached the centre of Thornton and rounded the last bend, the furious snarls of the Lupata became clear. Looking behind her, Felicity could just see the tops of the great gates above the hedges. They were closing. The day was almost over, and the town was preparing for the evening. In front of them, the arena awaited.

Georges thundered up and bellowed, 'Now you will see some magnificent contests, little Felicity.' His great nostrils flared, and he shook his head. Surrounding spectators stepped back as this great, snorting, outsized Taureau pranced into the arena.

Felicity looked about her in wonder. They were in a vast clearing. Its floor was sandy and dry. Large Thorns had arranged themselves to close off all entrances apart from seven openings. There were only two wide ones. The remaining five were narrow and dark. The spectators gathered in self-arranged groups between these entrances. They continually jostled to stay the furthest away from the gaps. Two young Lupata locked in a vicious wrangle rolled and thudded into the quest group, scattering them everywhere. The beasts sprang up and tore after each other, their blood-flecked saliva splattering Pippi and Felicity as they flew past. The larger one's eye flicked a glance at Pippi, and Felicity heard her softly growl.

'Not for you, you brute,' she said, her large eyes surveying the chaotic scene.

Felicity ran to the back and grabbed Reuben's arm. 'Is there no control?' she shouted above the noise. 'Can't you make them stop, Reuben?!' she cried out. But her voice was lost in the tumultuous sound of the giant wolves' battles. Pippi stayed focused on the action, and Reuben led Felicity to a quiet spot near the hedges.

'This is their calling, Felicity,' he said. 'The Thorns honour this great event by allowing their defences to be assaulted. The Lupata have travelled far to seek their Thorn enharmonic, and having triggered maturity, they must compete to find a good mate. It is the way of things and always has been. The competition is fierce, and the injuries may be great, but the rewards are great also,' he continued. He was looking at Felicity and found his eyes fixed to her mouth. It was a wide mouth, and her lips were pink. He inspected her face further. Her eyes were one of his favourite colours – a sort of blue-green. Her small chin jutted out. *A strong face, but with much beauty*, he thought.

Felicity stared back at him, annoyed but distracted from her fear. How rude! She may have peered at him now and then, like the first time she saw him–

And just like our first meeting, you are making me smile, he said, interrupting her thoughts with his silent words.

Felicity didn't know what was so amusing. The noise of these overgrown wolves was terrible, and the pungent smell of their sweat and blood was sickening. She was horrified by the violence. How could they all think this was

70

an entertainment? She wanted to rest and eat after today's travels, but here they were in some sort of Roman amphitheatre. She expected a gladiator to stride out, half-naked, at any moment. She narrowed her eyes, and Reuben's smile increased even further. It was impossible to stay angry with him, though, when he smiled so beautifully.

Reuben relented. 'The Lupata will soon stop. The diminishing light will make the sparring too dangerous.'

Felicity snorted inelegantly as a Lupata was helped away with its left ear dangling and a great tear in its throat flapping and gushing blood.

'Only a surface wound,' she heard it murmur in a small voice. Its victor stood proudly and let out a howl of glory that bleached all other sound.

'A great victory,' said Pippi to Reuben, loping over to them. 'It was a son of Lupatafourthousandth that was defeated. He will not be pleased.'

Felicity saw the victor literally grab a large grey female by the scruff of her neck and drag her out of the arena. The female allowed this. 'Charming,' said Felicity.

'She is very lucky to have this mate,' said Pippi. 'He will make good cubs. Our lands are harsh, and our young must be strong.' She loped away, carrying her head a little lower than usual.

Felicity knew she had a lot to learn yet about this simple, raw world.

A chorus of howls ended the day's contests. The light was fading fast. Competing Lupata stopped immediately and left by the narrow exits. The crowds and newly-matched pairs of Lupata left by the two wider gaps.

'Where are the single Lupata going?' Felicity asked Sib, who had sidled up. He was eating something that looked like a shiny stick. It smelt a little nutty and sweet. Felicity licked her lips. Sib grinned and ignored her.

'They are going to cleanse their wounds and rest for tomorrow's excitement,' answered Georges in his normal

71

bellow. His bulk ensured there was always a good space around him. Felicity decided tomorrow she would shelter by him. In spite of his large body, his legs were short, and it would be hard for thrown Lupata to clear his underbelly.

Cheered by her plan, Felicity asked Reuben, 'What was Sib eating? It looked like a stick but smelt good? I thought it was only stod balls in the Temperate North?'

'No, we do have a few variations,' he replied. 'That was a sticky bud. The Thorns produce them in vast piles for this annual event. Their recipe is secret.'

Naturally, thought Felicity. 'Can we get some?'

'Tomorrow,' said Reuben, 'in the arena.'

'Oh, goody, stod balls for supper,' she said loudly.

Reuben raised his eyebrow at her temper.

Georges snorted. His experience of Taurelles was silence is best at these times. 'Reuben,' he said, 'where will we sleep tonight, my friend?'

As the weary group wove their way through the narrow damp avenues once more, Felicity looked at the Thorns, who stood like sentries as they passed. They were tall with lovely swirls and patterns on their trunks. Their branches were close, and within them were slightly broad, flat spikes. She presumed the avenues of bush simply sat there all year. Their entire life cycle one of waiting. For what?

'They are happy to just be,' said a tiny Thorn who had rustled up beside her.

Felicity looked down at him. She wasn't quite sure where his face was so she politely looked a little above his fluffy bright green new growth.

'We perform our enharmonic duty with the Lupata at the matings, and then we are free to form our own alliances. The soil nourishes us, and we have the year to meditate in peace,' he said. 'The annual excitement of the matings is a time of great energy for us, and it is enough.'

His voice was chirpy and strident, like a bossy little boy, she thought. Felicity's dimple appeared as she smiled at him.

'Thank you,' she said. 'May I introduce myself? I am Felicity Isabel Penfold, and I am not of your world.'

'I know,' he said.

'And your name is?' asked Felicity.

'You couldn't pronounce it.'

Felicity's face wrinkled up as she made a face. The little Thorn jumped back, unsure of this new expression.

'Thorntenthousandth,' she guessed.

He laughed. Those around chuckled. His laughter was infectious, and Felicity found herself giggling too.

'No, no,' he said, breathless, 'try again.'

'Thornthreehundredthousandththirtythird,' said Felicity, her tongue thick with the tongue-twister.

'Nope!' he said. 'I am Thornsixthousandsixty.' He did a little bow as he said it.

Felicity bowed back and then said, 'May I call you by a name I can remember, Thornsixthousandsixty?'

The young Thorn nodded in acquiescence, and Felicity pondered on it as they walked along. The air was damp, and the sound of dripping water sliding off each rubbery leaf onto its neighbour created a backdrop of sound as they squelched along. Felicity sighed. It had been a long day.

At that moment, there was a shout and a scuffle behind them. Pippi knocked them aside as she rushed to the defence. Young Thorn planted himself between Felicity and the noises. *Defensive from young*, she thought, as the diminutive bush protected her. Pippi didn't return. Reuben and Gus set off to see what had happened, and Georges gathered the remainder of the group together. The hedge walls were high. It was almost dark, and other spectators were long gone to their homes.

Felicity shivered and watched Sib. He always stood alone unless she, Reuben, Georges or Gus talked to him. Pippi seemed to avoid him as much as possible. The Sibilin were not comfortable in this Old World. Perhaps these changing times would bring out a better side to the Sibilin. She walked up to him.

'Who are your enharmonics, Sib?' she asked.

He looked at her in the gloom. His small eyes grew smaller. 'The Colour Changers,' he finally answered.

'Gosh,' said Felicity. She appraised the Colour Changers who had been with them on this journey so far. They still looked like small balls of leaves. She looked at Sib, tipping her head to one side as if to make the two species meet better on a slanted view.

Sib watched her. He sighed. 'We do not question the laws of our world,' he said and half-dropped his eyelids as he continued, 'Our soul bondings are brief and we rarely re-seek our enharmonic.'

'Why would you, Sib?' she asked, confused. She had thought this part was pretty simple: one plant, one beast; they meet and trigger, (somehow) their maturity; then they go off and find a partner of their own kind for the rest of their life, or thereabouts.

'Why would you re-seek your enharmonic even if you wanted to?' she repeated.

'We can use our combined enharmonic energy in a time of crisis, if absolutely critical. But it is dangerous and rarely done. It saps us both and may end our lives.'

'So why would you?' said Felicity, even more confused. 'Why don't you just deal with the crisis with your own mate? Why return to a Colour Changer, or whatever?'

'Because the special combination of plant and beast is possible only with two enharmonics. They share a secret link, as you heard Gus explain. This draws from the energies of the world and its mysteries. This is the greatest energy of all,' Sib said. He sidled off, bored by her questions.

Felicity tried to picture Sib and a pile of leaves as they sort of squashed together. It didn't really work. She hoped never to see this mystical re-reunion between any of them if it spelt impending crisis, anyway. She had decided to name young Thorn 'Scratt' after a character in a book she had read once, and was just about to tell him when Pippi came running round the corner. Gus hung on to her tail, and Reuben was pounding behind.

'Quick, quick,' Reuben shouted. 'Move! Run! Follow Pippi. QUICK!' he screamed as they all hesitated. Reuben grabbed Felicity's hand and tugged her along. Her feet were only touching the ground every other step. She was panting, the blood swooshed in her ears, and she felt faint. Her jelly-legs were giving way. She was going to fall. What was happening? Reuben looked truly scared, and she was terrified.

Young Thorn cried out, 'There, Pippi, there!' He pointed to a gap in the hedge that was barely noticeable. The whole group tumbled through. Young Thorn wedged himself into the narrow opening, and the hedge seemed complete. Everyone stood in the secret clearing. Shoulders heaved, and breaths were gasping. But the thick wall of green occluded sound; they were safe.

Then Felicity heard them. Ugly, strange voices. A creaky language like the silly croaks she and Freya had made as children that had the whole family laughing as they tried to decode it. But why could she hear it? Was the hedge breaking down? Her heart jumped a beat. She took a shaky breath and looked to the others. Gus was standing totally still and listening hard. His big eyes looked at her, and she understood. He was mind-listening, and she was catching his thoughts. She looked at Reuben. He was frowning hard. *He can't understand.* It was up to her and Gus. She focused on Gus' eyes, and the ugly words were clear.

'A Toxic,' a voice said. 'A Toxic with this arrogant Orion. Trying to spoil our fun. A Toxic that must be caught and punished. A shame to his people. A betrayer to our cause; shame on him, shame on him.'

'Shame on him, shame on him,' a chorus of foul tongues chimed. The menacing voices passed on.

Reuben said, 'What do they say, Gus?'

'They know I am with you, a Toxic. They are not pleased,' replied Gus.

'How do they know?' asked Reuben.

'Why do they say betrayer?' interrupted Felicity.

'You understood?' said Reuben, looking at her with surprise.

'Yes,' she said.

Reuben seemed pleased. 'Thank goodness,' he muttered.

Gus looked at him. 'You chose well, Reuben,' he said with a reassuring smile.

What on earth are they talking about, wondered Felicity, not grasping Reuben's need for reassurance at this early stage of the quest. He took her ability to translate the Toxics' language through Gus as extra affirmation of her belonging in this quest. Even better – he could not! He smiled happily. *He's losing the plot with the stress*, thought Felicity, but she smiled in return, helpless as always when faced with his charm.

Gus returned them to the task. 'Only the Aquatics know I wished to join the quest. They must have a spy working with the Aquatics. It is beyond belief, but there is no other way,' he said quietly.

'But you are safe with us,' bellowed Georges, and Pippi rubbed her thick, furry neck against Gus' prickly body. Felicity saw a movement from Sib out of the corner of her eye. He had sidled closer to the hedge and seemed to be listening intently. He didn't see her watching him. Gus had flattened his spines with pleasure at Pippi's caress.

Reuben was chewing the edge of his finger as he thought fast. *Why are they here? Gus thought they were gathering in the Shadowed South ready to attack the caves. Why are they here?*

'It must be a small renegade group just looking for trouble,' said Pippi, catching his thoughts. 'We couldn't have communicated – their minds were black. We had to run. There was no light entering them.'

'They were evil,' said young Thorn.

'Uncontrollable,' said Reuben.

'This world has seen many, many things,' rumbled Georges, 'but let's sit and talk now the danger has passed.' As they all found somewhere comfortable to rest, Georges' deep voice continued, 'There have been other imbalances in the early days. It is recorded in the great Root that as we came into being, each new pair of enharmonic species tipped the energies up and down as they settled upon the terroire. So do not be scared, my friends. These Toxics have such anger and bitterness. Their hearts are black and ugly, but they were created on this world. This world let them down, and on this world will all be resolved.' He looked at Reuben as he said this.

Thank you, said Reuben, mind-sharing. He was so very glad of Georges. His buffoonery and vanity hid a wisdom born of antiquity. And calm. The group were at peace, and Reuben decided to make camp right where they were. Gus came close to Felicity.

'What would they do to you, Gus?' Felicity asked the unspoken question. All eyes looked down. Gus did not respond. Felicity thought again of those voices. They were truly ugly. Spiteful and full of malice. She could not imagine Gus sounding like that with his gentle voice.

Camp was set up, a small fire built, and Scratt showed them all how to toast the stod balls until they were crispy. As she crunched them, Georges and Gus entertained Felicity with descriptions of their world. From the high frozen parts of the Eastern Wastes, down to the deep caves and valleys of mist and moor, and across the seas to the damp Temperate North, they took her on a visionary journey. Gus lit up the inky black night with his tales of colour: the pastel perfection of the Fragrants, the bright green lands of the Orion, and the tiny, shimmering chime birds that populated the golden lands of the Western Isle. Georges spoke of baking plains where lived the great Taureau. Felicity learnt of the violent waterfalls that crashed and thundered down the softened cliffs, and of the rumour that their unattainable heights were the heavenly nests of the Strata.

She longed to see these things. In spite of today's drama. She felt her courage increasing each day, as if the world was slowly seeping into her. *I can't imagine not being here*, she thought sleepily.

As the small group fell silent, Reuben alone remained awake. Tomorrow he would actively seek the key member whose arrival kept them here. They must move on. Today had been a warning.

11

Little Green

A watery sun lit up their makeshift camp the next morning. Its first fingers of light touched Felicity's face and woke her before the others. Felicity stretched and quietly stood. Rubbing her eyes, she enjoyed the moment of peace as all slept. She noticed the sun's rays picked out the colours of the beasts' shelters; they had hung their wraps and capes over the available limbs and knobbles of the plants, so that the whole camp looked like a soft-shelled beetle of many colourful parts. Only Georges stood separate, snoring loudly as he slumped against the tallest Green. Many of the plants seemed content to simply sleep as they stood or lay. Felicity watched a pile of Colour Changers resting in the corner like an unused compost heap. A movement on the other side of the hedge caught her attention.

'Let me in! Let me in!' a voice said. Its sound was strange, hypnotic. 'Is there an Orion within? An Orion who seeks to make the quest of which the whole world speaks? Let me in; I must speak with him. Please, please let me in.' At these last words the beautiful young voice started to sob.

Felicity felt a tear slide down her own face, unable to avoid feeling its pain. She turned to fetch Reuben, but he had woken to the sound and was behind her. She stumbled as she bumped into him, and he held her steady as he looked over her head to the wailing in the hedge. Felicity wasn't sure she had ever been quite so close to him. She inhaled that wonderful spicy scent he carried and enjoyed the feeling of his rough body coat before he let her go and called Scratt.

'Scratt!' he whispered with urgency.

Scratt brushed across from his hidden shelter.

'It's a Green, but a very young one, I think,' Reuben said. 'Can you let him in now? Then close the gap again until I have sent Sib out to check the Toxics have absolutely left.'

Scratt whispered softly as he moved, and before the last murmurs of sound faded on the misty air, the little Green had slipped inside their hideout. He stood about the same height as Scratt, but his youth was evident. Felicity knew the size of the mature Greens, and this little sapling was clearly very young. She looked more intently: baby palm leaves trembled above a tragic little face. Felicity wanted to hug him. She had always wanted a little brother. But the camp was awakening, and one of the mature Greens cruised towards them. Its long droopy 'arms' encircled the little Green, and it gently lifted him aloft onto its shoulder. He seemed comforted by this and stopped weeping.

Reuben addressed him formally, 'We welcome you, little Green. I am Reubenfourthousandth. Please introduce yourself, if you may.'

'I am Greenseventhousandthseventy, and I am a Greenesse.' There was a murmur of surprise from the listening crowd.

'We apologise Greenseventhousandthseventy for mistaking you, but your youth and separation from home suggested otherwise. We are honoured to receive you – but why is a young female wandering alone?'

The little Green's face began to crumple again, and its protector made a warning sound to Reuben. It turned without a word and transported its charge away. Reuben followed meekly.

Scratt spoke quietly to Felicity, 'The Greens are the seniors in the plant families – their learning and knowledge bestows upon them the highest respect. Reuben must wait until the Greens accompanying us are ready for him to speak with her again. They will ease her pain. She should not be travelling at such a young age. And a female too!'

Felicity felt herself flush, but this wasn't the time to defend women's rights. She counted to ten in her head and went after Reuben. 'Reuben, her voice draws me in. Does it have special powers? I felt myself cry as she did,' she said, trying to catch up with him.

'Yes, I think she carries great harmony. Her spirit is vast. It shines out around her further than I can see,' Reuben replied.

'Well, I can't see that, but I love her musical voice. I thought she was a little male green. Why is everyone surprised he is a she?'

'The Greenesses prefer to stay in their homelands. They have much to teach their young, being the plants of great knowledge. A great responsibility befalls them – all Greens must chant the history of our world from the very beginning. The Stipple Greens, in addition, lay down everything that was, is and can be; a budding Stipple must take in ancient connections that other Greens will never possess.' Reuben hushed his voice at these last words.

Felicity raised an eyebrow. Just occasionally, she felt the desire to giggle at Reuben's reverence.

'Well, we must move on,' he said. He clapped his hands for attention. 'Sib will check if we are safe to leave,' he called out into the space. His voice echoed slightly against the thick, green walls.

All were packed and ready by the time Sib returned. Felicity was surprised at Reuben's choice of scout. Scratt released them from their shelter, and as they stepped out into the dense hedgeways, Felicity found herself holding her breath for a moment, but there were no more ugly voices.

The small band marched back to day two of the matings. As they approached, the snarls were loud in the early morning air. Georges picked up his pace, and Felicity felt the tremors of adrenaline in Pippi, who had kindly offered her and Scratt a ride.

Reuben was going to try to talk with Little Green once

everyone was inside the arena. He felt she was an important part in this puzzle and was determined to persuade the older Greens to loosen their protective hold of her. He had not forgotten the Aquatics' sense of urgency; the matings were a marvellous sight, but his path lay now to the west, and he was very keen to be there. Speaking with Little Green was essential. An immature Greenesse travelling alone – there was a reason she had found them. She might tell him where to find the next member. Why hadn't the new member presented themself? This waiting was hard. He picked up his step alongside the others and entered the arena with determination.

*

The scene before Felicity's eyes was as yesterday, but at this hour the crowds were thinner, giving her a better view. The Lupata came in a variety of colours: steely grey, ash silver, tawny brown like Pippi, fox red and hazelnut brown. A huge black Lupata in the far corner caught her eye. He was pacing the perimeter of the arena, and his colour and size made him stand out. She looked up at Pippi. She knew Pippi had seen him. Her friend was very, very still, and her head was raised proudly. Now that she had a better knowledge of the Lupata, she could see Pippi was actually quite small. But she was far more muscled and solid than some of them. The first two who had come to the east had been taller than Pippi, but more rangy. The black beast who paced ever closer was very broad, like Pippi, but tall too. *He really is quite breathtaking*, Felicity thought.

She edged towards Georges as she felt Pippi's attention leaving her. Pippi took one step forwards and then with a bound she was in a skirmish with another female who had sidled up to stand between her and the approaching male. The other female was considerably larger than Pippi. Her fur was silver. Felicity noticed some of the sparring males eyeing her in between mouthfuls of fur. The skirmish was brief and fierce. The silver female limped off elegantly. Pippi returned

to her proud stance. The huge black male was now so close
Felicity could see his muzzle was speckled with grey hairs.
She felt a slight shift in Pippi's stance. Then a pause and then
imperceptibly her neck straightened again.

From behind Georges' front leg, Felicity watched the
meeting. Pippi was beautiful. Her fur shone chestnut and
golden and red-brown in the strengthening sunlight. Her face
was broad, and her eyes deep and kind. Her full tail swished
in pleasure as they rubbed noses. The male bowed down,
and Pippi place her paws on his knees. The top of her neck
was now completely exposed to his huge muzzle. But instead
of lifting her up and dragging her off, he simply licked her
with rough strokes of his huge black-spotted tongue. Then
he walked away.

Felicity ran across the sandy ground. 'What happened,
Pippi?' she asked, excited. 'What was all that? Is he your
mate now?'

'I dealt with Silverback so that I could consider him,'
replied Pippi, with nonchalance. 'He is fine, but too old
to spar. Why he is here, I am not sure. I allowed him to
approach me. He is attractive to me.'

'I'm not surprised,' said Felicity. 'He is magnificent,
Pippi.'

'Yes,' Pippi replied and then was silent.

Felicity sighed; really, sometimes this world was just too
confusing. She wished for the tenth time that Al was here.
Oh, Al, we could have had so much fun. But Al was not, and
she was. She would tell Al the best bits when she got back.
When she was home.

Reuben strolled across. He looked very pleased at something. Felicity wanted to hold his warm hand, but couldn't
think how to manage it. If only it was as simple as it was
for the Lupata. A steely-grey beast was carried away at
that moment with its left foot dangling by a bloody thread,
and as Felicity swallowed the rising nausea, she quelled the
thought.

'Perhaps not,' she muttered.

'Perhaps not?' said Reuben, catching up her hands and swinging her round.

'Why are you so happy?' she said, laughing.

'I have spoken to Little Green, and my heart is greatly eased. Her story is a sad one, but we can help her now, and she is a strong young Greenesse. This is a great asset to our quest. She is young, but already her power is very advanced for her age. Her spirit of light and already considerable knowledge is our gift. I feel she is the key we were waiting for, but we must gain permission from her people for her to accompany us. She found her way to us, using the Aquatics as a guide once her family were lost to her. I think we must divert to the South East – her lands – for this permission. It is a long delay, but we need her, and we cannot take her without the elders' permission. Her family's flight was rash; we must heal the laws before we go west. If we set off shortly and travel through the night, we can be at the ocean by tomorrow evening. I will plot how we can avoid the Toxic lands as they will lie in our path, but we will find a route around them. Little Green is a wonderful gift from the world!' Reuben swept Felicity up then, and as they hugged, she closed her eyes to better enjoy the moment.

Georges looked across at their laughter and gave a bellow of delight. 'Time for your enharmonic, Reuben,' he boomed out across the spectators, making Reuben flush.

'What does he mean?' asked Felicity as Reuben placed her hastily down.

'I don't know,' he muttered.

Sometimes he seemed so young, Felicity thought.

A Thorn came by with a basket of sticky buds. Felicity's mouth watered. Reuben put up his hand, and the Thorn offered him a handful of the tasty sticks.

Felicity bit into hers. 'Oh, it's absolutely delicious!' she exclaimed. 'The best thing I have tasted yet – it's like an extra-salty, extra-sweet peanut crunch stick.' She sat on the dusty ground and leant back against the thick hedge, savouring every small mouthful of her feast.

The sun was high in the sky. It wasn't hot, but it was warm, and Felicity enjoyed the moment. Reuben relaxed properly for the first time since they had met. He joined her by the hedge, and they happily sunbathed, sticky treats in hand, and watched the rest of the day's sparring. It didn't worry Felicity now. This Old World, with its savage but beautiful traditions, had brought into her life a strange happiness. She recognised the honour and excitement of the participants. She hoped Pippi would find a mate...

*

She woke with a jolt. Someone was shaking her shoulder. Hard.

'Wake up, Felicity,' Sib was saying crossly. His tongue snaked out and in as he spoke.

Felicity jumped up. The light was fading. It was cold, and she shivered. The arena was almost empty. How long had she been asleep? 'Where is Reuben?' she asked Sib.

'He speaks with Lupatafourthousandth before we travel. He did not want to disturb you.' Sib was sidling away as he spoke.

'Where are we going?' she asked, scurrying after him. It was cold, and she pulled Reuben's shawl across her chest and knotted it behind her waist. She had discovered it was easier to walk fast like that.

'We gather by the Norgate to take sustenance, and then we travel tonight,' he said. Felicity and Sib crossed the arena and left by the farthest side. As they reached the other large exit, Felicity turned. She looked across the darkening, dusty space. The growls and snarls were forgotten echoes. Tufts of fur rose and dropped in the small flurries of wind, and only the drying patches of scarlet brown bore witness to the violence of the day.

'Goodbye,' she said to the silent space.

12

The Troupe of Nine

They had been travelling for hours. The moon was high, and the path hard to follow. Pippi stayed close to Felicity and nudged her unhelpfully. Georges brought up the rear with Gus in front of him. The two were becoming good friends, in a symmetry typical of this simple world, thought Felicity. The oldest and the newest; tradition and new beginnings.

Many of the followers had decided to stay in the Temperate North. The matings would go on for many weeks, and Reuben had suggested politely to each and all that a different way of supporting the quest might be to support the Old World's traditions – and honour the contests with their presence. He realised he needed to condense the quest group for speed and efficiency. Looking at the newly shrunken group, Felicity wished Reuben had consulted her. How could they defeat a small army of Toxics with just nine members? Furthermore, what was Reuben thinking of taking along two saplings, Scratt and Little Green? The only decision that made sense was the one to include Wolfgang. She couldn't remember when she had named Lupatafourthousandth 'Wolfgang', but everyone adopted the name instantly.

'Felicity, this group that Reuben has accepted make a good team,' said Pippi, hearing Felicity's anxious thoughts. 'Thorn may look small, but he will grow, and a Thorn is not to be underestimated. They are the enharmonics of the Lupata. Little Green has the promise of immense powers. All happens as it should. Even Wolfgang was probably supposed to join the quest. Would you like to know the strengths of the team?' she added.

'Yes, please. I have some idea, but I'm not entirely sure,' replied Felicity.

'Well, as you know, Reuben has agility – amongst his other attributes,' Pippi said, laughing, 'and Georges his immense strength and knowledge of the old ways. Gus has his spines and his ability to understand all languages. Sib has vast geographical knowledge, and his kind have a special relationship as messengers for the Aquatics.'

'I presume you and Wolfgang will be good fighters – if there is a fight?' Felicity asked, finally.

'There will be danger and maybe battles. Who knows?' said Pippi, sounding excited.

Lovely, thought Felicity. She tramped on, pensive, but became fascinated by Little Green's halo, which bobbed along as they travelled.

'Is that glow around Little Green useful? It fades and brightens sometimes. Reuben said something about her having a vast spirit or harmony or something. Is the light connected?' she said, her words loud in the night air.

Pippi hushed her. 'Do not speak of her spirit so lightly, Felicity,' she said in a whisper. 'The aura of the Greens is the very heart and life pulse of our world. We are all connected with it, but the Greens have a special connection. The ordained Stipple Greens carry the strongest pulse; it is laid along with the knowledge and keeps the cycle of energy and light flowing. They are the most spiritual of our world, and their light shines out in the darkness. Do you see how Little Green's glow lights our path, along with the moon?'

'Yes,' said Felicity. It was true; as the night drew in its dark cloak, so Little Green's phosphorescent glow shone ever brighter. 'But it dims when Scratt chatters.'

'Yes,' said Pippi, 'it does. Body and mind and soul are one. Scratt drains with his chatter, but the strength of Little Green's light suggests a young Green of great importance. The loss of her family will have further dimmed her light. I look forward to seeing her in full flame one day.'

Finally Reuben stopped marching. They were far from Thornton now. They had passed through smaller hedge towns and were in a broadly open expanse of winding rivulets. They had hopped and jumped over the tiny waterways for the last hour. Felicity was exhausted. Ravenous also, of course. The troupe gathered together. Georges was slurping the stream noisily, and Wolfgang growled at him to be quiet.

As Georges raised his dripping chin, Reuben said, 'Where is Sib?'

Everyone looked around. Little Green took a deep breath and concentrated. Exhaling slowly and smiling hard, her light gradually increased until it illuminated the patch of ground and its immediate surroundings. Looking behind her, Felicity could see Gus' three-pronged shape, and Georges' huge head, with little clouds of steam emanating from his nostrils in the damp night air. She, Pippi and Scratt stood close to Reuben. Wolfgang was retracing their steps, trying to pick up Sib's scent. Pippi joined him.

'He was not with us for the last stretch and possibly more,' he said as he returned.

Reuben looked at Felicity. She could not see his expression in this light. He was silent, and they all waited quietly.

'Okay,' he said finally. His voice was deep. Felicity went over to him. She tentatively laid a hand on his arm. He took hold of her hand with both of his and then surprised her by pulling her close. He held her tightly for a brief moment; then he raised his voice and said, 'Wolfgang and Pippi, you know what to do. Scratt, please source food. Georges and Felicity, you help him, and all three of you stay near this spot. Little Green, you're with me; I need your marvellous light. Don't worry, we won't be long,' Reuben said, and then he left.

'They won't be far, I'm sure,' Gus said as he and Georges trotted up to Felicity. 'Wolfgang is an experienced tracker, and Pippi is a fine young Lupata. If they can't scent him, no one can.'

'But it's so dark. Where would he go?' asked Felicity.

She felt vulnerable here in the open night without Reuben or Pippi. Georges was wonderfully brave but possibly not the most intelligent, and Gus was a Toxic, after all. Her fear carried to Scratt, and he began to whimper. Felicity tried to put her arms around him. He was about the same height as her but only because of his fluffy top growth. His face was somewhere on a level with her shoulder, and he was prickly.

'Why did I beg to come?' he sobbed. 'I am too young. I should be at home with my family. I want to go back. I want to go back.' He was really crying now, and Felicity was getting wet.

Georges rumbled, 'Thornsixthousandsixty! Where is your pride? You are on the verge of enharmonic manhood and you cry like a baby. What a story you will take home when this quest is over. You will be the Thorn of all Thorns. Your kind will gather around you on those quiet days when the Lupata matings seem a distant memory. Danger is not here, young Thorn. Be calm.' As Georges' deep voice rumbled on, Scratt subsided.

Felicity let go and feebly patted his scratchy, leafy back. 'My mother would say you always feel miserable on an empty stomach,' she said. 'Let's find some food for everyone when they return.'

So with Georges giving instructions in between noisy slurps, she, Gus and Scratt foraged for food in the dark. They found a different variety of stod ball, which hid under the ferns at the water's edge. The balls smelt fishy, but they were food. Her hands were freezing from the icy water. She blew on them loudly, trying to restore feeling to her numb fingertips, but Scratt stopped her.

'Sssh! I hear something,' he said suddenly. They all listened hard. They could hear splashing and shouting. Felicity thought she heard a howl.

'Over here, quick!' urged Georges, calling them to his side. He stood and faced the noise with his head lowered and his gnarled horns pointing forwards. Felicity and Scratt sheltered beneath him, and Gus stood on his right flank, spines fully out. By common accord they were deathly silent.

A faint glow appeared in the distance and grew increasingly strong. It seemed to dart to the left and right. With it came shouts and splashes, and finally, arriving in a chaotic bundle, came Little Green with Reuben holding one of her outstretched branches. He tried to speak but couldn't.

'Toxics!' he finally gasped, hands on his knees as he tried to fill his chest with air. Felicity felt fingers of panic tingle up her spine.

'Follow my light,' said Little Green. Her tone was calm and steady in spite of running. 'Come on, everyone, quickly. Reuben and I have seen a safe hide. Pippi and Wolfgang are leading them away, but they might double back. Please!' she begged.

Her hypnotic voice drew them forwards. Felicity grabbed her shawl, now full of stod balls, and they followed. Little Green held onto Georges' matted mane on one side, and Scratt held the other. Gus took big strides on his prickly long limbs, and Felicity found herself scooped up by Reuben in one swift motion. He was damp with sweat but warm, and it was lovely to simply be carried for a moment. She felt guilty. *He must be utterly spent.* But still he strode. They reached the place very soon. It was a meeting of streams that overlapped as the ground rose and fell, creating a natural bridge with a hollow underneath like a canal underpass. Except it was cleverly hidden from view by some large bushy ferns.

Reuben said, 'This is not brilliant. The Toxics may find us, so be prepared. Felicity and Scratt, stay well back if it comes to anything.'

They waited for hours and hours. Or so it seemed. Finally they heard the thudding of Lupata paws on the ground. The rhythm sounded steady as it approached. Without warning, a huge head peered around the corner of their ferny hollow. Reuben stepped forward.

'Welcome, and welcome,' he said to Wolfgang and Pippi with relief.

'We lost them about five hundredds away,' Pippi said. 'We should be safe for the night.'

'Was it the same ones who were in Thornton?' asked Scratt, his voice trembling a little as he spoke.

'No,' Reuben replied to him, 'there are obviously more travelling the Temperate North than we suspected.'

'This is not a good sign,' said Gus. His voice was sombre.

'No,' agreed Wolfgang. He was limping.

'What was the howling?' asked Felicity.

'I had to call Wolfgang to my aid,' said Pippi. She sounded irritated.

'You did very well, my little cub,' he said to her.

Scratt snorted, and everyone went quiet, pretending they hadn't heard him. Pippi nipped him sharply on the muzzle and then started licking his front paw with care.

They seem to have made friends, then, thought Felicity. She was smiling and thought Reuben was, too, as he said with a slightly odd voice, 'Let's eat.'

To everyone's delight he had secreted some sticky buds in his jacket, and he produced them with relish. Georges ate all the stod balls, and no one minded. He asked for a sticky bud, but Scratt threw a stick at him instead. He stomped off to sleep outside, as guardian whilst they slept. He claimed he could go three days without sleep.

'When I was in my prime,' he began, and they all told him to shut up. Politely, of course.

Felicity settled down in her favourite position, with Reuben on one side and Pippi on the other. She lay quietly, hoping they would reach the shore tomorrow without further Toxic scares. She still didn't really understand what it would be like to come face to face with these bitter beings. She looked at the outline of Georges standing firmly in the moonlight. Little Green had long extinguished her glow and was fast asleep beside Scratt. Gus stood quietly and sadly in the corner of the shelter, but his breathing was even. Felicity hoped for his sake they avoided any trouble tomorrow. She raised her head above Reuben's shoulder and could see the long dark slope of Wolfgang's back as he slept alone and fully stretched out between Georges and them. *Tomorrow I shall think of a better name for Little Green*, she thought. The moon passed over the top of their shelter and slowly sank out of view. A rustling in the ferns told of a night creature snuffling for food by the water. Then as the first bird tentatively trilled its early morning call, Felicity finally fell asleep.

13

The Strata

Reuben was up first. He went straight to the water's edge and peered intently each way along its banks.

'They are far, Reuben,' said Georges with a yawn.

'Thank you, my friend, for your safe guardianship,' Reuben said to him with a pat on his furry flank. Clouds of smelly dust rose as he did so, and he turned his head away, discreetly trying not to cough.

'Well, we managed to avoid discussing Sib last night,' said Georges. 'What will you tell Felicity? The mind-sharing worked well. Felicity was distracted by the Toxic scare.'

'Yes,' replied Reuben, 'but the minute she awakes, she will remember.' He chewed his lip absent-mindedly. He had to consider the possibility that Sib was now a threat to reaching the Western Isle safely. Furthermore, he was beginning to think it was insanity to try and reach the South East – homeland of Little Green. They would have to pass directly through the edges of the Shadowed South, home to the majority of the Toxics, now.

Last night's skirmish had shown the Toxics were completely out of control. The idea of violence for its own sake was a horrifying new development in this beautiful world. Territory and breeding issues might cause short breakouts, but these were never in vain; they would achieve a decision, and each side would accept it. They had the Banyan meets, the wisdom of the Oceanids, and finally the unbiased help of the Strata when issues were complicated. It had worked since the Old World began. Never, never, he thought, had any beast or plant sought violence for its own sake. It was horrific to him. Like wounding himself. Why would a creature seek to harm another for no reason? He could accept the Toxics' bitterness born of rejection. Even understand their abhorrent campaign to destroy the very heart of the world, the Roots laid down since time began, thousands of generations of work by the Stipple Greens, guarded so faithfully by the Taureau. Even in that violent threat was there some misguided motive, he thought. But what he had witnessed last night chilled his soul. He looked at Georges before mind-sharing. It was getting a little easier as they headed west. *Small gifts*, he thought.

Why, Georges, do we guard the cave? he asked silently.

You ask of things of which we do not speak, came back the reply.

Frustrated, Reuben sighed. Well, it didn't matter now. The caves and the Roots needed more than guarding. They needed defending. He curled up his hands into tight fists. He felt the tension travel up his arms as his despair grew. The answers to every question were contained in those Roots. They contained all that was and is and shall be. If the Toxics succeeded in destroying them in their utterly ignorant frenzy of hate, he thought angrily, what would become of his beautiful, loving world?

He looked up at the sky. There were about seven Strata circling and wheeling high in the early light. It was as if his despair had called to them. He went and stood by Georges as they gracefully descended. The flurry of wings and Strata song woke the sleepers, who scrambled up and stood quietly watching. Wolfgang's and Pippi's noses were raised, scenting their visitors.

'*Welcome, Reuben's quest party*,' sang the first Strata.

Felicity was mesmerized. They were incredible creatures. Sort of huge birds. They reminded her of the pterodactyl pictures at the Natural History Museum in London. Except they were quite stunningly beautiful. Their feathers were glossy and of so many rich colours. She had once seen some tiny birds on a wildlife programme. She remembered that nature man raving about their hues of infinite variety. *Well, beat this, Mr A,* she thought to herself, smiling. They had long beaks and a crown of feathers on their heads, which would have been comical if their eyes had not been so wise and serious. With their wings folded, they stood as high as Georges' shoulder. Their breast feathers were a marvellous concoction of curl and shade. With the first Strata leading, they began their lilting song of words:

There is not time for formality,
We are the strata of the West Sea.
We come to aid you on this new day.
Reuben the brave, hear what we say:
The Greens are calling, return their prize child,
But we see from our skies the Toxics run wild.
They spread from the south to the edge of the west,
They move in a wave and have heard of your quest.
They gather more renegades each passing hour.
We, the peacemakers, diplomats of power
Say tarry no longer; the Sib one has gone.
Watch us and follow; this quest must succeed.
We'll divert stray Toxics and call winds for your speed.

At the end of each phrase their wings lifted, and with beaks pointed to the sky, they let the harmonies soar into the humming air. Felicity squashed a giggle as she noticed Scratt swinging from side to side with the rhythm.

Their song finished, Reuben enquired politely, 'I cannot break the traditions of our world, most honourable ones. I cannot take an underage Green without the permission of her elders at a Banyan. I am forbidden to go west by this law. How can I proceed?'

The first Strata stepped forwards again. Felicity prepared for verse two. But he sang simply, 'Seven will send three to inform the Green elders that the child is safe. You will call a Banyan in your homeland, and there will gain your pass. Four will be your guides.' As he finished, the three were already taking off. They leapt towards the stream, and in the first bound their wings unfurled, gave a couple of massive beats, and they soared up into the pale blue skies.

Felicity was entranced by these powerful creatures. 'Wow!' was all she said.

They ate a hurried breakfast with the huge birds preening their glossy feathers a little way away. Soon they were off. Two of the four cruised at a low level, keeping close. The other two flew at higher altitudes, looking for potential trouble. Wolfgang and Pippi walked side by side. Wolfgang's furry back was twitching, and Pippi kept looking behind her. Georges was cantering gently along in the rear. Felicity was sure he was surreptitiously chewing on something as he ran. Gus and she walked in companionable silence, and Scratt and Little Green trotted along just behind Reuben, who led the column out of the tributary lands and towards the sea.

'How far is it to the sea?' Felicity asked of Gus.

'If we carry on this pace, we will arrive at some point in the night,' he replied, a little breathlessly.

'Where did Sib go, Gus?' Felicity asked at last. It was absolutely weird that no one had mentioned Sib apart from the Strata in their song. Why had she not last night? She tried to remember the sequence of events. She had just been glad everyone was okay and then too tired to even care? It was all becoming a bit of a blur. Her tummy rumbled. Breakfast had been short. No wonder Georges was scoffing something illicit back there, she thought. Gus had still not answered. Mum said she was like a dog with a bone when something was on her mind. Clearly Gus did not know who he was dealing with. She tried again, 'Gus,' she said in a firm tone.

He looked at her, big black eyes suspiciously vacant. 'Yes?'

'Where...is...Sib?' she repeated, pronouncing the words slowly.

Gus' spiky shoulders drooped, and he glanced forwards to Reuben.

Felicity followed his gaze. She looked back at Gus, huffed, and then said, 'Right!' and strode ahead to catch up with Reuben, arms swinging and panting slightly with the effort. Pink-cheeked and out of breath, she tapped Reuben on the shoulder. He ignored her. She tugged the back of his jacket. 'Reuben!' she shouted.

He stopped abruptly, and she fell into him. He turned and met eyes with Gus.

'I know you are mind-sharing, and that is even more rude than barging into my thoughts,' said Felicity. Her voice sounded shrill.

Pippi loped up and gave her a huge lick. 'It is time to tell her, Reuben,' Pippi said in her kind voice.

The Strata circled the group anxiously. Reuben called up to them, 'We halt for a short break.' At his words, they soared up to join the other two, without reply.

Reuben looked at Felicity. He took a deep breath and let the air out slowly. The rest of the troupe halted, glad of the rest. They had learnt of Sib last night. Reuben brushed Felicity's cheek with the back of his hand. Her skin felt warm and soft. He concentrated on the downy layer of blonde hairs that caught the light. He needed time to organise his words.

'Felicity, sit down,' he said. She sat. 'Sib has left with no communication. He was blocking his thoughts for the last few hours, so none of us can tell where he went. As you know the Sibilin can be disloyal, but I have told everyone and I tell you there must be a good reason for his sudden disappearance. He will explain when he rejoins us.' He glanced at Georges, and Felicity knew, she just knew there was more.

'What?' she said.

'I said nothing,' said Reuben.

'Yes, you did. I have lived on this world for long enough now to mind-share, a bit. I heard you, Reuben. I heard you say to Georges just then that the rest could wait.'

Georges snorted in delight at Reuben being caught out

and came to Reuben's aid. 'Felicity,' he bellowed, swallowing first. 'Felicity, we protect you for your own sake.'

'No!' said Felicity. To her huge embarrassment and frustration tears began to roll down her cheeks. 'No! That is not fair. I am dragged to this world of B-A-L-A-N-C-E', she said, 'and someone we trusted on our side of the B-A-L-A-N-C-E has run off. A great flock of flying dinosaurs arrive, and you all look terribly worried. It's not good enough. You have to tell me what is going on with Sib. What is so bad? I never trusted him anyway. Why is everyone so surprised he went off?' The rain which had been threatening all morning finally came, and as Felicity finished her rant, the deluge soaked them all.

'Felicity, there are many risks to us losing Sib at this stage, and the Toxics are more widespread than we thought. Please trust me, Felicity. I will never keep anything important from you. But we must gain the coast tonight. We will talk on the voyage.'

Felicity thought of the Oceanid journey and gave in. Reuben did look exhausted. She wiped her face, which was wasted effort as the cold water streamed down her cheeks now. The troupe marched on, and the Strata returned. The rain was miserable. Georges' woolly coat smelt like a zoo pen, Little Green and Scratt clung miserably to Pippi's back, and Felicity thought she would even ride on Wolfgang rather than suffer this muddy, boggy march any longer.

Night fell, and the exhausted travellers trailed up to the brow of the last dark rise of land. The vast ocean sparkled silver in the moonlight as they crested the hump. *Thank goodness*, thought Felicity. She was past tears or pain. She felt numb from the gruelling trek.

'We camp here tonight. Tomorrow we head for the Western Isle,' said Reuben. There was a feeble cheer. With no Colour Changers, they had to forage for food – sand shoots but they were a welcome change from stod balls. Gus passed round the ornate flask of amber liquid that Felicity had first tasted on her second day.

'Oh, spirit drink! Marvellous!' exclaimed Georges.

Gus wrestled the flask away from him as he sucked deeply. 'It will last us all, as you know, Georges, but even spirit drink needs time to replenish,' admonished Gus.

Everyone took a few large gulps. Felicity felt it warm her up and satisfy her thirst all at once. It was reviving and filling. Al would have loved it. *So would Dad*, came the unbidden thought. Little Green and Scratt passed round the sand shoots.

'Thank you' Felicity said and smiled at Scratt. His chirruping voice had been noticeably silent today. She looked at him again. He was taller, and by his side, Little Green had grown noticeably too. Could they grow so fast? Nothing in this world would surprise her, she thought. She wanted Reuben to come and lay beside her again. The fire had dried her soaked clothes, and the spirit drink had made her sleepy. Wolfgang and Pippi lay close. Her eyes closed, but as the peace of sleep claimed her, a huge spume of water rose out of the ocean and splashed down onto the sand between their dune and the sea. Everyone leapt up. The Oceanid had arrived.

14

The West

The second crossing was awful. With the moon hidden by the stormy weather, the rough seas were invisible walls of icy water that pounded and crashed with terrifying velocity. The outraged bellows of Georges sang out into the storm's rush.

'The Oceanid would normally swim deep below a storm like this,' explained Wolfgang to Felicity, shouting to be heard. He had begun to speak with her occasionally. Perhaps Pippi's burgeoning friendship with him helped.

Felicity wrung out her hair as a large wave emptied over them all with a roar. Reuben ensured everyone was well anchored and then joined her. He helped squeeze out her dripping curls and tenderly wiped her drenched face with something dry he had tucked inside his clothing. Felicity took it. It smelt of him. His familiar spicy scent. She tried to speak, but the storm was too noisy to talk properly. He nodded as if she had spoken. She couldn't tell if he was smiling. She tried mind-sharing. As she broke into his thoughts, she saw an image of a girl with a fat, stripy tail. The girl had her face. *Eew!*

'Are you ok, Felicity?' cried Reuben hoarsely, unaware as yet of her mind presence. And then he sensed her inside him.

Reuben, said her lively voice, *Reuben, where will we go when we land?* Felicity wanted to think of landing. She could only think of land, of heat and solid ground, as this lashing, crashing ocean claimed them.

Reuben's deep voice replied, and his eyes held her gaze as they continued their private conversation and he filled her mind with beautiful images: *We will pass through the country of Georges – baking dusty plains that echo to the sounds of the Taureau herds. Then on through ice-peaked mountains, whose pine-clad lower slopes look back south – land of the Fragrants and their forests in whose verdant canopies they sway with the thermals of the western skies, as they look forwards to the open plains, the mountain passes, and Orion Country. My homeland.*

I feel your love, Reuben. Your homeland must be a very special place.

You will see, little Felicity, whispered his voice in her head. He raised her hand to his lips and gently kissed her palm before moving away to see if everyone else was safe from the storm. Felicity settled down into a damp but warm spot next to Pippi and tried to sleep in spite of the howling tempest.

*

The next morning the storm had passed, and they were deposited on a golden strip of sand, already warm at this early hour. Further back lay a line of bush, into whose depths the others had disappeared in search of food.

Reuben had let Felicity doze after the dreadful crossing, but she jumped up now, uncomfortable to be alone in this open landscape. Hunting through the jungly thicket, she could hear no voices, only the clicking, buzzing, and raucous chatter of the forest life. She looked up, but could see no sign of the Strata. *I suppose they have done their job for now,* she thought. *They only said they would guard us to the Western Isle.* But she would have liked to have heard their beautiful singing again.

A branch cracked ahead of her, and she stopped walking and held her breath. Gus appeared with armfuls of a ribbon-like plant. They flowed over his elbows and trailed from his head. He looked like a popped party streamer.

'What are you doing, Gus?' She laughed.

Gus beamed. 'Reuben suggested we all find different foods to show you how abundant the Western Isle is,' he said. 'You were absolutely still. We all agreed you needed much rest after that dreadful crossing.' He came up to her and stood disentangling his spikes from the thick ribbons.

'In my world we have many plants, too,' Felicity said, helping him. She pricked her finger on one of his leg spikes.

'Oh, Felicity, forgive me,' said Gus. He looked truly sad.

'You are a gentle soul, Gus,' said Felicity, touching his arm carefully. She thought of his three top branches as arms and his two bottom ones as legs.

'I like the names you give to our things,' said Gus as he now began plaiting the ribbons skilfully. 'Your names are simple and interesting. Arms and legs?' He lapsed into silence.

'Are you so different from your own kind?' asked Felicity.

Gus took a moment; then he spoke. 'Well, I think there are many Toxics who would like to be one with our world, but they don't believe it possible. That there is no way they can mingle with other species and belong. They have given up faith, but perhaps not hope,' he said, 'and then there are those who have given up even wanting to belong and who live alone. They are the most lost.'

His eyes darkened, and Felicity felt the chill of total isolation wrap around her. She shivered. She thought of her family, her mother and even her sister. Her father. The smiling, scratchy face of her grandfather, and Al. She had people who she knew cared about her, even if they didn't always manage to show it. She imagined if they all disappeared. Just her alone on the earth with a load of strangers, cold faces who went home at night and forgot about her. Getting up each day and knowing whatever she did it was known only to her. Good times and bad times – who would she tell each evening? This was the world of the Toxic, she realised.

But Gus was different. *Yes, Felicity, and there are others like me. We crave company and laughter and love.*

'We admire beauty,' he continued aloud. 'We cannot accept our destiny, but we know destruction is not the way.

These dark Toxics are more than lost, they are vengeful and could bring this world down with their destructive intents for the Roots. The Ancients were right – they must be stopped.'

'Can you help the quest prevent them?' said Felicity, copying Gus, who was continuing to deftly weave the ribbons of plant into a firm, interlocking wand as he spoke.

'Yes,' he said in his handsome voice, and Felicity remembered how she had first seen him – such a mix of ugliness and beauty. So lost and yet so giving.

'There is surely a place for you in this world that claims such harmony,' said Reuben, who had silently padded up.

'You read my mind, Reuben,' said Felicity, for once happy to share it involuntarily.

'Yes, it is not hard here,' he replied, taking a deep breath of the warm, pure air. He flopped down beside them and unfolded a purple leathery leaf as large as a dinner plate. As his fingers neatly peeled back the edges, its contents were revealed.

'Oh!' gasped Felicity in delight, for on its glossy, veined surface were piled a collection of multi-coloured balls. They were divided in two halves like tiny meringues, and the filling in their tiny centres was of the palest cream. Felicity felt her mouth water. They smelt absolutely delicious. Reuben and Gus laughed as they watched her eager face.

'Not yet, Felicity,' said Reuben as her hand crept out to take one. 'We will wait for the whole feast to arrive. I promise you the patience will be worth it. These foods work together. Alone they are good, but taken in their correct combinations and order, they are truly magnificent.'

Felicity heard his stomach rumbling and realised she couldn't think of when they had all last eaten. She stood up.

'Is there somewhere I can bathe and take care of my needs?' she asked, a little embarrassed. This side of things had been tricky, but somehow Reuben had always allowed everyone time to make themselves comfortable and clean. If they couldn't eat yet, then Felicity was determined to wash her hair. Reuben led her into the forest. There was a stream with some flat stones at its edge. Felicity hoped Reuben was not going to stay. She stepped carefully to the edge of the water and began, with relief, stripping off the crumpled clothes she had been wearing since the day of her mother's school reunion. Her throat felt tight as she allowed herself to think of her mum. To her surprise, a sob broke the forest's hush. Worse, Reuben had not left.

'Felicity!' he said and clambered over to her.

'You were…supposed to…have…left,' she said in gasps. She couldn't stop. It was awful. Her eyes were screwed up, and her wails echoed back and forth across the little glade. Reuben said no more. He simply held her, firm and close. Slowly, slowly the spasms of grief backed down, and Felicity could open her eyes again. The birdsong and strange noises of the forest returned. She gave a huge, juddery sigh.

'Thank you,' she said to Reuben's damp jacket front. She went to step away, but he held her tight. She was unsure what to do, so she politely waited a moment. Then she tried to pull away again, but still his strong arms held her close. She cleared her throat and pulled her face away from his chest to see his expression. His hazel eyes were dark brown, the pupils large. His face was so close she could see the sunlight creating a teardrop of illumination down his nose. Very gently and looking straight at her, he lowered his face and kissed her. Warmth ebbed through her – it felt as if Reuben's breath filled her with sunshine. She remembered once as a tiny girl the perfect bliss of sun on her face, birdsong in her ears, and a warm hand holding her tight. Reuben's kiss returned her to this deeply buried memory, a moment of utter contentment. As he let her go, he held her face a moment between his hands. They were trembling.

'Please forgive me, little Felicity,' he said. 'I knew not how else to bring you back to the light.' He stepped back, smiled lopsidedly, and left.

Felicity melted onto the warm stones. She wasn't sure

how long she sat. She heard the water gurgling, and saw the green fronds swirling and dancing beneath the water, but she was detached from the scene. As if in a trance, she finally stood up, finished undressing, and stepped into the cold water. Its icy embrace returned her to her full senses.

'Flipping-flip!' Splashing all over and gritting her teeth before dunking her long tresses into the water, she washed fast and furiously. She washed out a few bits of clothing but didn't dare get the heavy things wet. The shawl Reuben had lent her seemed to dry miraculously with a shake, and she wrapped it around herself gratefully.

She sat for an hour or so, watching the clothes gently steam on the stones. She found since Reuben's kiss everything seemed to take on extra colour. She enjoyed watching a trio of tiny turquoise birds engage in a love fight. The cocky males sparred angrily as the female watched with apparent nonchalance. The victor claimed his prize, and Felicity looked away with a happy smile. It seemed only polite. Hunger had been replaced with pain, and she dressed in the damp but warm clothing, carried the outer layers, and returned to camp with hope of sustenance at last.

The quest troupe had reassembled. Georges was standing by the shoreline, looking back at the circle of friends gathered in anticipation of the coming feast. There was a trail of vegetation from where he stood back to the group. Felicity was astounded by the feast. Added to the plaits of leaf that Gus had by now piled up high were many more of the tiny meringue-things. Wolfgang and Pippi had carefully made a mat the size of a rug, of criss-crossed white rubbery shoots that wobbled where they lay. Scratt and Little Green had filled large, conical-shaped flowers with a pale-lemon coloured liquid and carefully placed tiny matching conical flowers by the side with which to scoop and drink. As Felicity approached, they all turned to her with pride.

'Wow!' she said, holding out her hands with wonder.

They all began to speak at once, until Georges bellowed,

'Silence! Enough talk! Let's eat!' To which everyone readily agreed.

Felicity sat next to Pippi and Wolfgang. Pippi tipped her head sideways, sensing a change in Felicity, but Felicity kept her face averted and focused on Little Green and Scratt, who were eager to show off the treasures of this Isle's pantry.

'We have plaited strape, thanks to Gus,' they said.

Felicity took one and looked at Gus to see how it should be eaten, but it was Reuben who called across, 'Like this, Felicity,' and with a mischievous wink, crunched his white teeth firmly through the whole plait before tearing off a large chunk and chewing hard. Felicity tried and was surprised to feel that the leathery ribbonlike plant had dried to this crunchy, slightly chewy consistency. It tasted almost meaty, she thought.

'Dip it, Felicity!' called out Gus with difficulty as his mouth was rather full.

Felicity watched him to see what he meant. He had taken a scoop of the liquid and dipped his plait into it. The liquid turned the plait pure white. Scratt passed Felicity a scoop, and Felicity dipped. *Mmm. It tastes salty now, like beef jerky*, she thought, swallowing noisily. She sipped the liquid, expecting it to be salty, but its flavour was simply refreshing. Like a good mineral water. She helped herself to a couple more scoops before trying the next offering. Georges had tossed a few of his leaves in her general direction, whilst hoovering up more than half of them himself. Felicity tentatively nibbled the edge of one. *Jacket potato.*

Rising to the pace of this feast, she walked over to the mat of wobbling shoots. Their appearance was a little unappetising, but she could not offend Wolfgang and Pippi. She knew they would have chosen something difficult to harvest, and therefore must honour their courage and hard work. She closed her eyes and bit into the shoot. It was absolutely disgusting. Felicity retched. Everyone broke into raucous laughter. She opened her eyes and stood, hands on hips, facing them.

'Eergh!' she said, discreetly spitting out the last traces of the disgusting plant. 'I am so, so sorry, Pippi and Wolfgang. I simply cannot eat those...things,' she said finally, dashing back and drinking some of the 'water'.

It was Little Green who saved her. She stopped giggling and said in her exquisite little voice, 'Dear Felicity, you must not eat the shoot; you suck out its syrup. Look. Like this,' and her pretty little mouth daintily drew the syrup out of the revolting plant.

Felicity took another from Scratt, who was still cackling, and bravely sucked. The syrup was delicious, of course. It tasted of sweet spice, like the precious amber liquid that Gus had in his leaf flask, but stickier. Felicity took another shoot. The flavour was perfect after the saltiness of the plaited strape. Reuben had been right. It was worth waiting.

Feeling sated, Felicity peeked a glance at him. He and Gus sat back to back. Gus had withdrawn his spines so Reuben had a comfortable back rest. Felicity knew he was aware of her. She felt Pippi's interest and tried to block her mind from everyone, but it was very difficult here.

This is the Western Isle, Felicity. We are far from the Toxics' influence. You must increase your mind's strength. Reuben was in her head. She looked at him. His eyes were closed. In fact, he looked almost asleep. Everyone looked drowsy. How many silent conversations were actually going on, she wondered. What a crazy world, she thought. And yet, was it? Reuben opened his eyes and looked directly across the clearing into her own. She felt that sunshine warmth spread slowly through her. They smiled at each other. Georges and Pippi exchanged glances.

Reuben handed round the tiny meringues, and Felicity gathered a few of the leaf plates and helped him. Everyone appeared to be excited that Reuben had found these delicacies of the Western Isle.

'Well done, Reubenfourthousandth,' said Georges. 'How did you manage to find these in just a few hours?'

'Remember, Georges, this is close to the habitat of my enharmonics,' replied Reuben. 'Orchadea is not far, and she sent help.'

Georges glanced at Pippi, but they concealed their thoughts. *How will she accept Reuben's enharmonic, Pippi? Not well, I think*, was the silent reply.

Unaware, Reuben walked up to Felicity and said, 'Close your eyes, and open your mouth,' so she did. He popped two of the tiny creations onto her tongue. The moment they touched down, they began to fizz.

'Ah!' she exclaimed. She closed her lips and let the fizzing explode on her tongue. It was such a funny feeling. She giggled and opened her eyes. Georges was trotting back and forth, throwing his head up and down and shaking it from side to side. Wolfgang and Pippi were sneezing and then taking more with little growls. Scratt was cramming three or four in at once and running around shouting. Little Green gently sucked one at a time, eyes closed, as if in meditation. Gus' method was to roll two around his mouth and keep a straight face. She and Reuben began feeding them to each other, two at a time, and spluttering with laughter as the fizzing, crackling meringues tickled their mouths and inside their noses.

The chaos could have gone on all afternoon, Reuben had collected so many fizzruffs. But suddenly there was a rustling in the forest, and everyone instantly calmed. Beginning to work as a pack, they lined up in their places. Wolfgang and Pippi stood out front, with Reuben centrally behind them. Felicity felt strong. She placed herself immediately behind Reuben and in front of the remainder of the troupe. Pippi looked at Reuben, and they seemed to agree. But Felicity heard Gus move quietly closer. Behind Gus was Scratt and Little Green side by side, with Georges bringing up the rear.

'Name yourselves, approachers of the west,' called out Reuben. His confident, deep tones hung in the air, but there was no reply.

'I am Reubenfourthousandth of the Orion, and I repeat, name yourself.' His voice was deep and strong. But still no voice came.

Wolfgang and Pippi stepped forwards. Wolfgang's dark fur rose up on his back, and Pippi growled, low and steady. Felicity felt the hairs on the back of her neck rise up, and a cold chill travelled down the back of her arms.

Gus took a step away and pushed his spines out to full length. There were some extra ones around his face that she had never seen. They glinted like steel in the light and clinked if they touched each other. He smiled at Felicity, and she heard him in her head, *Toxics, little Felicity, but fear not; all will resolve,* and then he turned back to look long and hard at Georges. Felicity glanced back at Georges and saw him as he once must have been. The greedy, bumbling buffoon had gone. A towering, dark beast with wild eyes and long teeth snorted and stamped. His yellow horns faced forwards, and saliva drooled from his mouth.

Little Green spoke. 'Fear not, Felicity. They are simply confused. Once we have them under control, I will calm them.'

Felicity could not see Little Green's aura in this bright light, but she felt it, and it eased her. Scratt stood tall, and Felicity noticed he was now taller than she. Strange things were happening even for this world, she suspected. His expression was serious but not alarmed. Felicity forced herself to turn back to the front.

'Get ready, quest family; they come,' said Reuben, and out of the forest stepped the Toxics.

15

Toxics

The line of creatures stretched the length of a hockey pitch along the front of the forest. Felicity felt her heart start to pound at the sight. They were foul, misshapen replicas of Gus, and their spines were filthy and blackened with dirt. They moved with a creeping, sideways sway, their features twisted with vicious anger. They were chanting in that unnerving language she had first heard in Thornton. Wheezing and spitting, croaking and hissing, they approached. Their spines faced forwards, and they held their limbs straight out in front of them, a grimy, spiked wall. Felicity watched. In this bright world she was growing to respect and love more each day, the creatures moved as a mindless, grey lump.

Reuben shouted instructions. 'Little Green, cover Felicity and Gus with your aura. Georges, please watch out for sidecrawlers. Scratt, cover Little Green. Gus, keep Felicity by your side. Wolfgang and Pippi, let's go–' but Felicity could no longer hear his commands as he was running with the Lupata, his right hand raised to halt the creeping line.

Felicity watched the brave trio diminish in size as they crossed the space to the forest's edge. Wolfgang and Pippi were snarling and growling as they galloped from side to side, containing the advance and giving Reuben time to identify any sort of leader. Finally a particularly disgusting gnarled pair of Toxics shuffled ahead of the others, who were jostling and whining as the Lupata held them back with sheer determination and courage.

Reuben called on the ground and the air as he ran full pelt, and his stature was as stone as he halted to repeat for the third time, 'Introduce yourselves, disturbers of this world of balance, and miseries of life.'

Felicity gasped. Surely now the Toxics would pounce. They held still, but the two leaders moaned evilly, and lumpy saliva drooled over their facial spines. Reuben looked directly at them. Their eyes were large like Gus', but in place of deep intelligence were black chasms. No light reflected in their pupils. The orbs of darkness turned towards him. He tried to mind-share. He could hear only wind. A rushing wind and the sound of whispers, low and malicious, then the smaller one spoke.

'We choose not to speak in the language of the world,' it said in voiceless grunts of air, 'but for the advancement of our cause, we will use the words of a world that is destined for change.' Strangely the hoarse whisper gave him comfort. Communication of a kind, he thought.

A group of about twelve had broken forwards further down the line. The two leaders turned their heads slowly and stared at them. The renegade group slunk back, weaving side to side and complaining with furious cackles. The two leaders slowly turned back to Reuben. Then the smaller one spoke again.

'I am Demet, of the first clan of the New South,' wheezed the grey mouth. A lump of black-flecked spittle flew out of its thin purple lips and sizzled as it hit the floor. Its lumpy colleague cackled at the look of surprise from Reuben.

'Do not underestimate us, Reuben the last,' said the small Toxic.

Reuben looked down at his left hand. A tiny speck of the spittle had landed on his third finger. Suddenly he felt excruciating pain. His flesh was burning and blistering. He felt the anger rise, and he opened his mouth to let the fire out. As he exhaled and inhaled one long deep breath, he felt the still pure air of the west travel down to the depths of his lungs. He blew gently on his hand. The pain was under control now, and he looked up straight into the black holes of the Toxic's eyes. He felt the strength of his world pour into his veins, and he let it saturate his mind. He focused all his energy into a solid ball, and then he simply emptied this ball of energy and strength like an arrow into those miserable vacant holes. He heard the Toxic whine and moan as the goodness of the world spread into its withered pores. It cowered back, and by its side, the second Toxic whimpered with fear at this silent adversary.

'I say to you, Toxics of many thousandths of our ancient world, do not mistake the silent strength of light, sun and harmony. Neither must you mistake dull ignorance and pointless destruction as containing any purpose. Your introspective lives have led you to stray far from the paths of hope. Our quest seeks to abate your hopeless cause. Why do you bring your lack of light to these lands? Come and learn from Toxictoxicth the true possibilities of our world and your place in it.'

The small Toxic straightened up again. It looked past Reuben to Gus, by Felicity's side. Its expressionless eyes stayed on Felicity for a few moments. Felicity saw Reuben's hands slowly clench and then uncurl as its gaze returned to Gus. Gus stepped forwards and started to slowly approach the line. Georges stomped closer to Felicity and Scratt, and Little Green moved to fill the gap Gus left. He walked slowly and surely towards the line of Toxics. Felicity heard the crackling, hissing noise of their mutterings spread through their lines as they all realised Gus was one of them.

He walked calmly to stand by Reuben. He faced the two Toxic leaders. Two pairs of empty eyes. He felt their walls of anger, and closing his eyes, he went into their minds. Through the hissing, ugly broken language of their thoughts he travelled. He broke through the second Toxic's barriers and reached its young mind trails. He found its memories. He saw it small and fresh, trying to find a friend in its land. He saw it confused and lonely as it realised friends were not available to Toxics. He saw it fully grown. Encased in bitterness that swirled around its memories and distorted them. He came back to its present thoughts. Its vacant pupils sharpened for a moment and looked at him properly. He spoke to it in the language of the world. They dulled. He spoke to it in the Toxics' chosen new harsh whispers. It listened. For a moment he knew it heard him. It shared his mind, and it saw his light. Then it retreated. It looked at him, and its eyes were pools of sadness as it remembered the hope. He spoke to it for the last time before it shuffled away, alone.

'Be calm. Toxic of hope. Be still, and be calm. Wait. Our quest continues, but be patient. Seek others like ourselves, Toxics of hope, and shelter with them. Leave this darkness. I saw your beauty. Find me when the quest has succeeded. Find me, new friend.'

At these words and at the desertion of his second-in-command, Demet became enraged. He darkened and blackened, and his foul features shrivelled up even tighter. He started spitting and hissing, and boils erupted between his spikes. He stood alone in the centre of the massive line of Toxics and simply fumed. His colleague didn't look back. It calmly walked away, past the quest group and on along the shoreline, as if in a trance. The rest of the Toxics were crowing and cackling, hissing and spitting. The whole line of them began to advance with their praying mantis shuffle, led by the postulating leader.

Reuben and Gus looked at each other.

'Well done, Gus,' said Reuben, and then they turned and ran back to the group.

'Run!' said Reuben, laughing.

Felicity decided he had definitely gone mad. They were backed up to a frothing sea, full of so much food they could hardly jog off, and a line of misinformed, blackened, melting Toxic die-hards were approaching fast. Seeing the blisters on Reuben's hand was not reassuring, either. Wolfgang and Pippi broke their defensive patrol and galloped back. Before Felicity was aware of what was happening, Pippi had grabbed her and tossed her onto her back. Wolfgang had snatched Scratt and Little Green onto his. Gus was hanging onto Georges' mane, and they were off.

Reuben took the lead. Felicity saw him anew. His long legs that she had surreptitiously admired found their pace. He was running at full stride along the shoreline. The water splashed up into their faces. Felicity licked her lips as she bumped along and tasted its saltiness.

'Hold on, Felicity,' said Pippi, and she lurched ahead in huge bounding leaps. The quest troupe just cleared the end of the line of Toxics. They flew on for about another four hockey pitches' length, and then Reuben called a halt. Looking back, Felicity could see the swaying line of Toxics had reached the sea. But they simply continued on. They entered the water, and their moans were muffled as they bobbed in the water like a scattering of ugly corks.

'Oh!' She giggled, horrified and fascinated at their end.

'Not their end, I'm afraid, Felicity,' said Reuben. 'They will float with the tide and reach the Shadowed South, which I think was always their leader's intention before they ran into us.'

'I wonder why so many were here in the Western Isle,' said Georges.

Wolfgang and Pippi were panting, but Wolfgang stopped for a moment to answer him. 'I think that may have been the final gathering of strays from the west.'

'Yes,' confirmed Reuben. 'Sib talked to me of the gathering of the Toxics in the regions. He said the Western Isle was the last region to turn. I think Demet, the leader, was sent from the Shadowed South to harvest the final lost souls and take them back with him.'

With Sib's name, just at that moment, floated a small wave of despair; Felicity felt it like a thin tissue hovering between them. It was almost visible. Sib had still not returned; his sudden departure remained unexplained. The Toxic party had been dark. So very dark. The sun slid behind a large cloud, and Little Green, from Wolfgang's back, held her slender arms up and began to sing. As her gentle, young voice crooned its soft melody up into the sky, the shapes of the Strata could be seen high above. They were still there, protecting from up high, realised Felicity, and gradually felt her shoulders relax as Little Green's magic renewed their hopes.

Reuben came over and put his arms around her. She leant her tired head on his chest. He smelt strong and a little sweaty, but she didn't mind. His courage was magnificent, and her heart felt big enough to hug them both, at that moment. Reuben kissed the top of her head. As the sun came back out, he lifted his head and looked to the edge of the forest. A movement caught his eye.

'Not more, surely?' he muttered to himself. But out of the forest stepped the most exotic creature Felicity thought she could ever have imagined, even in this surprising, mystical world. It was tall and yet so delicate. It was a plant, and yet its features were clear on its petal-framed face. It floated gracefully over to them across the sand. As it reached them, Felicity saw it was a beautiful woman. Well, a beautiful woman plant, she thought.

'Hello, Reuben,' said the plant.

'Hello, Orchadea,' said Reuben. He let go of Felicity and went to touch Orchadea. They touched foreheads, then noses, then lips.

Enough, thought Felicity, studying this interloper. Orchadea was mainly tendrils apart from her face. She reminded Felicity of an orchid her mother had once received from a secret admirer. Her face was the largest flower; tiny flowers seemed to denote her hands and feet, and the rest of her was a swirl of delicate, downy tendrils. Like a chiffoned ballet-dancing orchid. Felicity ground her teeth. The rest of the troupe seemed delighted to see Orchadea. Reuben turned back to Felicity, and he and Orchadea looked down at her from their lofty heights.

'Orchadea, may I introduce Felicity Isabel Penfold,' he said, and as Felicity faced this exquisite, fragile plant woman, she heard him continue, 'and Felicity, may I present Orchadeafourthousandth, my enharmonic.'

16

Orchadea

Orchadea led the group into the forest. Reuben kept close to her side. Georges, Pippi and Wolfgang walked and talked at the rear, and Felicity found herself listening to Scratt and Little Green's conversation. There was a buzzing in her ears as she glanced repeatedly at Reuben and Orchadea. A shaft of sun lit up Orchadea's pinky-lemon petals. She sighed and glanced behind her. Wolfgang and Pippi were having a heated debate. Pippi gave a snarl and shot off into the forest.

They walked for the rest of the afternoon. It was hot and sticky, and Felicity wished she could bathe again. Memories of that morning returned. Felicity swallowed noisily, and Scratt heard.

'Are you thirsty, Felicity?' he asked and began to rummage through his branches until he pulled out a little cup, with delight.

'Where on earth did you find that?' said Felicity. It was a small, blue cup made of hard plastic. It looked like the teacups she had left Al arranging at the school reunion. Felicity grasped it. It had a familiar plastic smell. She held it against her cheek and closed her eyes. A longing for home, for her kitchen and her mother sitting typing as supper burnt swept over her. Home. She opened her eyes and looked at this beautiful forest trail they walked. She saw these magnificent creatures who had become her friends. But home was always there, in the background. I will come home, Mum, she promised, but as the silent prayer left her mind, she found her eyes fixed on Reuben.

'Is it no good?' said Scratt, concerned at her silence.

'It's perfect,' Felicity said. 'It is for drinking; you are right. It reminded me of my world for a moment.'

'Do you miss your world?' said Scratt, with interest.

Felicity looked at him. In the days they had been travelling, he had grown from a small childlike Thorn to an almost adult height. He was still very slender, but he was taller than her now. Little Green was also visibly maturing as they travelled. *Why?*

'Yes and no,' she replied. 'Your Old World is a magical place, and I am beginning to feel I belong here.'

'Nothing happens without reason,' said Little Green, joining in their conversation.

'What caused you to be stranded, Little Green? What happened to your family?' Felicity scrutinised Little Green's face to ensure she had not offended.

The ferns cracked under their feet, as Little Green considered her reply. 'We were travelling to find Reuben's quest,' she said, after a pause. Her voice was quiet. 'My family had been told by the Aquatics that I had a part to play, in spite of my age. My mother was not happy to travel, and was angry I had been called to help when so young. But she accepted the wisdom of the elders, and we set off.'

'Where are your lands?' interrupted Felicity.

'Deep in the South East. Down, down, below the Sacred Caves you will find my lands. They are so beautiful, Felicity. I wish you could see them. Like here, we have forests of tall trees and flowers of every shade, and the ground is full of life. But we also have dusty open spaces similar to Reuben's land, where the elders form long tunnels of shade. Here are held the most respected Banyans of the world. These Banyans can go on for many months.'

'What exactly is a Banyan?' asked Felicity, fascinated.

'At a Banyan, all matters are decided. Knowledge is brought, questions are asked, history is consulted, and elders join the gaps. It is a time of quiet, of thought, and of calm energy. It shows the best of our world, in some ways,' said

Little Green. Her light had begun to softly glow with her words. Its phosphorescence gently sparkled as the dappled sunlight shone forest green in the early evening.

Felicity changed her mind; she did not want to know, now, what had happened to this young Green's family. Felicity imagined never seeing her own family again. She could not. She looked at Little Green's wrinkled eyes. They held such knowledge. She stopped walking. Reuben noticed and left Orchadea's side. She was surprised he had noticed. A spasm of cramp overtook her right thigh.

'Ow!' she exclaimed, rubbing her leg.

Pippi came crashing through the undergrowth and skidded to a halt by her. 'Felicity, what ails you?' she said, licking Felicity's face with her long tongue.

Felicity smiled in spite of the pain in her leg. Reuben tried to mind-share, but she wouldn't let him. She blocked him with satisfaction. Another pain shot through her leg.

'Ow! Ow!' she said.

'Felicity, Felicity, relax. Your anger is not helping,' said Pippi, smiling.

'Well, as everyone has stopped, we better make camp here tonight,' said Reuben.

'Is that okay with Orchadea?' asked Felicity petulantly.

Orchadea took Gus and Scratt to help collect the green drink this forest provided. When they returned, Scratt offered Felicity his little blue cup to drink from. Felicity dipped it into the pale green liquid that they had collected in more conical flower heads. It was just like the drink she had tasted in the last forest. It quenched the thirst immediately. Felicity took a second cup and sat back.

'Felicity, come for a ride, and we will fetch food,' said Georges with a snort that raised the pale pink birds from the surrounding canopy.

Felicity jumped up. She had missed Georges' antics. She climbed up carefully onto his furry back. Her legs stuck out sideways across his wide torso. Breathing through her nose

119

was best as he was rather smelly. But his infectious love of life soon cheered her up as he cantered through the forest, shouting and bellowing.

'Cheer up, little Felicity. Look at the flowers; aren't they so magnificent? Hear the evening chorus of the air's finest creatures; is not their song heavenly? Smell the herbs as we tiptoe through this fine carpet of green.' And he inhaled so fast Felicity nearly slipped off his back. The creatures of the forest scattered, and the plants were crushed by his massive hooves, but Georges remained happily unaware.

'On evenings like this I turn to thoughts of love,' he said. 'Love with a pretty little Taurelle so trim and lively.' His nostrils flared.

Felicity thought she would like him to calm down, so she feebly patted his neck and tried to distract him. 'Where do we go tomorrow?'

'We pass the infinite, earthy lands of my youth,' said Georges. 'There I shall find my next wife. She will be caramel-eyed, and her coat will be of the softest fur.' He tossed his head and bucked.

This was not going very well, Felicity thought, clinging on with all her strength.

'My pretty, pert little Taurelle to console me from the memory of my first dear love,' he said, 'my dearest love with whom I spent so many years. But she has passed on, and I am still a fine Taureau who needs a companion.' Georges was now so agitated he was carrying Felicity under branches that were swiping her in the face.

'Georges!' she shouted.

'Eh?' he said. 'What is it?'

'Please stop going so fast.'

'Oh, dear Felicity, forgive me. My homelands beckon me, and I feel vigorous. I apologise. I will behave.' Georges fell silent.

They found some strape, and he showed her how to gather the ribbons. They peeled the pliable strips of plant from its large trunks. Later, as they returned to the others, Felicity thought about Georges. She had understood him to be extremely old. He clearly did not think he was past mating age. She looked at the faded colours on his muzzle. She remembered the glint in his green eyes. He was obviously an exceptional Taureau.

Back at camp, a small fire had been lit. They all shared their treasures of food and drank as much green drink as they could. Reuben confirmed that tomorrow they would leave the forest and traverse the great Taureau plains. Georges was challenging Orchadea, who insisted they could not go deep into Taureau land. She insisted that the Aquatics, like the Strata, had recommended they reach Orion Country as fast as possible. A Banyan must be held to safeguard the future of Little Green, and Reuben and she had reached their time, and they needed to soul-bond. It was essential Reuben become mature for the successful outcome of the quest; she had come now to help him achieve this.

Reuben looked across at Felicity as Orchadea spoke. For the first time he had not chosen to sit by her at the campfire. Felicity was devastated. She watched Orchadea smooth some balm onto Reuben's blistered hand.

Georges backed down. The quest's resolution was more important than any of them individually. He had pledged to put the quest above all else, and so he would. 'But I will have a good look for my little Taurelle as we pass,' he said and went to lean against the largest tree for the night.

Felicity found solace in the shadows of the trees. Pippi came over, and Wolfgang too. They sat on either side of her.

'You speak, my lady,' said Wolfgang in his deep growl. Pippi gave a little whine, and he growled again. Their wolverine noises passed backwards and forwards for a few moments. Finally Pippi licked Felicity roughly on the back of her neck, pushing her over.

'Stop being so childish, Felicity,' Pippi said. 'Your anger confuses and worries Reuben. Why are you being hostile to Orchadea?'

'Am I?' said Felicity. 'I haven't spoken to her yet.'

'We do not need words to communicate, as you know by now,' said Wolfgang, and Felicity stepped back in alarm as his huge head swung round. 'Your thoughts upset the quest troupe morale. You are a key member, and the quest relies on you. You must rebalance,' said Wolfgang angrily.

'Wolfgang is right, Felicity. We need you,' said Pippi.

Felicity gave a huge sigh and sat down. Pippi lay by her, her furry nose neatly arranged on her paws as she stared deep into Felicity's eyes. Wolfgang elongated his black frame and closed his eyes. *Women talk*, he thought.

'Well, I don't quite know how to begin,' said Felicity. She was too embarrassed to mention the feelings that were growing between her and Reuben.

'You want to mate with Reuben, and you see Orchadea as a threat?' said Pippi.

Felicity gasped, and big purply patches appeared on her cheeks. This fascinated Pippi, and she sniffed gently to assess the cause, her nose wrinkling from side to side.

'Well, I suppose that is…um…one way of putting it,' said Felicity, clearing her throat. Oh, God, this was worse than talking to her mother about…stuff. The ridiculousness of the situation overcame her, and she snorted down her nose.

Wolfgang opened an eye. Was this stranger part Taurelle? He shifted his position to peer at her more closely. He needed rest. His Lupata would be his true mate within days, he knew. Her time was approaching. He felt good. He had not expected to breed again. His many cubs were long-grown, and his mate gone to the earth; he was happy to be himself. He had heard of this quest. He had come to the matings to seek Reuben. He knew he could help. He still had the strength that had made him a leader, some years ago. This Lupata with the strange name, Pippi, was an unexpected gift, and he felt excited at the prospect. But he was not in his prime. He needed rest. He rolled over with a grunt and went back to sleep.

Pippi was waiting patiently for Felicity to communicate. Felicity tried.

'I come from a different world, Pippi. In my world we cannot simply choose a mate and breed. Well, in some ways we do, but there is a bit more to it.' Felicity chewed her bottom lip. How did she explain society and morals and religious beliefs. Certainly Pippi and Wolfgang's world also had rules and traditions. She tried again. 'Um. You see, I must be of the right age, in my world, and my people ask me to be joined in a ceremony once I have found my life mate.'

Pippi tried to understand. 'It is not so different. We have ceremonies. You can follow our traditions once you and Reuben are ready,' she said, 'but he must become mature first, and that requires his enharmonic bonding. You must not be threatened by Orchadea. That is the way of our world.' But even as she spoke, Pippi sensed Felicity would not like the maturity ceremony that Reuben and Orchadea would perform once they reached Orion Country.

Felicity was wondering what Reuben thought of all this. He had never spoken of it. It's true he had kissed her; he wouldn't deny the attraction that pulled them together. But–

Wait and see. Pippi's thoughts spoke across her own. *Trust our world, Felicity. Trust Reuben. Let go of these angry thoughts.* Pippi stood then and went to lie with Wolfgang.

Felicity went back to the fireside, but it was too hot. She couldn't find anywhere to settle. She was huffing and puffing. O-r-c-h-a-d-e-a was draping herself across Reuben, who was talking intensely to her. Georges was snoring loudly. The Lupata slept soundly. She looked at Gus. He winked at her. She was sure he had just winked at her. She went to him.

'Felicity, go to sleep. Tomorrow we cross into Taureau country. It is dusty and hard tramping. Sleep, Felicity. Worry not. Sleep,' he said. He drew in his spines, and she slumped against him. Little Green and Scratt scuffled over. Felicity closed her eyes. She suddenly felt very tired. She was floating on waves, and they were so, so soft, she thought, smiling. But it was even too much effort to smile anymore. As the pale moon of the world slid silently up to hang in the navy blue sky, Felicity finally fell into a deep sleep.

*

By mid-morning, dust filled Felicity's mouth and nose. The heat rising from the orange, desiccated ground wrapped its strength around her throat and squeezed. Georges had left. At first light he had told Reuben he would go ahead and had galloped away, leaving a feeling of great emptiness. Reuben came to her side.

'Hello, Felicity,' he said, with a smile.

'Oh, hello, Reuben,' she answered, focusing on the shimmering horizon.

'You do well to stand this heat,' Reuben said. 'But you are gaining too much colour on your face, Felicity,' he said, leaning over and peering at her.

His head provided a moment's welcome relief from the searing heat. Felicity felt like a spit roast, gently frying on all available surfaces. She supposed they were all immune to the weathers in their world. *Perhaps they just call on the wind to cool them.* No doubt now something horrid would happen due to her mean thoughts. Reuben started softly laughing, and she was pleased to see his face looked pink, too.

'Felicity, Felicity, stop being so cross,' he said, laughing even louder. He leant closer and gave her a soft kiss on her hot cheek. His lips felt velvety and cool.

She closed her eyes and squeezed her lids so tightly she could see small white spots. She would not cry. She would NOT cry. Reuben stopped walking. He turned and put his arms around her; then closing his eyes, he took a deep breath and blew a steady stream of cool air across her face. It lifted the sticky tendrils of hair that clung to her temples. They both opened their eyes and looked into the centre of each other's pupils.

Reuben entered her mind. *Patience, Felicity. Patience. Funny strange Felicity.*

Felicity felt a small ease in the knotted ball deep inside her stomach. She leant forwards and kissed him quickly on the bump of his nose. That tantalising scent, she thought. She inhaled it and smiled tentatively at him. Reuben seemed satisfied and, ruffling her hair, moved back to the front of the line, and Orchadea.

No one spoke much for the rest of that molten day. In the early afternoon Reuben declared them close enough to the mountains to pause. They rested and drank the refreshing green drink of the forests. The plants all formed a small bivouac of shade, and Orchadea handed round a tiny bark pot of balm. It smelt like salad dressing, but Felicity smeared it on gratefully. Her face was burning now, and the bark balm gave almost instant relief.

Then as the sun passed its apex and imperceptibly crept to the horizon, they reached the mountain pass.

17

The Pass

Felicity looked up at the towering chasm. The walls of the pass were sheer cliffs of stone. There were a few dry plants clinging bravely to their hostile surfaces, but their main faces were smooth. As they stood, exhausted and silent, a low, familiar shape scuttled across one of the higher slopes. Reuben gasped. Gus stepped forward beside him.

'Is it him, then?' he asked as if continuing their silent conversation.

'Yes,' said Reuben. He turned to the troupe.

'Georges will join us tomorrow. He uses today to seek his Taurelle. His urge is strong, and we must honour him this time. We will make camp once through the pass. The walking will be cooler now. He handed round some strape that they had brought with them for lunch. No one had been able to eat much at their midday meal, in the explosive heat. Felicity wondered how long Reuben thought it would take them to reach camp.

'A couple of hours,' he replied, his mouth lifted at one corner with amusement. He knew how it annoyed her when he jumped without permission into her head.

Felicity felt a yearning for something unnamed as she looked at him. He was unfairly good-looking. Even now, covered in the day's dust and with cracked lips, his hazel-brown eyes glowed a pale amber as they looked directly at her.

Gus and Reuben led the way. The Toxics should not be here, she knew, as they were all heading to the gathering in the South, but the quest party had been surprised once.

The Toxics' behaviour was unpredictable, and this pass was narrow. Felicity found that even the sound of her breath felt too loud, as they turned the first narrow bend within this stony tunnel. Looking up, she tried to glimpse the scuttling creature on the higher walls, but the overhang prevented any vision apart from chinks of fading light as darkness descended.

Cold came, and the last light left. Reuben now asked Little Green to walk with him. She failed to reach him, so narrow was the passage. Eventually Wolfgang had taken her gently in his huge jaws and lifted her over Felicity. Gus helped her settle just behind Reuben, who needed her phosphorescence, but the oppressive atmosphere and her own exhaustion affected her aura, and she was only able to push out a small green light. This was enough, however, for them to move slowly ahead. Felicity was quiet. From the original crowd with whom she had begun this journey in the Eastern Wastes, they were now down to just seven. She missed Georges. Even his awful smell, she thought. And still no one mentioned Sib.

He is here, Felicity. Scratt's voice entered her head. Felicity peered at his outline in the gloom, surprised. He had never intruded into her mind like this before. Beginning to understand the rules of this world, she realised he must feel adult to take this liberty. He towered over her now. A fine, tall, young Thorn. His branches had strengthened over the days, and she could imagine him at the Lupata mating ceremonies providing a wonderful shield, alongside the strongest and tallest of the young, male Thorns.

'Thank you, little Felicity,' he said aloud now, in his deepening voice.

'Hey! You might have grown up, but you're still chirpy little Thorn to me, so don't you dare call me little Felicity!' she replied, laughing. Then she remembered what he had said.

'Who is here?' she asked.

'Sib,' he replied quietly.

At that moment there was a distant sound. It began like the sound of huge waves crashing on a sandy shore. Felicity was delighted. The sea and fresh air tomorrow, she thought. But it changed. The rolling sound became more fractured. The waves changed and became a tapping rumble now. The knocks and tapping crescendoed. The approaching noise clarified. It was rocks, not water, she realised with terror. She felt Scratt grab her arm.

They were all running now. Running in the darkness and hitting their sides on the sharp walls. Little Green's light glimmered erratically as she ran. Felicity didn't want to see this noise. She didn't want to see this terrible thing. *Just let it be over. Let me wake up, at home, in my bed,* she thought as she ran. Teeth crashing together, she gasped for breath. She could smell the dust of the falling rocks now; the wind of the avalanche tossed it along their narrow gorge. She could hear nothing but the roaring, thunderous sound of mighty rocks tumbling and smashing.

She screamed, 'Mummy!' but her cries were swallowed by the roar. A firm grip snatched her sideways, and she fell, winded, on the damp ground. Orchadea had found a hidden cave, and they were safe. The sound was still tumultuous, but it passed outside the solid cave entrance. They could still be blocked in, thought Felicity as her heaving chest began to find air. *We could still be blocked in and die in this cave, only to be found in thousands of years, a pile of bones and fossils.*

She turned over and lay on her back. Her chest still laboured, but the spots had stopped in front of her eyes. She rolled her head to one side, feeling the hard ground pressing against it. Reuben sat, his head in his hands. His breath was steady, but he would not look up. Gus stood by Thorn, both still. Little Green had her eyes closed and her graceful arms wide as she murmured thanks and peace to the spiritual place she seemed to reach so easily.

Finally Felicity looked at Orchadea. It was Orchadea who had saved them, Orchadea who had pulled her out of danger. She would have run on, oblivious. Straight into a stony death. Orchadea turned her petalled face quietly to Felicity. They looked at each other; blue-green eyes met green-blue. Pippi sat by Wolfgang and watched intently. Felicity knew something was expected of her. She felt strange inside. She recalled the words of her mother, 'Never be a coward, Flissy. Never be afraid to say sorry.' Felicity looked at Orchadea again.

'Sorry,' she said. She couldn't phrase the rest, but she hoped that was enough.

Orchadea smiled, and it was the sunshine rising after a storm. The cave felt full of lightness as the two faced each other. The lemony-pink petals framing Orchadea's face trembled slightly.

Pippi came over and nuzzled Felicity. Her breath was warm. Felicity didn't look at Reuben, but she felt him stand. He went to the entrance of their sanctuary and looked outside. The avalanche was over. He could hear a few small pebbles rolling intermittently down the steep sides of the chasm a little further ahead, but the roaring had stopped, and the dust clouds were settling. It was time to move. They must not stay here; it could become their cage. He thought of the sighting of Sib. He was determined not to jump to conclusions. *Unreliable and secretive, yes. Killers, no.* He sighed.

'Let's be clear of the pass before we make camp,' he said, turning to the others. 'We will discover soon enough any obstacles left by the avalanche, but we must not stay here.'

Everyone got up, brushing off the thick dust and coughing. Reuben led them outside, with Orchadea smoothly following. Wolfgang and Pippi yawned in unison and quietly padded behind Felicity as they stumbled into the dark pass once more.

*

They had been travelling for a couple of hours. The stars shone high above them. As they scrambled over fallen rocks, Felicity heard a tired shout ahead.

'We are out!' She staggered round the corner with Scratt, Wolfgang and Pippi. Wonderful fresh air flooded her nose and mouth even before her eyes captured the panorama below. They had exited the narrow pass, but with the view now lit up by the full moon, Felicity realised the land in front of them had dropped away. They were standing on a high ledge, and the path fell steeply to the dark prairie below. Felicity could see a tiny reflection at the bottom of the valley floor, and she realised it must be water.

'Reuben,' she called, excited. 'Look, a river.'

Telling everyone to stand carefully, Reuben edged back to Felicity, and as they looked down together to the glinting ribbon of water, he reached out to hold her hand and squeezed it tightly.

'My lovely Felicity,' he said, and she felt the effort it took him to speak, as exhaustion claimed him.

'Well done, Reuben. We are all safe, no one was hurt.' She lifted their entwined hands to her cheek and held them there a moment.

There was a wider point on the ledge, with just room enough for the entire troupe to huddle together and rest. No one could eat, but they shared the amber nectar juice from Gus' flask. Felicity was sure they had already drained it in the forest.

'We will eat well with first light,' said Reuben, and they all agreed.

He came and lay close to her, and Orchadea gracefully elongated on his other side. Scratt and Little Green rustled off to a corner, and Gus stood behind them, protecting them from the drop. Felicity could hear Wolfgang and Pippi quietly grooming each other, but they had moved out of her vision. They seemed to need privacy tonight. There was no need for fire, and it would have been a beacon to unwelcome guests. As the quest pack fell silent, preparing to sleep, a slithering and scuffling noise approached. Reuben tensed, and Felicity felt her heart bang. She was almost too tired to care. But Reuben stood stealthily. Wolfgang and Pippi came to his side.

'Welcome, quest members!' said a familiar voice, loud in the darkness. The scuffling stopped, and in the light of the moon, Felicity saw the silhouette of Sib. Head raised, feet out, he stood boldly, facing them.

'Welcome, Siblinsixteenthousandth,' said Reuben, as he left Felicity's side to approach the interloper of the night.

18

River Day

Under the ceiling of starlight, Sib spoke. It was the Aquatics who had told him to leave, he said, and the opportunity had arisen by chance the night they travelled west. Felicity didn't care. She tried to sleep, but the sound of his wheedling voice made her cheeks burn. Why had he not sent a message? Why did no one challenge him? She took some deep breaths to calm her anger. Surely Reuben would not accept Sib's pathetic story. Sib turned his head in the moonlight, and his beady eyes peered directly at Felicity. She felt sick. She couldn't see his expression, of course, but she knew he had heard a tail of her angry thoughts. She blocked her mind and continued to listen.

'I travelled far, far west, as instructed by the Aquatics. My mission was to shadow the Toxics gathering in that area. The Aquatics and Oceanids knew they were collecting en masse, and they wanted me to seek information for them before they left the Western Isle for the great gathering in the Shadowed South. They knew I had an understanding of the Toxics' new language.'

Felicity tried to remember if Sib had revealed this when they had first heard the ugly language, in Thornton. She didn't think he had.

'So I lived stealthily, staying on their edges and listening to their ideas and plans. They had become great in numbers, and it was hard not to be seen, but I managed.'

Felicity made a small noise, and Reuben turned to look at her. She quickly closed her eyes, as if asleep.

'Their main aim was to try to gather recruits from all

Toxics, even those opposed to change,' he said, 'but the Oceanids told the Aquatics that they had heard worse. The Strata had begun to suspect, watching from the skies, that the Toxics were actually trying to recruit other Old World species to join their cause. A changed world might benefit others, in some cases, and it was this that worried the Aquatics and Oceanids greatly.'

At these words, Little Green moved towards Sib. His eyes glinted in Little Green's glow as she gently approached. She was also taller, Felicity noticed. Her phosphorescence surrounded the small circle of Little Green herself, Sib and Reuben. Sib took a small step back.

'You grow fast, Little Green,' he said, bowing slightly in respect.

'Your story concerns me, Sibilinsixteenthousandth,' replied Little Green in her dulcet tones. 'To whom else would it benefit my world for the old ways to be lost and destroyed?'

Sib's eyelids flicked down and up before he replied, 'The Sibilin live in the hostile deserts that lie within the Central Lands. Our terroire is not fruitful like those of the Western Isle, or the South East. It is not green like those of the Temperate North. Our enharmonics are not a good match for our kind.' His speech rose to a whine as he answered Little Green.

Reuben said nothing. He felt Little Green's growing strength. It was good. He needed her to help him with Sib. He was pleased with the way the troupe were developing. With his guidance, this quest would succeed. It must succeed. The moon was dipping; it would soon be dawn. He stepped forwards and interrupted, 'Forgive me, Little Green. I welcome you to continue this discussion, but we must sleep first. Dawn is close. Tomorrow we descend to the prairies that border the lands of my people.' He touched her arm gently and felt her respond.

She entered his mind privately. *Be careful, Reuben. I feel disruption in Sib.*

Yes, thank you, Little Green, I feel it too. We will discover more in the morning. Rest, my dear friend – we need you strong.

Reuben went and lay by Felicity, who had genuinely fallen asleep and was softly snoring. Orchadea was silent. Reuben lay on his back, his hand reaching out to gently hold Felicity's. Little Green rested quietly as Sib lay down. She ensured he slept before joining Scratt's side. Gus touched her arm, and she felt lightened. In him, perhaps, was the hope for the Toxics.

*

The first rays of the sun touched the sleeping face of Felicity. She opened her eyes and was astonished. The little river she had spotted in the moonlight was actually a broad blue expanse of water flowing through the valley's centre.

Reuben wanted to move on, but as they descended the root-bound track, Reuben looked back. There were many large boulders piled up in a crevice, which he presumed must have been the main fall of the avalanche. He could see the tops of the craggy mountains, but they were so jagged in appearance it was hard to tell where the landslide had begun. It had not, in the end, impeded their way, and he was glad of that small mercy.

A sense of urgency pushed on his thoughts. He must get home now. It was all he could think of. He needed to clear Little Green, to bond with Orchadea, and to receive his further instructions. He was tired of the trail. Tired of leading them all when the picture was not clear to him. The reliability of his beautiful world was shifting. He understood what the Aquatics meant now. He needed every ounce of Old World strength. He needed to become a mature Orion male. His eyes were on Felicity, but he was not even aware of it.

Orchadea spoke silently to him. *She is strong, Reuben, but not of our world. Can it be possible – that which you seek with her?*

There is more to our world than we know, Orchadea. Felicity was sent here for a reason. I was made different from my kind. Why could these things not balance?

Orchadea sighed, a stream of floral-scented air that wafted past Reuben. *We will see, dearest Reuben. Let the elders discuss these things at the Banyan, whilst we come to our intended maturity.*

As Orchadea was speaking, Felicity had her eyes fixed on a plume of smoke that was travelling towards them far ahead on the valley floor. Gus, Scratt and Little Green saw it too. Wolfgang and Pippi cantered down the path ahead of the others. Their four legs were a definite advantage on this treacherously narrow track. Sib's technique was to scale the rock side; he was able to cling on in some way. *Like a giant newt*, thought Felicity. The trail of smoky dust was clearly coming their way. Felicity had to concentrate on her footing, but each time she looked up it was closer. The hairs on her arms rose. She knew a Toxic could not move so fast. She looked at Reuben. He was smiling. The dust cloud enveloped the Lupata as they galloped into it, way below.

'Georges!' said Gus and Reuben together.

'Oh!' said Felicity. 'Oh, thank goodness.'

The troupe were finally reunited about an hour later; the bellows of Georges being audible for the last thirty minutes.

Sib was grumbling, '...enough noise to make another avalanche.'

Reuben looked at him. But everyone was glad to be together again. Georges regaled them with his recent adventures.

'I look forward to introducing my lovely Taurelle. The cutest little black lady on our plains,' he was saying. 'She was not mated – her size is larger than most Taurelles. She is the perfect size for me, and she loves my great maturity,' he added, tossing his head as he pranced back and forth.

'Um, Georges, where is she?' asked Felicity, adoring his ridiculous pomposity.

'She will not travel with us. She will join us later,' Georges said and would not explain further.

'We welcome your return,' said Reuben.

The sparkling river drew them on fast. Georges had taken the lead, for a change, so Wolfgang and Pippi brought up the rear without discussion. The sun rose, and with it came the heat and the flies. Felicity had hoped they might not be present in this world, but she was disappointed. The fat insects, more like a bumblebee, buzzed around their sticky, dusty faces. Georges' tail swished in front, a hypnotic pendulum that only seemed to bat the bugs from side to side. They hovered about Gus, who seemed oblivious to them, and pestered the Lupata without pause. The cool water offered relief, and Felicity could hear other minds chanting tiredly, *Ah, water...cool drink...diving...Stipple Greens beware...*

Felicity stopped walking with a jolt. Who had said that? She watched each of them. Some were walking, some brushing away the bugs. She tried to listen again, but it was clear whoever had said it was now blocking her. Her forehead prickled. They knew she had heard. Fear clawed inside her stomach. Perhaps they thought she had heard more. What had they meant, anyway? She chewed her bottom lip. She must look calm. Perhaps they didn't know who had tapped their thoughts. Her thudding heart slowed down. Perhaps she could listen in again later. Be of more use to Reuben. Felicity the diviner. She fell flat on her face as a plant root caught her shoe.

'Felicity the blind,' she cursed herself softly. Sib tittered. She looked at him with dislike. His eyes went white. She shuddered. He had dropped his second lid to conceal his pupils. His opaque, milky-white inner lids concealed all. *He is really beginning to give me the creeps. Why is he here?*

Little Green came and lightly touched her arm. 'We all have our places in this story, Felicity. Do not be so quick to judge. We learn more by remaining open.' Felicity was still frowning, so Little Green said, "When we reach Reuben's homeland, there will be many creatures of our world there. All the plants and beasts favour Orion Country for it is a land of great bounty and joy. There you should seek the Colour Changers. For they are the enharmonics of the Sibilin, and maybe they can help you find the tolerance you need.'

Felicity said nothing. She knew Little Green meant well. There was always someone to help, she realised. First Reuben – currently consumed with Orchadea. Dear Gus seemed more withdrawn since the Toxic attack on the beach, and Wolfgang and Pippi were mainly busy with each other these days, when not on duty. Georges had been full of Taurelle thoughts, and Scratt just kept busy growing! Little Green was a consistent friend. Looking at the tall plant in front of her, Felicity could not imagine the young Green she had been when she first joined them. Her steady light in the darkness had been unwavering.

A large splash made her look ahead. Georges had reached the water and plunged in without hesitation. His huge displacement caused a succession of small waves. They all ran laughing towards the inviting river and jumped in. The plants floated on their backs, trailing arms and tendrils. Georges had his own stretch, and they stayed clear of his thrashing legs and horns. Sib paddled at the edge, his long tongue lapping the water. Wolfgang and Pippi swam hard and fast up and down; channel swimmers focused on their muscular strength. Their large noses pointed out of the water, nostrils flared to breathe with their aqua-exertions. Felicity was reminded of her own darling dog Pippi. She admired the Lupata again. *Wherever Pippi now is, may it have rivers like this*, she thought. Orchadea sat elegantly on a fallen branch, trailing her hands back and forth in the water. Where was Reuben? Felicity trod water and spun around. She could not see him.

She dipped her hot head into the icy water, and opening her mouth, let it fill up. She had seen the others drinking it, so she swallowed a little. It was delicious. It tasted like aniseed, and even when cupped in her hands, kept its turquoise colour. She swam a leisurely backstroke, looking up at the blue sky. The sun was high, and the wisps of cloud stretched out, forgotten ribbons of moisture, abandoned by the wind. She closed her eyes. She could hear the lapping of water in her ears. She lifted her head a little. A bird was calling in a distant place, and there were flurries of wind that dappled the river's surface where she swam. Suddenly she was underwater, gasping for air as her nose and throat filled with bubbles. She fought with the enemy and thrashed to the surface, choking. Reuben bobbed up, looking pleased with himself.

'Caught you, Felicity Isabel Penfold,' he said, laughing. Then he cried out as her hand swung with all the force she could muster and slapped his cheek. He looked horrified.

'How dare you!' she said, beginning to cry. She swam to the bank and hauled herself out. As she lay steaming with her face buried in the grass, she heard him climb out and lie beside her.

Reuben wasn't quite sure what to do. He was silent. Perhaps she would speak, but her pitiful sobs disturbed him. She wouldn't let him mind-share, so he reached out and stroked the wet curls back from her face. It was all blotchy. He looked at the plants on which she squashed her face. Was she allergic to them?

'No, I'm not, you stupid man,' she finally gurgled and sat up, wiping her face with his shawl. She hiccoughed as the tantrum left her and looked at him. How could he under-stand all the feelings that were raging through her? He wasn't even a human. At that thought she began to wail again. Sib and Orchadea glanced at the disturbance from the opposite bank. The others swam up, and Felicity felt embarrassed.

'I am so hungry after that swim,' she said, hoping no one would mention the tantrum.

They didn't. Their minds shared fast – *a strange behav-iour of her world*, they all agreed. Georges surged towards them in the river, and they all scaled the slimy banks as fast as they could. The waves announced his arrival. He heaved his mammoth bulk out of the frothing water with great difficulty. Looking around the group, Felicity saw them struggling to contain their mirth. Scratt held his lips pursed tightly together. Reuben was biting the inside of his cheeks. Even Orchadea was trying to concentrate on the ground beneath her.

Georges stood, sides heaving on the soggy ground, and announced, 'You saw, I hope, my streamlined physique cut through the water like a young Oceanid. My Taurelle, Tatania, is a lucky woman.' At these words, the whole gang exploded in snorting, gasping laughter. Georges was outraged. He galloped across the prairie roaring, 'Ill-mannered whippet generations...Ignorant young pups of unknown age. Rude, ungrateful limpets of the world...' His bellows caused basking birds to rise, and scattered the small deer-creatures grazing in the afternoon sun.

It took the diplomacy of their combined strengths to tempt him back, with Wolfgang and Pippi as emissaries carrying profuse apologies. The troupe settled down to eat the fat chive-flavoured river reeds that grew in abundance at the waterline. Then refreshed and invigorated by their day, they set off for Reuben's land. Felicity looked back at the sparkling water as they cut a trail away towards the hills in the distance. She felt a need to memorise the images of this adventure. To tell Al and Mum. Then, shoulders lifted, she looked ahead.

19

Orionwood

Orion was humming with the news that the quest company had arrived, and preparations were in full swing as the troupe awoke. Looking up, Felicity gazed at their shelter. It was similar to the tepees she had seen in pictures of the Native American Indians: tall and made of some sort of thick cloth. It was probably animal hide, but Felicity didn't like to ask. A hole at the apex allowed smoke to escape from a centrally situated small brazier. The beds lay around the edge, filled with soft feathers, and had felt like bliss last night. Vents above their sleeping heads had let in the sounds of the wild, and someone had laid a fire that smouldered sweetly overnight. It smelt marvellous, thought Felicity, and had ensured them a deep, restorative rest.

This morning they ate outside the shelter, so Felicity was able to watch the activities with great curiosity. There were mainly Orion bustling about, but scattered amongst them were all the beasts and plants of this exotic world. There were a group of Colour Changers carrying food and drink, and bringing all their glowing colours of autumn into this green settlement. There were tall trees encircled with Fragrants that swayed and murmured, adorning the trees in a multitude of rich pastel petals with their columbine faces. Looking up at them, Felicity could see the fragile Fagrants preferred to be raised out of the noise.

The Taureau cantered about, raising dust and making the ground shake. Thankfully none of them were as massive as Georges, but even so, they stayed out of the thick of things. Seeing a Taurelle knock over a group of Thorns like skittles, who had ventured into her path, Felicity understood why.

There were Thorns lined up, subconsciously forming hedges wherever they congregated. Felicity looked for any Lupata. She spotted a pack resting under a tree farther off. There were not many Sibilin, and those that were lay silent and still, tongues flicking as they observed matters with a wary eye. There was a pale green one that Felicity guessed might be female. She was smiling at a group of young Colour Changers who were fighting over the honour of carrying drink to the quest company.

In a large clearing, a group of tall, elderly Greens were forming a tunnel with their long arm branches. Their aerial roots formed dangling long curtains. Three Orion that clearly carried some sort of authority were walking up and down the tunnel, tweaking and closing the gaps of the sides, whilst talking earnestly to the Greens that they were helping. Two Thorns were brushing the ground in the tunnel to make a smooth, clean floor. A large ginger-haired Orion approached Reuben. He smiled and held out his arms, and they embraced.

'Welcome home, my son,' said Reuben's father. Running up behind him came a gaggle of four small Orion. Two had Reuben's eyes. They jumped all over him with glee.

'Ouch!' he exclaimed. 'Wow, you four have certainly grown since I left,' he said, giving each of them a strong hug.

'Where is Mother?' he asked his father.

'She wanted to prepare you a feast for this evening. She left early to gather the foods. But let us discuss your progress and your plans,' said his father, brushing away the little brothers and sisters.

'First, Father, I must introduce to you my friends,' said Reuben.

Everyone stood up to meet Reuben's father. Before Reuben could begin, however, he saw his mother running across the clearing towards them. She was laughing, and with a happy smile, he stepped forwards to meet her. She wrapped her arms around him tightly. Felicity was fascinated by her. She was quite tall, but smaller than Reuben. Her hair was dark and silky like Reuben's but flecked with grey. Her eyes were huge yellow-amber orbs. She moved with a grace that Felicity envied. She was truly a beautiful creature. Felicity felt shy. Reuben stepped back and took her hand. He pulled her in front of his parents.

'Mother, Father, I introduce to you Felicity Isabel Penfold. She has come from a world apart and is the stranger I was first sent to seek for the quest.'

The two Orion bowed with dignity, and Felicity found herself trying to curtsey. She had only ever seen people doing it to the Queen, and it wasn't the same when you tried it yourself. She gave up and simply smiled the biggest, politest smile she could muster.

'How do you do, Mr and Mrs Orion,' she said.

Reuben laughed. 'Felicity makes names for us all,' he said. 'She finds ours too long. I like them well.'

'So do I,' said Reuben's mother, with a gentle smile that made Felicity feel welcome immediately.

'Welcome to Orionwood,' said Mr Orion, with a mischievous smile. She liked him.

Reuben introduced all the others and pointed to Georges, who lowered his head in acknowledgement from the edge of the settlement.

'My, what a fine old Taureau. I haven't seen one like him since I was a small boy. He is truly of the old ages of our world,' Mr Orion said, awed by Georges. Little Green smiled with delight. Felicity remembered the Greens and Taureau were enharmonics.

Reuben's mother clapped her hands, and the bustling village gradually fell silent and stopped moving. Two little Orion continued chasing each other until a tall Green picked them up and planted them on his shoulders. Mrs Orion spoke aloud to the crowd, her strong face commanding silence.

'Our son Reuben returns with his quest company. The

Aquatics inform us they may stay for one week. There is much to resolve before they depart for the Upper North. We, his family and friends, must aid the company in whatever way we are able. My son was chosen, along with the other quest members that we are honoured to receive, to heal our world. They need our support.' There was a murmur of approval from the crowd.

Mrs Orion continued, 'Today the Banyan will commence to decide the fate of the young Greenesse that travels with them. Please do not bring your own grievances to this Banyan. It is solely for the elders of the world to resolve the breaking of one of our laws. As always, however, all are welcome to bring their energies and strength to aid these discussions. There is a village feast this evening to welcome and nourish the weary travellers; would all who are able please offer their services to the Orion women for instructions.' At this she nodded sideways, and Felicity noticed a long line of Orion women, young and old, patiently waiting to begin preparing the feast.

They really were an attractive people, thought Felicity. It was only their luxuriant stripy tails poised behind them that separated the line-up from a beauty contest final. She twisted a lock of hair and stuffed it in her mouth. It tasted dusty, and she longed for a bath. Gus, Scratt, and Sib stood together. Wolfgang and Pippi sat quietly, listening to Mrs Orion, but their eyes scanned the village perimeter constantly. Felicity saw Pippi and Georges meet eyes. She focused with her growing skill and managed to tune in.

No, none have been seen for about a week, Georges was saying. Felicity knew he spoke of the Toxics and felt herself shudder involuntarily. Reuben took her hand, aware of her anxiety. Mr Orion's eyes watched, but he said nothing.

In silent agreement the whole village bestirred itself. Felicity could still be surprised by the unspoken communication. Here in the west it was so strong. To see them all move instantly like that was quite disconcerting. For a moment she felt a stranger to this peculiar, wise world. She took a big breath and let it slowly out. She would not cry now, not here in front of all these people. A warm glow spread through her, and she knew without looking that Little Green had come close.

Thanks, her mind whispered as the calming energy flowed through her.

You are not a stranger to us, dear Felicity, Little Green echoed back into her mind, *and I would love you to show me your lovely world*. So as the village fluttered about, the tall plant and the beautiful young woman stood immobile in its centre, sharing their thoughts. Felicity pictured Earth. She thought of its oceans and its forests, of its snow-capped mountains and its icy tundra. She thought of the glorious creatures of so many varieties and of the plants that held all the secrets of life. *I see it, Felicity! What a magnificent place*, said Little Green in wonder.

'But we have many problems, Little Green,' said Felicity aloud, lowering her head.

'Show me, dear Felicity,' said Little Green. Felicity made herself think of them: The polluted cities, the poisoned land, the savaged rainforests, and the starving people. Tears poured down her cheeks as the images flooded her mind. Little Green's eyes went dark with pain.

'To all there is balance, Felicity,' she said. 'Show me more, and we will find it together.' So Felicity made herself think again. She saw the passion of those who fought to stem the tides of destruction. She saw the love and unquenchable hope of mankind at his best. She saw the creatures running wild that had been saved by the dedication of those who sheltered and rehomed them. She heard the laughter of all the voices that defied the darkness and found the light. Little Green followed her thoughts and images.

'Hope is light. Light is love,' she said. Together they stood, the hope of the Old World, and the hope of the new, and Felicity allowed Little Green to ease the pain she had carried in her heart for so long. Like an arrow striking her, all became blissfully clear, and for a moment her very essence touched the light. *My life has been leading me here for as long as I remember.* Her father had thought her odd, strange. Her mother had known and loved her for it.

Reuben turned around, and their eyes met. He smiled, and watching the corners of his shining eyes crinkle, Felicity knew she had found her place. *Soon*, said his voice, deep inside her mind. A shout broke the spell of the moment, and they all turned.

'The Banyan commences! The Banyan commences!' a chorus of young Thorns rustled along pronouncing the news. They were giving away sticky buds, to Felicity's delight. Her stomach rumbled loudly. Reuben laughed.

'You said they were only eaten in the Temperate North,' said Felicity.

'There are always exceptions!' Reuben replied and called over the Thorns.

They took a handful and shared them out with the others. Georges raised his head with interest, and Felicity ran over to him. He took six. She ran back to the group, concerned they might lose her.

'Come,' said Mr Orion. Mrs Orion had long left to begin the feast, and Felicity felt a little guilty going to the Banyan. She hoped Mrs O would understand.

The quest company was organised by two tall Greens who peered down from wizened faces. Little Green was asked to stand in the centre of the tunnel, alone. She stood erect and calm. Reuben kept Felicity by his side, and they, Gus, Scratt, Wolfgang, Pippi, and Sib sat on each side of the tunnel, close to the centre. The musky scent of the old Greens made their noses tingle. Felicity heard the bellows of Georges as he tried to come close. A Green placated him, and he was allowed to stand at the entrance, thereby blocking everyone else from entering. Two Orion opened up the far end as an alternative. The Green and Orion elders debated how to overcome the law that disallowed a young Greenesse to travel alone. The voices rose and fell as the point went back and forth all day. Disconcertingly, a thread of conversation would suddenly disappear as the participants wove in and out of verbal and mind language.

Felicity felt dirty, tired, and excluded. It was stuffy, and the droning voices were hypnotising. She closed her eyes.

Instantly Scratt's clear voice jerked them open as he piped up, 'But, sirs, the Old World has solved the problem if only you could see. Greenseventhousandthseventy and I have matured unexpectedly. We are full-grown and need only our enharmonics to reach full maturity. The world has provided us with our answer. No rule is broken if Greenseventhousandthseventy is no longer a child. It is unusual but not disallowed for females to travel.'

There was total silence as all eyes turned to this adolescent Thorn. Reuben and Mr Orion looked at each other. The silence stretched out. Felicity held her breath. Outside, noises of beasts and plants filtered through the shady canopy. Finally, the eldest Green broke the silence. The power of Little Green's phosphorescence had been noted. It was not usual in such a young female. Peering down at the adolescent Thorn, his mouth was a thin line as he spoke.

'Our world has been changing for a long time,' he said. His voice was like a low rumble of thunder. 'We have been slow to embrace these changes, but the anger of the Toxics causes us to listen. If this brave group think they can rise to the task the Oceanids have created, then we must rise to the challenges these changing times present.'

There was a murmur of voices, but all were silent as he spoke again.

'We, the Greens, hold the knowledge of the world in our Stipples. We have sent them since the first Green to lay down the knowledge in the Roots. The elder Greens and I believe the answer for this world will be found with the success of this courageous company. They fight to protect our Roots and yet to realign the Old World with the dark Toxics – to find their place and heal their curse. Our laws were made to protect us and keep the balance. But our forebears did not lay them down to hinder us. If my learned Orion agree, then with conditions we should be able to allow Greenseventhousandthseventy to travel and fulfil her destiny and the destiny of our Old World.'

The Orion gathered together, and the talks went on. Their elders were not going to accept the fact that Little Green was tall as evidence that her childhood had ceased. The sun dipped down and shone over Georges' head, bathing one side of the dark tunnel in a deep red glow. Felicity longed to escape. *This is worse than end-of-term assembly.* She slumped on her prickly seat.

Eventually the elders turned to the Banyan attendants, and a tall Orion said, 'The young Greenesse must pass maturity tests, beginning with new sun tomorrow morning. If she succeeds, her enharmonic will be found. If this is as it should be, it will also have matured early and be ready for the soul-bonding.'

An excited murmuring began as he finished speaking. But he interrupted them, 'It has been agreed, however, that the young Thorn, in spite of his fast advancement, must wait until the proper time to seek his enharmonic and fully mature. We do not accept his speedy growth as significant. There is knowledge of Thorns achieving adolescence far in advance of usual expectations.'

Felicity looked at Scratt. He looked winded. As the Banyan broke up, Little Green went to comfort her friend. She soaked him in her light, and at last he raised his head with a sigh. Plants and beasts brushed past as Scratt, Little Green, Felicity, Reuben, Gus, Wolfgang, Pippi, and Sib clustered round. No one spoke, but each in turn patted Scratt on his branchy shoulder.

Sib raised his legs to their highest position so he could look at Scratt. 'The Old World can be hard.'

Scratt looked at him and then turned away.

The aromas of the evening feast floated in, and the group went in search of Mrs O's grand repast. Reuben was quiet as he walked by Felicity's side. She realised Orchadea hadn't joined them for the Banyan.

'No, she prepares for our bonding,' Reuben said, reading her thoughts, as always.

'What about you?' asked Felicity. She tried really hard not to sound upset, but her voice wobbled. She cleared her throat and spoke more loudly. 'When will you prepare, Reuben? When is it to be?'

Reuben stopped walking and turned to face her. He lifted his hand to her cheek, and she turned her face to meet its gentle touch. He didn't need to reply. She knew the answer. It would be tonight.

20

Enharmonics

Reuben and Orchadea had gone. The elders came to their tepee to collect Little Green, and turning over, Felicity realised Reuben had left. The dent in his feather cushion showed where he had lain, holding her until she slept. She couldn't think of the evening now. It was like a party she hadn't wanted to attend. All the eating and dancing had led up to the moment when Reuben and Orchadea would leave. *Like a wedding banquet.* Felicity stood up, restless, and walked to the opening of the tent.

Georges was going to spend the next few days on the outskirts of the village, now the welcome banquet was over. He said at his age he deserved a couple of days' good sleep after the long journey. Wolfgang had suggested it was meeting Tatania that necessitated the rest.

Gus had much to discuss with the elders. They wanted to know all he could tell them of these destructive, new Toxics. Felicity was astonished they held no fear. Only curiosity. Remembering the face of the Toxic, Demet, at the landing beach, she wondered if their lack of fear was ignorance or wisdom. She didn't want to listen to Gus and the elders, even if they had invited her, which they clearly hadn't.

Wolfgang and Pippi were going to spend the time here mating. Pippi said her pups would not be born until long after they had defeated the Toxics. Felicity imagined Lupata cubs and smiled.

'What are you smiling at?' said Scratt, coming up behind her. The others were stirring now.

Felicity turned to him. 'I was thinking of Lupata cubs.'

'Ah, truly beautiful balls of fur,' said Scratt. 'As our enharmonics, we do, of course, take special interest in them. Wonderful little beasts. Nippy, though. Even a four-week-old Lupata can give a fair bite.'

Felicity wondered if she would still be here to find out. How she would love to take one home. A gurgle of laughter welled up inside her; what would Mum say if she took one back?

'Mummy, I brought a Lupata cub for us to keep. He will chew up most of the furniture and needs walking at least eight hours a day. He will grow to about the height of our conservatory, but that's okay. He can sleep outside.'

Scratt left to chat and breakfast with a group of young Thorns. If he couldn't mature, then he would have some fun. He approached them with a half-smile.

Felicity flopped onto the rubbery, bright green grass. A flurry of Colour Changers brought over some drink. It was the pale lemon water. Sib poked his nose out of the entrance and then shuffled over. A stray feather was clinging to his scaly back, but he hadn't noticed. Felicity needed to talk; she didn't want to think about Reuben. And Orchadea.

'Have you bumped into your enharmonic since your soul-bonding?' she asked. She still had no trust in Sib, but he was with them for now.

Sib's tongue flicked out as he composed a reply. His eyelids half-covered his orange eyes as he replied, 'No, as I told you before, there is no reason. Our use to each other was finished. Our lives are now ours to lead alone or partnered.'

'But if you are so important to each other?' said Felicity.

'There would only be one reason to seek out our enharmonic during our lives, as I explained before.' Sib opened his eyes wide and looked directly at her. 'It is dangerous and could kill.'

'I forgot. Thank you for reminding me,' she said.

Sib looked away.

Felicity surveyed the camp. Little Green was in the

Banyan, bravely meeting the challenges the elders had devised. Deciding to escape Sib, Felicity walked across and tried to peek inside. A large pair of Thorns shielded the interior view. Felicity tried tapping one of them on his branchy arm. No response. She tried pushing her face through the lighter green bits, but that hurt.

'Hmm,' she said, annoyed by their silent defence. She was a quest member, after all. She strolled slowly to the corner, where their bodies met the wall of Greens forming the tunnel. She really wanted to know what poor Little Green was having to do in order to gain permission to travel on. She prayed for Little Green's success. Meanwhile she was going to find a way into the Banyan tunnel. There was not even a chink of light at the corner, but Felicity discovered if she went round the side of the Greens' walls, she could at least hear.

'My knowledge was passed to me by my mother before she died,' Little Green was saying.

'Yes, child, but you cannot have taken in all the knowledge needed for a mature Greenesse at such an early age,' replied the rumbling voice that Felicity recognised as the elder Green of the previous day.

'I assure you, I am no longer a child. Look,' said Little Green, and then all was silent. Felicity thought they were mind-sharing. This was pointless. If they didn't speak aloud, she would have to give up, but as she turned away, the light pulled her back. Even through the dense curtains of the Greens outstretched arms, Little Green's phosphorescence shone. Looking up in amazement, Felicity saw that the entire Banyan tunnel shimmered with a blue light. She heard a collective gasp from the judges. Then Little Green spoke again, as she concealed the true power she had developed, and the blue light faded.

'Furthermore, please listen,' she said firmly, and all was quiet once more as their minds connected within.

After a long time, Felicity heard the elder Green say in a

hushed voice, 'Surely, you cannot be?'

'It is impossible,' said another voice.

Little Green replied clearly and loudly, 'I am, and my parents believed it was intended. My mother used my capacity to shed all the ancient knowledge she held from her family, my ancestors. They were the First Stipples of the west.' After a pause, Little Green continued, 'We passed through the South East, and my parents used their combined skills to bring us safely past the edges of the Shadowed South. But we were overcome as we touched the shores of the Temperate North. It was as if my mother knew our time was limited.' Felicity heard the grief in Little Green's voice, but she went bravely on, 'She gave me all her knowledge. I was able to take it, as you see; I am a Stipple, and I had the strength. I am the first Greenesse Stipple since our world began. I descend from the First Stipple created by the Old World, and I have matured. Let me honour my parents, soul-bond, and finish this quest.'

A crescendo of voices met this statement. Felicity could not hear who was speaking. She wanted to ask Reuben what all that meant, but of course, she couldn't. She left the meeting as two Thorn patrol approached with a look of intent. She was going to be courageous too. She was going to find Reuben's mother.

*

Reuben and Orchadea had travelled until the sun was at its fullest. They understood what they had to do. Neither of them spoke. The presence of the stranger, Felicity, had unsettled Orchadea. Felicity was not of their world, and her jealousies had affected Orchadea's balance with Reuben. But Reuben's need was strong, and Orchadea knew when the moment came, the Old World would ensure there was perfect communication. They walked swiftly. Reuben smiled at Orchadea. Her pale green-blue eyes were clear and calm.

'We should make our union here,' he said finally. They had been following a broad, calm river, which, as it turned a corner, had started to pick up force, and they saw that the now bumpy water had reached its drop. A cascade of green-blue water tumbled down into a deep lagoon below. It was not a huge waterfall, but still a place of potency and yet serenity. Above them wheeled two large birds, wings outstretched, and below lay the smoky-blue water. They scrambled down the sides of the fall and found a small path that ran behind the great wall of water. It was slippery but wide enough to tread. About halfway along, the cascade had a break that allowed the now lowering sun to pass into the secret cavern in which they stood.

Staying within the sunlight, they walked to the back of the space. It was peaceful. They sat facing each other, legs crossed and arms relaxed. A perfect circle. Reuben focused on Orchadea's face until it became a blur. Orchadea closed her eyes as he did, and they mind-shared.

Let the ground and the water and the air take us.
Unite us together, and within this Old World,
May we now become complete.

Reuben saw images of his world, of the great rivers of Orion Country, and of the dell in which his mother had given birth to him. He saw himself as a baby, and then flashing pictures of his life flowed until his mind was filled with Orchadea. He saw her as a tiny Fragrant, clinging to her mother, and then growing tall into the beautiful plant she had become. He knew she was with him, seeing all this at the same time. They were together and yet apart.

And then he felt a pull. He felt himself pulled down as if falling. He was lying flat on the ground, and Orchadea was too. They were connected to the earth and part of the earth. He saw the roots of the plants and the fissures in the rocks until he touched the molten core. The heat burnt his skin, and he tried to come out of the trance, but the bonding with Orchadea needed them there. He was aware of her fear, too, and he tried to calm her. *Orchadea, trust it*, he tried to say. Then, quite clearly, whilst the fire scorched him and he learnt to conquer the fear, it happened. It was as if something had been bolted on to his innermost being, and he knew the deed was done. The heat abated, and he felt himself pushing through the earth until he broke out of the ground like a vast, free bird.

Looking down, he saw the immobile figures of a young Orion and Fragrant lying flat on the earth. Their colours disappeared to insignificant specks as Reuben and Orchadea attained the heights and soared over the world's surface. They flew free and cooled their burnt faces on the cooling winds of the thin air. The flight was glorious, something Reuben would never forget to his last day. Then gently, gently, like feathers falling after a fight, the two free spirits came slowly back to earth and reclaimed their quiet bodies, fully mature at last.

21

Flight

Felicity had spent the afternoon with Reuben's mother, whom she had found organising the village stores of food, braiding her daughter's hair, and giving counselling to a young heartsick Orion all at once. It was a lovely day, and Mrs O had broken off to show Felicity where she could bathe in private.

When Felicity returned, Mrs O shared with her some delicious liffles. Felicity had tasted these on her first night. The vast curly leaves of all different colours were not only delicious but full of energy too, Mrs O explained. They broke like an extra-thick poppadom, and each colour had its own special taste. Mrs O said green were her favourite, but Felicity preferred the pale violet ones. Like sea salt and raspberry vinegar flavour, she decided. She and Mrs O spent the late afternoon just talking. It was lovely. Felicity felt her strength and energy coming back to her in this wonderful place. Mrs O spoke a lot about Reuben and his growing years.

'He was always special,' she told Felicity. She described the moment he was born, and without his tail.

'His father and I trusted we would understand the reason one day. When he was called to the quest, we wondered if this was its meaning. Reuben had grown into a calm and brave young Orion. His leadership qualities were not in question; he had led most of the young Orion into deep waters on far too many occasions! Now that we see him with you, Felicity, we believe we may understand.'

Felicity had not really known what Mrs O meant. She

wished Reuben were back. *It is all so confusing. What does his mother mean? And what on earth happened in the Banyan? Suddenly Little Green had been let out, beaming. That's it. No hard obstacle courses or exhausting puzzles to solve. Out. Free to mature. Not many of us – the immature – are left now*, she thought.

It was Georges who heralded Reuben's return. His whoops of celebration broke the still evening air as the troupe were preparing for sleep. Peering into the fading light, Felicity could see the outline of Reuben, but no Orchadea. As he walked towards them, Felicity felt strangely shy. She stepped back behind the cover of Little Green. She needed time to compose herself. She was glad she had bathed today. Deep in the recesses of her rapidly dissolving jeans, she had found a lip balm. The adventures so far had miraculously not spoilt it. It was a stubborn little tin and normally broke at least one nail before opening. Felicity fought with it desperately now.

'Open! You stupid little tin!' she cursed, knocking Little Green as the lid gave way. She jabbed a bit onto her lips, rolled them around and stuffed the tin back into her pocket. The familiar smell of the balm was intoxicating. For a moment she was back with Al, getting ready to go shopping. Al constantly stole Felicity's make-up, but Felicity always forgave her. Al would lend Felicity any of her clothes without question, which was essential as Felicity could never find the great clothes Al did. She blamed her mother, but secretly knew it was probably her own fault for never being quite sure what she liked.

'Hello, Felicity,' said a deep voice.

She looked up, thoughts of her bedroom gone as her eyes looked straight into Reuben's. His expression made her toes curl up. Literally. She had to force herself to uncurl them as it was hurting. She took a big breath to steady herself. He was quite changed. He was taller, broader. His face was shadowed with new growth around the jaw. His voice dropped to a rich bass. If she had written this in a story, people would have said it was ridiculous. But he had overnight become not just a male Orion but a huge, glorious one! He smiled as she stared without shame. She began to be aware of the others' amusement as they watched her reaction.

Pippi entered her mind. *Yes, transformation is an amazing thing, isn't it, Felicity?*

Felicity felt a lurch inside her. She looked away.

'What's wrong, Felicity?' said Reuben as he saw the flicker in her expression.

Sheer panic flashed across her face. Reuben reached out, alarmed, but he was too late. She was running. Running anywhere, but not to be faced with this man who had taken away her friend. She couldn't go far as it was becoming so dark. She collapsed on the opposite side of the village to the Taureau. A few Lupata on guard moved discreetly away as Reuben ran up and nodded to them.

'Felicity, don't ever run from me again. My lovely, strange creature. Why? Why do you run?' Reuben's voice was so deep it vied with Wolfgang's now. She supposed she would just have to get used to it. She took a shaky breath, fighting back the inevitable tears.

'You have grown up, Reuben. You are a man,' she said. She couldn't say the rest. She hung her proud head, and her freshly washed golden tresses slid across her face, protecting her. Fat, silent tears oozed out, and she squeezed her eyes together tightly, angered at their betrayal.

Reuben said nothing. He simply took her in his arms and hugged her until his strength and warmth reached her deep inside. When he felt her calm, he said, 'Felicity, we do not always have the answers in our lives. We must have faith. If we really seek something, the answer will come when we are ready to hear it. Yes, I am full grown. You are still a sapling.'

Felicity giggled soggily.

'But you will mature, and I will be waiting. Felicity, dear Felicity, if there is a way for us, if it is the will of both our worlds and of the Great Spirit who is of all worlds, I will have you with me forever. Will you?' He released her carefully and waited. He took a great risk. He might terrify her. But he had to know.

Felicity was unable to speak. This was all so unreal. She knew she loved him. She didn't see how that was possible, but she knew she did. She was Felicity Isabel Penfold from the centre of England. She was not quite fifteen, and last week she had been making biscuits with Al.

'Reuben,' she said, and her voice sounded odd, small, 'I have strong feelings for you – I think we both know that. But–' Her speech was cut as a crowd of Strata eclipsed the rising moon and landed with a beating of their massive wings, right in the middle of the village. Tepee doors were thrown back as everyone spilled outside to see them. Reuben grabbed Felicity's hand, kissed it, and pulled her with him as he ran back to find out the news.

'They don't like to fly at night, usually,' he said with difficulty as he dragged her along.

Felicity could feel the new strength in his arms as he pulled her off the ground a couple of times. *Good*, she thought, *we are going to need that new strength.*

They reached the crowd, and Felicity stood with the others. Georges had barged in and stood by their tepee, his breath scattering the Colour Changers once again. They squealed and reformed. The Strata began their song.

We come in strength, twelve abreast,
To tell you, key members, dire news for the quest.
The Toxics, in error, have caused a great sin
And swayed to their darkness some Sibilin.
The Oceanids, from Upper North, request you come at once.
We fly at dawn, the band entire; for Taureau there comes a plunce.

As they finished singing, Felicity heard a swishing sound, and a huge airborne sled appeared, carried by eight large Strata. It was huge. In the moonlight it was hard to see how it was made.

Georges lowed indignantly. 'My dear sirs, I am not, I repeat NOT flying in that contraption. They were invented only five hundred years ago. They are not tried and tested. In any case, my muscles are too heavy.'

Felicity heard a Thorn snort that sounded suspiciously like Scratt. The tall, beaky Strata with the red eyes peered over his crooked beak at Georges. His eyes flared with light, and Georges blew two streams of hot air from his dilating nostrils. All were silent as the battle of wills continued. The diplomacy of the Strata must have won, for the tall bird bowed briefly, and Georges said, 'All right. In the name of this quest I will allow your most respected and strongest Strata to carry me to the Oceanids. I accept the honour graciously.'

Reuben now stepped forward and bowed in greeting. 'Welcome again, honourable peacemakers of our world. Your news is not unexpected. We had heard rumours,' he said, glancing at Sib. 'I am eager to meet with the Oceanids. We answer your call. Please take your rest in my homeland. The Colour Changers will bring you all you need. We shall prepare, and we shall be ready.' Reuben's grave voice rang out over the settlement. All who heard knew this was the last time they would see this valiant band. The future for all rested in them.

There was silence as his words sank softly into the night air. Then the Green and Orion elders spoke out. 'We are honoured with your presence. Please carry word to the Oceanids that we, the Green elders, are satisfied all laws of our world are in balance.'

The Strata leader dipped his head in acknowledgement of this request, and they lifted gracefully away to the outer edges of the village, taking the plunce with them, Felicity was glad to see.

All was activity and chatter as the entire village rallied to help prepare. Reuben watched Sib as he trundled across to the other Sibilin currently staying in the village. Reuben knew this must be a great shock, that their own kind could betray the world. He was pleased to see Gus joining the group, his understanding would help them. Reuben looked forward to the full facts when they reached the Upper North.

It seemed fate had intervened for him with Felicity. *Well, we needed time*, he thought and sought out his mother. He found her and his father by the food stores.

His mother turned to face him. *He has transformed*, she realised with pride. Their eyes met, and he heard her voice gently cradle him. *My son. My beautiful, fine son.* Her eyes glistened in the moonlight. He stepped forward and let her hold him tight.

His father stepped forwards. 'We have taught you all we can, my son. With your travels you continue to grow in wisdom, knowledge and strength. Use your mature power wisely. Harness fear to keep you safe. Continue to find the strengths in your friends. And never abandon the energy of our world. It is your guardian and your ultimate protection. The Toxics are strong, and they are dark, but you have the light. Light vanquishes darkness. Remember that.'

As his father finished speaking, Felicity approached. 'Reuben, the others are not sure what we should take. Will we need food? Do we need protection from the cold?'

Mrs O replied, 'Yes, my dear, it will be colder than the frozen wastes of the Lupata, although at this time of year the midday sun will make it tolerable. At night you must smear yourselves with the flubbum I will provide. You must also take some bark balm; it will heal any wounds your party may sustain. It is usable by all beasts and plants when space is limited.' She held out her arms to embrace Felicity. 'Keep my son safe, Feli-ci-ty,' she said, stumbling over Felicity's name.

As Felicity and Reuben headed back to the others, his mother gazed after him with longing. Would she see him again? Mr Orion held her for a moment. They looked at each other. *Trust, my beautiful lady.* Her husband's words were firm in her head. She breathed deeply to calm her spirit and then took his hand, and together they made the necessary preparations for their son's final adventure.

22

The Upper North

Georges stood with stoicism as the plunce scythed the air. Its balance depended on the skill of the eight Strata designated to carry him. *This is unnatural! What would Elfrida think if she saw me now?* His mind slipped subconsciously back to his first wife in his distress. As the eight changed direction, he roared his disapproval.

The Strata were flying at a height of about ten thousand feet. The air was cold, and the fluffy clouds drenched the passengers as the birds cut through them. Felicity, Reuben and Little Green sat on the leader Strata. Felicity was placed at the back, and she focused entirely on not slipping silently off. The wings felt powerful as the bird pulled the air past them with its strong, muscular action. When it was climbing to its cruising height, the three leant forwards instinctively and gripped hard with their knees.

The Strata smiled to himself. He had no intention of losing his precious cargo, but their concentration would keep them silent and allow him to fly as swiftly as he was able with such a weight. He felt the aura of Little Green flow through him. He was proud to carry such a learned plant. As he flew, he thought serenely about this problem of the Toxics and their threat. The perspective of distance gave problems clarity. He washed his fiery eyes with a blink of purple eyelids. He and his kind lived in territory unknown to all the other creatures. They remained separate; impartial observers that were so essential to the balance. He thought of the cliff top where he had been raised, and of the forest canopy which sheltered his latest fine brood. The Toxics were lost. It needed intervention; he agreed with the Ancient Oceanids. Their recent tantrums were ultimately only going to destroy all the answers they sought. It was time. He heard Georges bellow and chuckled.

Felicity felt the leader's tremor of laughter beneath her. The ground was terrifyingly far below, and the shuddering she felt under her bottom wasn't good, she thought. She daren't look, but she knew behind her were the other three Strata. Strata second held Sib, Strata third Gus and Scratt, and the last free Strata carried Wolfgang and Pippi. The eight tethered Strata bravely pulled Georges, whose complaints she could hear in spite of the wind. Felicity was inclined to think he was actually scared. Not surprising, she thought, as they disappeared into wet blindness yet again. She leant forwards and tried to relax. How long was this interminable journey going to be?

*

To her horror she had nodded off to sleep. She was shaken awake by Little Green.

'Felicity, Felicity! Look!' she said.

Felicity looked. They had reduced height and were now soaring over vast stretches of snow-topped ground. Felicity could see a white fox running low as he darted amongst the vast shadows the Strata created. The land gave way to an ocean broken with small lumps of ice.

'We are in the Upper North,' said Little Green. 'Home of the Oceanids.'

Amazed she hadn't slid silently off in her sleep, Felicity was glad to have arrived. The Upper North was magnificent in its bleached starkness, but absolutely freezing. She thanked Mrs O silently for her extra clothing. She and Reuben had numerous tops of soft hide that felt like velvet as she slid them on, and over that they wore soft fur that fell into all the right gaps. The others had to liberally smear themselves with the flubbum, even Wolfgang and Pippi applied a little to their extremities.

The plunce was strapped with small packages that each of them would carry; they were all the same except the one for Georges, which was twice the size. It seemed only fair. In each package were carefully selected skeleton provisions that Mr and Mrs O had debated long and hard. There must be enough for survival in the hardest days when no food could be found. It was a challenge; the Old World foods were not designed for storage, but Mrs O always kept a variety in her stores for visitors.

Felicity thought of the foods she had seen being bundled into her package, and her mouth watered. Some banished sticky buds at first; Reuben had asked his mother especially for her. There were river reeds, sand shoots, forest peas, small chicanes, earth balls, strape, plunts and chiclas. The gaudin cheese would not store, and Mrs O said the arctic rolls were better fresh too, but there was plenty of Felicity's new favourite, liffles, crushed and mixed together in a rainbow of crunchy colour. For drink there were tiny non-porous flasks of amber and nectar, and Orion river water of palest blue. The flasks came in a myriad of shapes, and the Orion children had enjoyed selecting the perfect size and shape for each nook and cranny of the packs. Mrs O had apologised for any missing foods. Felicity was particularly relieved the stod balls had not been included.

The Strata flew evenly between two icy peaks, and as they emerged from the glacial walls, Felicity drew a breath of icy air in surprise. The white, frozen ground had become a vast lake. It shone to the furthest horizon: a black abyss of depths unfathomable. They flew over it for the rest of the day. Georges was grumbling intermittently. Reuben risked turning round to wink at Felicity and Little Green. Just when the whole troupe couldn't take any more of the feathery bumpy ride, the Strata dropped suddenly to the water's surface.

'Help,' shouted Felicity.

'Merdes!' shouted Georges.

'Wheeeee!' cried Scratt.

The others said nothing. But with his keen eyes, Strata one had seen the beach, and he led his flock to the ground. The beach was small, and behind it was a cave. That was all. Water, grey beach, and a cave.

As the Strata landed gracefully, the troupe dismounted clumsily. Their limbs were stiff and awkward after the long flight. The landing of Georges went especially badly; he tried to launch himself to the ground before his team had balanced. The plunce tipped as he leapt, and only with sheer luck did the packages not disappear into the black, watery depths. The Strata bowed to each and all of them, and then without song, but in perfect union, they took off.

'Thank you,' Reuben said and stood watching them disappear from sight. 'Come on, gang,' he said. 'Let's see what's in the cave.'

Felicity thought that was a stupid idea and wanted to stay on the beach.

Pippi came and licked her face. 'Come on, little Felicity. It will be warmer out of this wind,' she said. 'We must make a large fire for the night and apply flubbum.'

Wolfgang padded over to them. 'Pippi, my little cub, you must not take the chill.'

Pippi nuzzled him.

Then together they loped, with Felicity between them, to the cave. Sib, Scratt, and Gus were gathering some driftwood, but Reuben was concerned it would not last the night. Little Green explained that the flubbum would act as a sort of long-burning oil if they smeared it generously over the wood. Georges offered his pot to use, as his muscles would keep him warm, but Reuben said it was better they all donate a little.

As the large moon swung up into the starry sky, the glowing fire crackled with promise. They were all exhausted, in spite of no activity. The flight had been a trial of endurance. They ate a few sand shoots from their provisions and chatted softly amongst themselves. Reuben asked Little Green what she would do about her enharmonic.

'In view of our hasty departure from Orionwood, I will simply have to wait,' she said, 'but I feel strong, Reuben, even without my final transition.'

Reuben felt differently and told her to keep her mind open to contact from her enharmonic.

'We should discuss the problem of the Sibilin,' announced Gus unexpectedly. They looked at him with surprise.

'Not now, Gus,' said Reuben.

'I apologise, Reuben, but it must be before we sleep tonight,' said Gus. His eyes were dark in his spiky face. Wolfgang and Pippi sat up. Georges trotted closer, disturbing a pile of driftwood they had prepared for the night. It slithered flat. Sib's hooded eyes were unreadable.

'All right,' said Reuben, 'I understand.' He stood and inhaled deeply. *I am so tired.*

Felicity heard him and responded, *My darling Reuben, you can rest soon.*

Reuben looked at her nestled between the two Lupata. Her face was pale, and her hair frosted. *She is so brave.* Felicity intercepted the thought and smiled. It lit a fire within him, and his vigour returned.

'We will talk until the moon sits on that tallest peak,' he said, 'and then we sleep. Tomorrow the Oceanids will come.'

He came closer to the fire, and Gus began his subtle interrogation. Sib made monosyllabic answers. The Sibilin wanted a different enharmonic, one with more respect. They wanted a different homeland, less arid. Felicity wondered why it was so important to Gus to hear Sib's opinions. The moon travelled down to the peak, and Reuben drew an end to the discussions.

'Soon, we will discuss further this idea that the Colour Changers are less respected,' he said. 'For like the Toxics' misjudgement that they have no place in this world, so is any belief that there is lower esteem for the plants that work so hard to keep us all comfortable. I worry that the Sibilin have so lost their balance of perception.' Reuben's voice was loud.

Felicity knew if it was day, his downy, tanned cheeks would be flushed a deeper shade. She took his hand and squeezed it, feeling his response. After a small pause, he thanked Sib for his patience and ended the discussion.

They settled down in the flickering firelight. Felicity was happy to be in Reuben's arms, but despite her warm, Orion hides and her furs and even the sticky flubbum, she was still very cold. Reuben opened his fur outer, and she shuffled inside. They lay close and listened to the muted sounds of this chilled spot. Only the odd fire crack and the water lapping gently on the shore could be heard. Reuben kissed the top of Felicity's hair. She could feel the tension in his body.

'Please, please, please let me mature,' she whispered.

Reuben felt her breath but not her words. The scent of Felicity's soft hair was delicious. He shifted a little away from her warm body and swallowed. 'Please, please, please let her mature,' he prayed in an innocent echo. And the night wind carried their prayers up, up and across the deep, cold water to a place unknown even to the world's inhabitants.

23

Ancients

A deep rumbling woke Felicity. She felt the ground beneath her shaking as she opened her eyes. Facing the cave was the water, and in the water were eight towering beasts. Eyes wide, she tried to take in their immensity. They had arranged themselves with grinding, juddering precision to face the quest band, leaving three quarters of their bulk submerged in the dark lagoon from whence they came.

Reuben and Gus stepped forward, leaving the rest of the troupe fanned out in an arrow to meet these mighty beasts.

'Welcome to our waters, Reubenfourthousandth, Toxictoxicth, Taureautwothousandthfivehundredandtwenty-fourth, Greenseventhousandthseventy.' After a pause, the Oceanid continued, 'Sibilinsixteenthousandth, Thorn-sixthousandthsixty, Lupatafourthousandth, Lupatafour-thousandthforty-four, and welcome Felicity Isabel Penfold.' Its voice was muffled, like someone holding their nose when they speak. Felicity suppressed a smile. Its eye swivelled up and around in its head until it focused on her. She remembered the age of these ancient beasts and was humbled. Its eye moved back to Reuben.

He replied, bowing to each one as he addressed it, down the line. 'Welcome. Welcome Hyperiononethousandth, Theiaone-thousandth, Coeusonethousandth, Phoebeonethousandth, Oceanusonethousandth, Tethysonethousandth, Themisone-thousandth, Mnemosyneonethousandth.'

'These Oceanids are the oldest living creatures to inhabit the Old World,' said Pippi.

Looking at the scarred, barnacle-encrusted body of the

one who spoke, Felicity could believe it. They were staggered along the shore like ships coming in to dock, and all were a greyish colour. She supposed their energy had gone into their size. It was not polite, she knew, but it was hard to find something beautiful about any part of them. They had tiny eyes and an indistinct mouth right at the bottom of their square-shaped heads. When they spoke it dropped down onto the sand like a ferry ramp. She had not really thought about the first two she had met. There had been so much else to focus on, like surviving. But now, in this bare place, and faced with eight all looking her way, it was impossible not to notice details. Especially as she had discovered the shallow cave behind offered no refuge.

The first Oceanid, Hyperion, was speaking again. 'So for today and tomorrow we will each take one of you for instruction. Your assigned Oceanid holds kinship with you. We have been listening with great interest to the progress of your quest.'

The second Oceanid, Theia, took over, and her voice was even more muffled, and Felicity could see barnacles clinging all over her mouth. Poor old thing, she thought.

'We heard of the resolution for Greenseventhousandth-seventy,' she said, giving a regal nod to Little Green, who responded with a dignified curtsey.

Please don't let them speak to me, thought Felicity, panicking now about her curtsey problem.

Coeus took over, 'And we are very pleased to see Reuben-fourthousandth fully mature,' he said, his voice deeper, but clearer than the other two.

'And we welcome the key member, Felicity, with the aura of her world sitting so gently on her shoulders,' said Phoebe. What did she mean? But already Oceanus was talking. He was the largest of the group. He was too far away to see well, but Felicity heard the amusement in his voice as he spoke. 'We heard the bellows of Taureautwothousandthfivehun-dredandtwenty-fourth,' he said. 'We are pleased to welcome

169

such a mature Taureau to our lands. If time was with us, we would share many memories.'

Georges bowed his great head down to his knees. And so they continued. Tethys addressed Wolfgang; Themis, Pippi; and Mnemosyneone concluded the selection process by addressing Scratt.

'We are honoured to receive a Thorn to our land,' she said. 'It has been a long time since a Thorn has come. She spoke from the furthest end of the beach, a disembodied voice carried on the wind.

Gus and Sib alone had not been addressed. They stood patiently. Gus had his head bowed low.

Hyperion, the leader, spoke out as much as his voice would allow. 'Toxictoxicth, we welcome you, friend to our world and saviour of your kind. Your courage and wisdom goes before you.'

Gus lifted his head. With sparkling eyes, he looked directly at Hyperion. 'Thank you. The Old World has many ways that still hold value. However, my task is not only to heal my kind and help prevent this destruction, but also to ask the Ancients of the world to be tolerant of change. The quest believes there must be a better solution, if we can save the Roots.'

Reuben looked uncomfortable at Gus speaking out so directly. He stepped forward to soften the words, but Hyperion, after a pause, replied, 'Toxictoxicth, we have heard you. Let that be enough for this time.'

It was time to approach their allocated Oceanid. Sib was left unconnected. Reuben looked back at him, concerned. He walked to Coeus and spoke quietly; then he beckoned Sib to join him by the head of the giant water beast. Felicity walked slowly up to Phoebe. She was horrified at Sib's exclusion, but Oceanids were not something you questioned. She was proud of Reuben for his courage. Phoebe, on close inspection, was not so frightening. Her skin felt quite dry to touch. She invited Felicity to touch her head as they communicated silently. All the others were doing the same.

Good morning, young Felicity Isabel Penfold, said Phoebe's voice in her head.

'Good morning, Phoebe...' Felicity's mind blanked – what was her generation? Panic set in as she couldn't remember.

'That is all right, Felicity,' said Phoebe, giving permission by using only Felicity's first name. 'Phoebe is a good abbreviation. We have been amused by your names for the company.'

'Do you hear everything that happens in the world from up here?' said Felicity, forgetting to be in awe of this friendly giant.

'No, but all we need to know, we hear,' replied Phoebe. 'Now please be calm. We have only today and tomorrow to equip you with all you need for your difficult task. Listen carefully,' and she began.

*

The first day was mainly taken up with rules. They must not share their information, even to a quest member. They must not listen to any change in direction apart from the authorised Aquatics.

'Who are they?' Reuben asked Coeus. His responsibility as leader meant he must doubly understand the rules.

Coeus voice droned in his head: Reuben, Felicity and Little Green held the final pieces of the jigsaw. But the ending would not be wholly revealed even to Reuben, for his own safety.

How can I protect my troupe and ensure the quest's success without knowing its ending?

Coeus heard his anxiety. 'Fear not, Reubenfourthousandth. You will succeed. You must succeed.'

*

The moon rose in the sky, and the Oceanids dismissed their charges for the night. As the giants retreated noiselessly back into the dark lagoon, Reuben realised Sib had not returned. He had boarded a ninth Oceanid, summoned by Hyperion, which had carried him away. As they prepared the fire and shared out some orsi left by the Oceanids, Sib's name bounced between them.

'He maybe will not remain with us for the quest,' said Georges, spitting some orsi as he spoke.

Wolfgang jumped out of the way of the soggy missile and loped to the back of the cave with Pippi. It was noticeable to Felicity that Pippi was thickening around the middle. They all ate with relish. The Oceanids had provided a mound of the seafood. The orsi looked a little like spiky razor shells on the outside, but when cracked open, they revealed bright orange flesh that tasted like sweet potato, Felicity decided. If it hadn't been for Sib's mysterious absence, it could have been a relaxing supper.

'I think the Oceanids had not expected Sib to rejoin us,' said Gus, after chewing for a while.

'But their resources would have informed them he had returned to the quest's cause,' said Reuben, frowning.

Little Green had been silent. Scratt was far too hungry to care much what the others thought about Sib. He was relieved to have a break from him. Sibilin and Thorn did not mix well, and he was not impressed with Sib's behaviour so far on this quest. He knew it was an honour to be here, and he would never have been so rude as to mention these thoughts. But, he thought, stuffing the entire cavity of his green mouth with orsi, it was less tense without him. Little Green touched him lightly on his arm.

'Don't dim my light, Scratt,' she pleaded. Her aura was pale in this cold place, but it was still present. A small, blue glow in the shadows. The fire flared up in a minor collapse. Felicity couldn't understand how there was wood in this icy place. *I suppose the Oceanids arranged that, too*, she thought as she ate hungrily. After a day of inactivity, they had enjoyed collecting the wood, and the resulting bonfire was huge. It lit a beacon to the sea animals that quietly slid past in the dark water.

'What other creatures live in the seas, Reuben?' she asked, as she concentrated on cracking open her twelfth orsi. The skill was to crack the thing like a very large pistachio nut.

'Hyperion spoke to Sib. I know not what he said,' murmured Reuben. He completely ignored Felicity. She didn't think he had even heard her question. She sighed.

'Reuben,' said Little Green's musical voice, 'the Oceanids are wise. They expected Sib. It matters not that they waited to summon the ninth Oceanid. That is between Sib and Hyperion. Worry not; he will return.' As she spoke, a large black shape loomed up onto the beach. Sib scuttled off its tall back. Little Green smiled. Sib slithered towards them.

'Well, well, I don't suppose you were expecting me back,' he said.

Felicity was surprised to feel sorry for him. She still didn't trust him, but she had never liked to see anyone mistreated. Al had had a nasty time when she first came to Felicity's school. No one wanted to be friendless. Al joined Flissy and Sandrine, and their friendship was cemented with three unspoken rules. They always meant what they said. They never lied to each other. They never kept secrets. Then one day, Sandrine went back to France, leaving Al and Felicity to remain firm friends. It was three years now, since she had first met Al, with her ridiculous bunches. She smiled.

'Felicity, Felicity!' Reuben was nudging her. 'You were miles away. I can't break into your thoughts tonight. Were you blocking me?'

'Sorry. No, I wasn't. I was thinking of home,' she said quietly. 'Reuben,' she said, 'I don't like Sib being left out.'

'I know,' Reuben said. 'I will talk to him.' He took a handful of the spiky food, and standing carefully, so as not to prick himself with their little needly spines, he walked over to Sib, who lay by the fire.

'Well, Reuben, this adventure is beginning in earnest,' said Sib, as Reuben approached him.

'Yes, my friend,' said Reuben. 'Has your Oceanid prepared you well?' He did not like to ask more than that.

'She took me to the land of the Aquatics,' replied Sib. His hooded eyes were wide open tonight. Everyone had been listening surreptitiously; they all gathered round the fire now, not pretending anymore. He laughed. Felicity was instantly aware she had never heard Sib laugh before. It was okay. Actually, it was infectious. They all began to giggle at their nosiness. It was hard not sharing their instructions. Intimacy had become second nature to them all.

'You know I cannot divulge information,' Sib said, following their thoughts. 'But I can tell you where I went. I do not think that is a secret. The land of the Aquatics, as I told Reuben. Some of you will have visited there, perhaps. Not many do. It is far, far to the west. In seas so warm they bathe you and caress your skin.' Sib's voice was warm. He was unquenchable this evening. He ate little of Reuben's offering. This was his passion, realised Felicity. His admiration for the communicators of the world was unmistakeable.

'Their centre is a vast web,' he was ranting. 'As far as the eye can see is a network of leaves and connecting tendrils, interspersed with raised flowers that sit on the infinite mat of humming plant. There is a constant flow of messaging in all directions.'

'Yes, and it makes a very irritating noise,' muttered Georges, who stood dozing in the shadows of the flickering fire. Sib's lids lowered a moment. But not even that halted him long. *Perhaps he has been affected by the great energy, thought Felicity.*

Yes, it is possible, someone said in her head. Eventually Reuben had to stop Sib's tirade of words.

'Sib, we are glad you have been returned to us for a second time,' he said. 'Of course, we wondered if we would lose you. Thank you for sharing with us the wonders of the Aquatic fields. They remain relatively unknown. You are lucky to have visited them.'

Sib nodded graciously and sidled away from the fire. Scratt came and lay down close to Little Green. Felicity fell almost immediately into exhausted sleep and dreamt of giant flowers sitting on large, green mats stretching to the horizon. They whispered to her, 'Felicity, Felicity, come join us. Felicity, come join us in our bed,' but the flowers had faces, and the faces were evil little gremlins that cackled as she lay down between them. She tossed and turned in the nightmare.

Reuben put his arms around her and stroked her hair. Gradually her thrashings ceased. She sighed in her sleep, and the little frown between her eyebrows smoothed out. He held her and felt the pulse in the base of his throat throbbing. Sleep claimed him at last, and the camp fell silent. The embers of the fire burned an orange-red in the black night air, a tiny glow of colour in the midst of the dark waters where the leviathans took their rest, patiently waiting to launch the quest.

24

The Quest

A trumpet of wails throbbed across the turbulent water. The wind had risen, and the waves crashed onto the tiny beach. Pippi and Wolfgang brushed the ashes of the fire into the sand, and the grey ground mirrored the stormy sky.

The Oceanids called from the sea, and the words of Coeus chilled Felicity. 'The Toxics have begun. They march for the caves. No time for explanations. We ride immediately.'

Reuben ran to the edge of the foaming waves to hear the rest of the instructions. 'The Strata will lift us to the Oceanids. The Oceanids will not risk us mounting in these conditions,' he shouted, his hair whipping his face.

'But we don't have our instructions, Reuben,' said Gus.

Reuben didn't reply. His face was strained, and Gus said no more.

The sky became black as the Strata returned. Barely had they been set down from the air before the Ancients moved off, surging into the high walls of stormy sea. Hyperion and Theia went first, followed by Coeus and Phoebe. Themis and Mnemosneione were just behind, and finally Oceanus and Tethys, who had to swim hard to catch up with the others. They had been delayed by the battle of boarding Georges. Each quest member sat aloft their allotted mentor. Only Sib remained above, carried by the first Strata. He had already received his instructions.

The gargantuan creatures cruised skilfully out of the lagoon and across the northern seas. They were unperturbed by the storm. This world had been their home for many centuries. As they ploughed through the water, they delivered their message. The final instructions were the same for Georges, Wolfgang, Pippi and Scratt: 'Defence of the key trio. At all costs – even to your own end. The three are Little Green, Reuben, and Felicity.'

Georges was glad. He would have done this without being told, but it was good to have the key members confirmed.

Gus' instruction from Hyperion was very short. 'Remain open to all possibilities. That is all we can say. It will, therefore, be enough.'

To Little Green were given the longest instructions. Her friends could see her still listening with concentration long after their Oceanids had ceased.

'You are a key member of the final stages of the quest,' said Theia. 'You are the Stipple who will rebuild the laws of the new Old World. Your mother knew this. Go to the core of the caves. There you will lay your Root. There you will live your life. Listen to the other Stipples. Bind your new Root to the old. The world needs to remember its origins, but they must be joined with the history of the Toxics so there will never again be imbalance or misunderstanding. You and your descendants will ensure this. But listen carefully, Greenseventhousandthseventy – you must succeed in opening the Old Root. The new and the old must be bound from the very first growth. For this you need Reuben and Felicity.'

'How will I open it?' asked Little Green, determined not to forget anything.

'You will know what to do,' was Theia's short reply.

Fighting to keep his vision clear from the splashing waves, Reuben watched Theia and Little Green. Precisely how much had Felicity and Little Green been told? His own instructions from Coeus had been simple but quite clear. 'You are a key member of the final stages of the quest. You must ensure Little Green reaches the core of the caves. Your allegiance is to Little Green, and she only. Nevertheless, Felicity is the third key member, and you need her with you when you and Little Green enter the innermost cavern. You are needed to help open the original Root. You will know what to do once you reach it.'

Felicity knew she should share the courage of her friends. But Phoebe's words had terrified her. All at once, this tale into which she had been dropped was real. There was no one to wake her up from a dream. No Al to tease her for her ridiculous imagination. No mummy to stroke her hair, and even if she wanted to, no father to call. She was astride a creature bigger than a whale, in the middle of an unknown ocean, gripping a lump of barnacles that scraped her blood-less hands, and surrounded by a storm that isolated her from any communication with her pack. She hadn't the energy to cry. She was ashamed of her fear. She remembered all Reuben had taught her, in times of anxiety. Feel the world, he would say. Feel its strength, and have faith. She thought of Phoebe's instructions. The fear flickered, locked inside.

Lifting her strong little chin, she shouted into the wind and the rain, 'I am Felicity Isabel Penfold. I am here because the Old World called me, and I will not let this quest down.' The salty water filled her mouth, and her eyes, and stung her cheeks, but she cried out again and again until her words echoed back to her, and her valour returned.

There was a shout from Sib, above, and Felicity peered through the driving rain. Far ahead, the rocky shores of the Temperate North drew a shape on the horizon.

25

Leets

Standing on firm ground with relief, the troupe gathered together.

Reuben said, 'We will have to take our refreshments on the march. That last sea passage was further than any we have done, and yet, in spite of heavy seas, we are here at–' he looked up at the watery sun, '–about midday.' He smiled briefly at Felicity, and they set off.

As they tramped, Felicity considered Phoebe's words. 'You are the third key member of the final stage of the quest,' Phoebe had told her. 'For this you were called from your world. You must keep yourself safe, using all the skills you have learnt here. You must stay with Reuben and Little Green. You will know what to do at the end. Before we leave you, Felicity Isabel Penfold, we have a gift. You lack protection to face the Toxics alone. They use the strength of our world and turn it to their advantage. You do not have the skill to draw the full strength of Our World in defence. Maybe one day. Meanwhile, we offer you a gift – the shield of the Aquatics. If in danger, seek them, touch them. They will protect you. You will be safe.' *I hope never to need that gift*, thought Felicity now. She decided to walk by Reuben, in the lead.

'Where are we going today?' she asked, panting as she tried to keep up the pace.

Reuben did not slacken his stride as he said, 'The eastern coast of this land. I want to be there by night. We will travel southeast, crossing Thornton in early evening. If you are lucky, we may have time to grab some sticky buds as extra sustenance for the night.' Smiling briefly, he reached out to touch her, as if in apology for his lack of attention.

The day's travelling was hard and dull. No one spoke much. Georges thought about the challenge. He knew his strength had been legendary. But if he was honest, he also felt the thinning of age within. The travelling had wearied him. He hoped what was once impossibly great was still good enough.

Gus, walking by him, patted his neck. 'You remain a legend, Georges,' he said. Gus reflected on his part. He prayed for the courage to stand up to Arrass. *I must use my love and loyalty to the Old World to draw strength*, he decided. *Arrass weakens himself by his rejection of the Old World.*

Little Green caught the end of his thoughts and said aloud, 'You will not fight him alone, Gus. We stand as a team.'

At this Sib, who trundled silently behind her, said, 'To the end,' and Scratt, hearing him, snorted rudely. 'And the end will be the beginning,' he said, frowning at Sib.

Wolfgang and Pippi, who had become less gregarious recently, spoke in perfect unison, 'This quest will succeed. We will, with all of you, ensure it.' Pippi trotted ahead after that, and Wolfgang followed. They went out of sight, but Reuben said nothing.

*

Passing speedily through Thornton at supper, Felicity was shocked by its change. There were only silent walls of Thorn, resting and ruminating. But Scratt said this was perfectly normal. Once the Lupata mating ceremonies were over, the Thorn did what they did best; they stood and slept, mainly. Apart from the young males and females who found quiet corners to form their unions.

Scratt dashed off and prised some sticky buds from his family. Felicity realised Thorn bonds were different once adulthood was reached. He was pleased to have seen them, but eager to rejoin the troupe as they marched on. Reuben agreed they could eat the sticky buds on the move, which they did. Felicity absently sucked her tasty snack, her mind thinking of what lay ahead.

As night fell, Reuben urged them on. Georges, Wolfgang, and Pippi were fine. Scratt, Little Green, and Felicity were flagging. Even Gus tripped repeatedly as his tired legs dragged across the dunes. *We have been walking across these dunes for too long*, he thought. The moon was high as they finally reached the shore. In the moonlight were two long boats.

'Ah, the leets were left, as requested,' said Sib.

Reuben looked at him in surprise.

Sib smiled. 'The Aquatics shared many things with me, Reuben,' he said, in his nasal voice.

'I am greatly relieved, Sib,' Reuben replied. 'I was going to find a stream once we arrived. I need clear instructions from the Aquatics on the sea crossing. Your knowledge saves me the task.'

Felicity glanced at Gus. *We could end up in a sea-hole!* She had heard of these from Scratt. But there was no chance to speak.

Reuben continued, 'Into the leets. Georges takes the first, with Sib as his guide. We follow.'

At this, even Little Green looked worried. She would never question Reuben, but she hoped the strain had not, on this occasion, led him astray. Sib smiled his half-smile, which Felicity thought looked particularly suspicious in the moonlight. Too weary to organise a sensible objection, they all climbed in. The leets were made of wood. They were like long fishing boats, but with very deep sides. As they climbed in, they found someone had left provisions for them to enjoy on the journey.

Georges' upper body still stood tall from their boat, and Felicity heard his booming voice, 'I shall not be able to eat a thing. I am a sensitive Taureau in spite of my size. I suffer from sea-nausea. No, I cannot eat these.'

Felicity heard the rustling of leaves as he unpacked the mouth-watering delicacies they had been left. Without warning, the leets began to move of their own accord.

'Sib,' called out Reuben calmly, 'could you please share the information you have been given by the Aquatics?'

Sib hesitated, but then he called back, 'The Dauphs pull us from beneath. Worry not. They take us to the mainland by morning.'

Reuben looked at the sky. The weather was fair. The stars were clear and bright, and the air was cold with the lack of cloud. This was a bonus. He thanked the Old World from his heart. 'Then let's enjoy our unplanned meal and a good night's sleep, my friends!'

Felicity heard the joy in his voice. She reached out and stroked his hand. He pulled her close, and as they sat side by side on the bench, he held her head and kissed her. She stopped hearing the water splashing and the sounds of the strange creatures beneath them. Georges' munching and Pippi's murmuring were lost. Reuben kissed her again. The moon above lit up his face as their eyes met. She felt a warmth spread through her, as she looked right into his shining eyes. It was the most sensational feeling. The darkness and the cool wind. The rocking of the boat and Reuben's warm face. His mouth on hers. She pulled away, overcome.

'You two had better eat,' said Wolfgang's deep voice from the front of the boat.

Felicity heard the amusement in Pippi's voice as she said, 'Yes, take your strength now, Reuben and Felicity. We face uncertainty tomorrow.'

Reuben sat back as their words cooled his ardour. He had not meant to kiss Felicity. He knew his mind should be focused on the quest. It was. But just for a moment he had needed to connect with her. 'I am sorry, Felicity. Please eat something.'

Georges called across, 'I can hear your antics, Reuben.

Eat and build up your muscles for the battle. There are arctic rolls in this feast.'

Felicity started giggling. She remembered the arctic rolls her granny used to make. Daddy was always rude about them. But she and Mum loved the mix of ice cream and sponge. Her laughter was infectious, and the whole troupe started tittering. She could even hear Sib sniggering, from their leet.

The laughter upset Georges. 'I don't know why you all think that is so funny,' he said in his sternest voice.

'Well, he can't run off this time,' whispered Reuben in her ear, his breath tickling.

The tension of the day dispelled; the entire troupe of nine ate as much as they could before sleep overtook them. The arctic rolls were not ice cream and sponge, but they were very tasty. More like chocolate roulade, thought Felicity sleepily. The creamy filling was rich and revitalising.

As she was drifting into sleep, she heard a loud belch from Georges, which set everyone off again. The boats started to rock precariously until Reuben said, 'Come on, everyone, sleep now. No doubt tomorrow will bring its own challenge.'

So they slept, not needing any further encouragement. And as they slept, the Dauphs gently towed the leets across the calm water and directly into the path of the Toxic army.

26

Sib

When they awoke, the Dauphs had gone. The leets had been nudged into a narrow inlet, where they drifted. It was the smell of burning that woke Wolfgang and Pippi.

'Up! Up!' they growled, leaping out of the leet and rocking the sides.

Georges bellowed as Sib tipped their boat, jumping out. Georges tried to balance, but fell, splintering the leet with his weight.

'Well, we won't be returning,' said Reuben, as Georges looked dismayed. He stood up, and the water reached his shoulders, so he forged through to the rocks that fringed the inlet. He carried Scratt and Little Green on his back. Gus bobbed along, and the others swam.

'What is it, Reuben?' asked Little Green. Reuben stood still, shading his eyes from the glaring sun, as he stood on the highest rock to look. Even at this hour, the shimmer of heat rose from the ground.

'Wolfgang and Pippi have powerful noses. The smoke is still distant. I can't see what is being burnt, but it spreads out in a line. I suspect the Toxics are burning trees or perhaps a little forest,' he said, climbing back down. The Orion eyes were keen. It had looked horribly as if the trees could be Greens. He blocked his mind. They had been too tall for the scrubby trees that grew in this barren land. He felt sick.

Little Green sensed something was terribly wrong. She looked at the others. Georges had his head raised; he stood tall, ready to face this unknown enemy. Wolfgang and Pippi were growling softly, deep in their throats, and Scratt stood alongside Gus. Sib's hooded lids were half-lowered. Felicity thought he looked uncomfortable; he was swallowing rapidly. It suddenly struck her he was mind-sharing with someone. Someone who was not here.

She scanned the horizon. They had landed somewhere to the east of the mainland, but by the heat, she knew it was further south than expected. She tied Reuben's shawl around her waist. Her curls stuck to her neck, and she lifted them, trying to fan air upwards.

'Follow me!' Reuben said and set off, running fast.

Felicity hardly had time to close her mouth before Wolfgang's jaws grabbed her and slung her on his back. Felicity clung on to his coarse fur. The Lupata were fast, but Georges in a charge was matching them. Little Green and Scratt had legs so long they simply took huge strides and kept pace. Gus trundled admirably along; he would have been last, but for Sib. Sib could close a gap in a disconcertingly short time, but distance running was not his strength.

'Reuben!' she called.

Reuben looked back. He looked ahead again. They were heading for a small hill; he prayed for shelter beyond. For coming at them from the west was an army. He didn't want to know how many or what. It would be large – Sibilin mixed with Toxics. He puffed out as he tried to concentrate his mind. *Think fast. Think!* Sib and Gus couldn't keep up. The hill was not attainable if they waited. He remembered his instructions, 'At all costs it must be Little Green.' But he couldn't abandon the stragglers. *Please not yet.* He stopped running, and Scratt fell into him.

'Ouch!' exclaimed Reuben. 'Little Green, Scratt – go with Pippi and Wolfgang. I will wait for Gus and Sib.'

'And I will stay with you, Reuben,' said Georges, creating a dust cloud as he skidded to a halt.

'No, find shelter behind that hill, and help Wolfgang defend it. We have no idea how many Toxics there are. They may have subdivided. They know of our quest. Arrass, their leader, I suspect, will head straight to the Sacred Caves. It would seem a good plan to let Demet destroy us while he tries to destroy the Roots.' Reuben's voice faltered as he finished this speech. He was looking past them.

Felicity spun round. In the time he had spoken, the Toxics had reached Sib and Gus. She watched in horror as the ugly creatures swarmed around their friends like ants.

'Go!' screamed Reuben, and as Wolfgang carried Felicity away, she looked back to see Reuben streaking towards Sib and Gus. *He moves like a cat*, she thought, but saw no more as they rounded the hill.

'Here!' cried Pippi. She had found a small hollow at the foot of the hill. It was not ideal, but it left them free to run if needed, and provided temporary cover. Gorse-type bushes that survived in this hostile terrain partially concealed its entrance from above. *Well, it will have to do*, thought Pippi. The cubs were strong inside her now, and they kicked in complaint as the adrenaline coursed through her body. *Not yet*, she thought, in an unknown echo of Reuben.

Felicity had dismounted. She was fighting with Scratt and Little Green, who held her firmly. 'I want to see,' she wept. 'I just want to see what is happening to him.'

'No, Felicity,' said Scratt, 'we must obey Reuben. We fail the others if we are seen.'

'Felicity,' said Little Green, and she expanded her aura and phosphorescence until all of them were bathed in a blue pool. Her silent words flowed into all their distressed minds. *Calm yourselves. Think of Gus and the light he has followed all his life. In spite of Toxic shadows. Think of Reuben, his courage and conviction. We are here to heal the scars of the past. We must defend and change the present. Be still, my dear quest companions. Reuben and Gus will return.*

'But not Sib,' said Georges, and in the instant his words broke the silence, they felt the change. Little Green's light extinguished, and an unutterable sadness hit Felicity like a wave of pain. They heard a fiendish cry from the leader,

Demet, in the Toxics' gross, new language. Wolfgang and Georges ran out to see what was happening.

*

Sib felt the Toxics around him. It was so dark. In his blindness, he heard Gus.

'Sib, I am here. Keep still. Let me speak to them. Their spines will hurt, but try not to move. Speak to me, Sib,' he urged. 'Are you there?'

'I am here, Gus,' said Sib. His voice was small.

'They don't know what to do without instructions. Keep listening to me. I will try to locate their leader. It is he they will follow,' said Gus.

'What will they do?' asked Sib. 'What do they want?'

'We want to kill you, of course,' said a terrible voice, in the ugly, spitting creak and spits of the Toxics' new language.

'Demet,' replied Gus, in the foul tongue, 'I was trying to find you. Your companions are crowding us.'

'Silence!' said Demet, and the other Toxics moaned and hissed and popped as they heard their leader.

Like blind offspring searching for their feed, thought Sib. He was trying not to cry out, but the pain was intense. The spines of the Toxics had stabbed him in many places, and their venomous sting was making him dizzy. He breathed deeply, willing his head to stay clear. The smell was terrible. Like rotting meat and warm, fetid air they surrounded and suffocated him. He tried to look up to the sky, but they were too tall, and even lifting his head caused more piercings in his back.

'Oh,' he moaned involuntarily.

Demet cackled at his suffering.

'Demet, listen to me,' said Gus. He spoke quickly. Sib would not survive this onslaught for long. In these numbers, the venom of their spines would be fatal. Gus had to get him out. As he searched to communicate with Arrass' second-in-command, he couldn't believe how distorted and corrupt Demet's mind felt. He had to find something of light within this defiled Toxic. They were the same, once, thought Gus. He tried again. Moving towards the sounds of Sib's feeble babbling, he continued, 'Arrass is misguided. Do not be misled. You are strong, Demet. I sense it. Be strong–'

'You vile sycophant and nurturer of all that has betrayed us,' screamed Demet. 'Arrass warned me of your honeyed words. The Old World is finished. The time of the Toxics is here. Exclusion and disrespect; loneliness and isolation...'

As Demet ranted, Gus reached Sib. He touched his lowered head and spoke quietly. 'I am here.'

'Go, Gus,' whispered Sib. 'I deserve this...I knew the Sibilin were planning to join the Toxics. I knew, Gus,' he said. 'From the beginning, I knew, and I said nothing until it was too late.'

'But you came back, Sib. You came back.'

'I love the Aquatics,' Sib whispered. 'I couldn't let their world be destroyed,' he said, softly, and then his breath exhaled for the last time.

In the jostling, spiny space, Sib's spirit left and rose to form his skytrail of departure. It streaked the blue sky in a divine, white crescent. Gus felt the heaviness of loss, but he could not afford to grieve yet. He was going to bring Sib back to the others. To the only family Sib had ever known, in the end. He forged on, ignoring the poisonous punctures of the diabolic creatures. The venom stung, but could not harm him like Sib. Now his eyes had readjusted to the filthy mass, and Gus could see more. He saw Demet standing at the side. Demet could not see what he was doing, but he could see Gus moving.

'Halt, scum and traitor!' he spat in the new base language. 'End him!' he commanded to his mindless mob.

There was a cry of joy as they leapt for Gus. Their monstrous mouths were black slashes of putrid breath that set the ground hissing and bubbling with their lost spittle, and their dirty spines were aimed directly at him, claws of destruction seeking their prey. But Gus had heard the intention before Demet uttered it. Amongst the dark whispering and bleak hollow spaces of Demet's broken mind, he had found thought. With a huge shove he broke the lines and ran for freedom. He scooped Sib up, fear giving him strength. He sucked in the clean air and felt the energy of the sky give him wings.

*

Wolfgang and Georges, watching from the crest of the hill, saw his dash for freedom, and they shouted to Little Green, 'Gus has broken away! He carries Sib's body.'

'Send him your aura, Little Green,' said Felicity.

'It's too far,' Little Green replied. 'Sib's departure has drained me. I'm sorry. Gus will have to use his own strengths.'

'Not without me, he won't,' bellowed Georges, and he pelted across the rapidly closing space to bring the body of their departed member home.

27

Athen

Reuben helplessly watched the scene unfold. He was trapped. The anarchic Sibilin surrounded him. The deadly effluents of the Toxics enforced them to march separately, and as Sib and Gus were swarmed, the rear wave of Sibilin had wrapped itself around Reuben. They did nothing; they seemed confused. Reuben spoke to the largest Sibilin, who appeared to lead this creature arm of the Toxic movement.

'Welcome, Sibilinofunknowngeneration,' he said.

'Do not use the terms of the Old World,' the Sibilin replied. 'My new name is Athen.' So Arrass had given this Sibilin the name of his ex-third-in-command. *The first convert for Gus.* Reuben's smile was sad as he thought of that day at the beach.

'We await instructions from Demet,' continued Athen the second. 'Do not move.'

Reuben was pleased to hear the Old World speech. He wondered how Athen could understand Demet's vile talk.

'He uses the old language if necessary for our cause,' replied Athen.

'It is good you still mind-share,' said Reuben, surprised. *The Toxics seem to have lost the ability. Communication is no longer a strength for them.*

'Arrass and Demet need us to continue the old skills,' said Athen aloud.

Reuben sighed. He must reach Gus and Sib. The Toxics were lethal. He heard the coarse, uvular clicks of Demet as he spoke with Gus. What was happening in there?

'Why have you betrayed our beautiful world?' asked

190

Reuben. He felt hope for the Sibilin; their betrayal was not steeped in centuries of bitterness.

'What a ridiculous question,' spat Athen. 'We have been restless for years. Sib the disloyal knew of our unease long ago. He agreed our lands are harsh, and our enharmonics of little consequence—'

Reuben interrupted him, 'Your enharmonics are treasured and utterly essential to the balance of the world. You are honoured with enharmonics who support all creatures and plants at the very foundations of our culture.' Reuben was mottled with anger. His fondness for the gentle Colour Changers put him in danger.

'Orion of no hope – be silenced!' cried Athen, and he snaked out his long tongue. It wrapped itself around Reuben's leg, and he fell, winded, to the ground. The other Sibilin cackled and sneered. Reuben thought of Sib.

'No use thinking of him,' said Athen, leaning over Reuben with his bloodshot eyes.

Reuben lay still. He heard the truth in Athen's words. He was sickened with himself. *The quest is failing*, he thought, for the first time. At that moment all the Sibilin looked up in unison. They looked to the sky. Their faces faltered, and Athen stood back to let Reuben up, without thinking. Warily Reuben stood. He felt it too. Sib was leaving. His death was like a silence. Reuben knew Sib had not been a popular quest member. He had seen the dislike of Scratt and the mistrust of Felicity. But Reuben had never given up hope. A Sibilin is not designed for loyalty, but for circulation, he thought. They circulate the matters of the world, serious or small.

Athen picked up his thoughts. 'Yes, news and information. We are the gossips and the prattlers, the lovers of all things new,' and then he paused.

The other Sibilin looked at him. Something was wrong. The death of Sib had shaken Athen badly.

'Sib the traitor was my brother,' he said and turned away. He looked at his followers, and he looked up at the skytrail of Sib for the last time. He half-lowered his eyelids, deep in thought.

Reuben recognised the expression, from Sib. They heard Demet issue his order to destroy Gus.

Athen threw out his tongue, and it cracked like a whip. 'Reubenfourthousandth,' he said in a very different voice. 'Will you present our case to the ancient Oceanids if we leave?'

Reuben could not believe what he was hearing. His heart soared, and he looked to Sib's trail. He knew that with this last act of dying, Sib had saved the quest company. Without the Sibilin wing behind them, the Toxics were back to their original evil but containable form. The Old World's harmony would reshift, and the crisis was swinging in their favour again. *Well, not exactly*, thought Reuben as he looked at the filthy creatures chanting their curses. He noticed Gus near the edge. He saw him break out from the hoard, carrying poor Sib's body.

'Thank you, my friend,' he said to the last, vanishing traces of the skytrail, and then, having reassured Athen, he left and ran to join Gus. Together they united with Georges and Wolfgang, and all four streaked over the hill. Wolfgang took Sib as they ran, and Reuben and Georges lifted Gus off his spiky feet.

'The quest continues!' cried Reuben as they reached the others, panting but safe.

28

Felicity

The day's heat was over. The troupe reached a slender belt of trees, and Reuben decided to set up camp. They had marched without rest, stopping only to transfer Sib's body from Georges to Wolfgang. Felicity was subdued. She had not liked Sib, but in the end, his love for the aqueous webs of the world had saved his soul. Little Green had said his skytrail was a good one.

Gus heard her thoughts and said, 'He died in honour, Felicity.'

Gus looked awful, she thought. His spines flopped against his sides, and his big dark eyes were encrusted with a pale green dust. She hadn't realised the plants could cry. Each member mourned Sib in their own way. Georges trotted, head down, and wouldn't eat. Reuben stayed far from Felicity. Gus had simply wept his large green tears silently and continuously. Little Green was unreachable. Her aura shone dimly but constantly as she called on her energy to heal. Scratt took comfort from the Lupata. He had walked between them all day.

Felicity felt alone. She needed Reuben. It had been a horrible day. She had a sudden overwhelming desire to be at home. She could picture her bed and her squashed bear, his eyes replaced with buttons by Mum when she read a headline of the danger of toys and their loose eyes. If she concentrated, she could almost remember the scent of her mother's perfume. But it was getting harder. *How long have I been here?* she thought, panicking. Her tears came at last, but whether they were for Sib or for her, she wasn't sure.

They buried him on the bank of a small stream, and Gus said a lovely prayer about Sib's love for the Aquatics.

After the speech, they gathered together. Reuben said they didn't need a fire, and he didn't want to alert the Toxics to their position, in any case. Demet and his gang had left them alone so far. Felicity suspected the dissolution of the Sibilin army had thrown them into chaos.

Felicity looked across at Little Green. It was hard to remember her as a young plant. She had grown so tall and mature.

'Will you find your partner when we arrive at the caves?' asked Felicity.

'No, I must bond with my enharmonic first,' said Little Green, smiling.

'Oh, of course,' said Felicity. 'I forgot. Have you heard him? How does it work? Orchadea and Reuben seemed to already know each other.'

'Well, we hear them talking to us, sometimes. They are a familiar voice in our head. I hear him. He is a young Taureau. I need him to mature fast, as the elders said. I hope he can. I look forward to meeting him,' said Little Green.

'Do you know his name?' asked Felicity, fascinated.

'Of course! His name is Nathaniel.'

'That's a name from my world,' said Felicity.

'Maybe our worlds are not so far apart, then,' said Little Green, eyes twinkling.

Reuben appeared. 'Come on, Felicity, let's go and gather food.'

Felicity jumped up and took his hand. They walked along the dusty track that ran through the spinney. Reuben walked head down.

Felicity tried to reach him. 'It is very sad that we lost Sib,' she said.

'It is my fault. I should never have left them behind,' he said, the simmering anger spilling out. 'I put the entire quest at risk through careless action. I knew they had not our speed. What was I thinking of?' He kicked a tree root and stumbled as it lifted to catch his toe.

Felicity was shocked. 'Reuben, you have led this quest unfailingly since the day I first met you. You are a good leader. Your steady guidance has kept us all going. Sib played his role, and he finished it well. He worked against his instincts, and that is very hard.'

There was no answer.

Felicity spun round and grabbed his arm. 'Reuben!' she cried. 'Reuben, please. It – is – not – your – fault.' She repeated the words slowly, staring straight into his eyes.

His mood had darkened their colour to a navy-brown. His muddy gaze cleared. His breathing had been tense, shallow, but as his focus returned to her earnest, sparkling eyes, he took a deep breath and exhaled slowly. He could not forgive himself quite so fast, but he heard her words, and he knew all was probably unfolding as it must. Perhaps with time he would understand why they had to lose Sib. Felicity saw his expression lighten.

'You are hurting me, Felicity,' he said, with a crooked smile.

Felicity looked down and noticed that her hands were squeezing Reuben's skin so tightly it had gone white. 'Sorry, Reuben,' she answered. 'But you were lost. I was scared. We need you.'

Reuben looked at her, and then he frowned and inspected her more closely. 'How do you feel, Felicity?'

'I am sad, too, of course–'

'No, I don't mean about Sib,' replied Reuben. 'How do you feel in general?'

Felicity was confused. 'What do you mean?'

'Have you not noticed anything strange?' he asked her. His eyes were glowing golden-brown in the evening sun.

'Reuben, I am very tired, and I wish you would stop being so weird. No, I have not noticed anything strange. Well, apart from an army of poisoned cactus attacking us.'

And falling in love with a man who lost his tail, she thought, blocking it as soon as it came to her.

Reuben burst out laughing.

Felicity was not amused. She had been very worried for him, and now he was being personal. Was this normal for Orion males, she wondered. She turned to leave, but he caught hold of her arm.

'Felicity, look,' he said, and something in his voice made the world still.

She heard her heart pumping, and was mesmerised by the pulse at the bottom of his throat. They were beating in perfect unison. She raised her eyes.

'Look,' he said again, using his eyes to explain.

Felicity broke the moment and looked down. 'I can't see anything,' she said. It seemed disrespectful to play games today, Sib's day, she thought.

Reuben frowned. 'Don't be so bad-tempered, my strange woman.'

'I am not a woman. I am 14 ¾, and in my world that is not quite a woman. Well, I am a woman, and of course, in a tribal situation I could have a couple of children by now, but actually I still have my GCSEs to pass yet.' She was rambling. Reuben's close scrutiny was embarrassing. But his smile lit up his face, and in spite of her annoyance, Felicity smiled and forgave him. It was good to see him happy again.

'Well, you are in my world now, Felicity,' he said, 'and you have matured. I imagine you don't need an enharmonic, do you?'

Felicity felt that warning prickle on the back of her neck. She looked down more carefully. Her clothes were shorter and there were definitely tighter. She had presumed it was all the rain or the food. Her mouth went dry. She hadn't been prepared for this. It was one thing, helping this mystical Old World change, but she had not given it permission to change her. She felt herself trembling. How could she go home now?

'Please leave me alone,' she said.

Reuben sighed. 'Of course. But please, my darling Felicity, listen to me before I go. I have seen you weep tears for your special world and its mistakes, but you keep faith. You have brought your gift of hope to our world. You were called here, and your open mind absorbs all. Hear this, then; there is no oddness in your maturity. It is the harmony of the Old World. It is the balance of us – we can be together when the time is right.'

When he had gone, Felicity felt herself all over. She looked at her hands. They looked like her mother's, a bit. Was that a slight wrinkle on the top? If she pushed the skin, it definitely puckered up for longer than normal. She had got old, she thought, horrified. She tugged open her jacket and peered inside. 'Oh my God,' she muttered. *How could I not have noticed what was happening? How old am I? Eighteen? Thirty?* She touched her hair. Well, that felt the same, at least. She breathed in and counted to ten. The panic slowly subsided. *I suppose it could be worse.* In this Old World, who knew what it may have decided to do. She sat for a while, letting the revelation sink in. As the evening air started to dampen, she walked back to camp. She was hungry and needed female company.

'Pippi, may I speak to you?' she asked as she walked up to the group. As Pippi loped across, Felicity could see that her belly hung low. 'Pippi, you've been getting fatter recently. Are you pregnant?' asked Felicity, direct as ever.

Pippi saw Wolfgang's head go up. He growled softly.

'I will talk of it later,' Pippi replied to Felicity. 'Help me share out this food. Is that why you called me?'

'No...um...well, have you noticed anything different about me?' said Felicity.

'Well, your scent has been of breeding for the last two days, but nothing else,' said Pippi, as they gave Georges his triple portion of stod balls. He was snoozing again.

'What!' exploded Felicity. 'What's breeding scent? Eew, that's disgusting,' she exclaimed.

Pippi laughed, and Little Green, who had heard Felicity's squeal, laughed too.

'It's hardly noticeable, Felicity,' Little Green said. 'The Lupata nose is extraordinary. This ability is crucial for the Lupata. At the ceremonies the males must know they have a mature female, and the females must know who is their competition.'

'Well, I am Felicity Penfold, and I am not a wolf,' Felicity said. She went and sat down on her own. Pippi and Little Green exchanged glances.

*

Reuben and Wolfgang returned from a last scout before they settled for the night, and Scratt came back with some wonderful amber nectar. Gus had been in an exhausted sleep from the moment they sat down. Georges was still snoring and had slumped sideways onto a skinny tree. Reuben clapped his hands, and Georges jerked awake, snapping the sapling with a crack. Little Green admonished him and then said they should at least make a clean break, so it could rejuvenate. When they had tidied up the mess, Reuben suggested they have a tiny fire, as the night air was cold. The flames curled and swirled and warmed the tired band, inside and out.

They shared some of the powerful amber liquid, and Gus raised his flask in a toast. 'Let's eat and drink tonight, with a thought for Sib.'

Reuben continued, 'To his pure love for the Aquatics, his bravery and his spirit's help at the end.'

The final words fell to Little Green, in her sweet-flowing voice. 'To a Sibilin who will go down in the knowledge of the Roots for the future.'

They all raised their little flasks and drank. 'To Sib!' they said together.

29

The Sacred Caves

They arrived at the sacred caves on the last afternoon of the Taureau contests. The journey had been arduous, but the loss of Sib hardened their determination to reach the caves. A pair of Strata had come and offered respect to the memory of Sib from the Ancients. They had also brought news that Arrass and Demet were now united and marching together. Arrass had detoured to try to regain control of Athen.

'But failing in his evil intents,
He joined with Demet to combine their strength,' they sang, wings outstretched. They warned the quest company that the Toxics were less than twenty-four hours away. Felicity quelled the flutter in her stomach.

This close to the Sacred Caves, the energy of the Old World was strong. After the grim trek, this fertile land overwhelmed the senses. A turquoise river thundered through its gorge, birdsong filling the forest, and glorious scents swirled in the dewy air as they came through the verdant pass. Reuben spoke earnestly with Gus as they walked.

'He is concerned for the aftermath of the quest,' Little Green said to Felicity.

'I know what he is saying,' Felicity replied. 'He wants to make sure someone can look after his beautiful world if anything happens to him.' She had a big lump in her throat, but she wasn't ill.

'Reuben's wisdom stretches far,' said Little Green. Her thoughts turned to her own future. The idea of being shut up in the Stipple chambers to make Roots for the rest of her life was appalling. 'For now we must focus only on stopping Arrass,' she said.

Felicity was not going to think any further than the end of the day. She was still getting used to her new body. She wished she had the equanimity of Little Green and Scratt, who said he was approaching his time now. He had been saying that since they left Thornton, though, she thought, smiling.

'Why are you smiling, my lovely Felicity?' said Reuben, stepping up beside her onto the thick, white stone upon which she stood.

'I didn't hear you,' said Felicity.

'I am silent as the night,' he said.

'That sounds like Georges,' she said, laughing. It was such a relief to know the travelling was over.

'Yes, isn't it?' said Reuben.

'You're hijacking my head again.' Felicity giggled. *How I love him*, she thought.

Reuben leant over and kissed her. No hesitation. Felicity knew her cheeks were burning. They were all standing in a line, ready to descend, and absolutely everyone saw the kiss. Georges, Wolfgang, Pippi, Scratt, and Little Green. Everyone. She forced her eyes to open as Reuben released her mouth. They were all grinning. No one looked surprised.

'Congratulations, Reuben and Felicity,' Georges said in his growly voice.

'What does he mean, Reuben?' asked Felicity. But a shout from below claimed his attention.

'Welcome, quest party. We have been expecting you. Come join the final hours of this year's contests. The biggest and fiercest ever,' said the voice.

'I know that voice,' said Georges, charging off. But as they watched him canter down the hill, they saw a small Taurelle cut him off. She charged into him from the side, and he staggered, in spite of his size. They all started to run towards the commotion.

'You detestable, irresponsible old beast!' the black Taurelle was shouting.

'She is a very pretty Taurelle,' said Little Green. 'I wonder what she wants.'

Georges looked unharmed, if shaken, so his friends decided to sit and watch. Some Colour Changers came rolling and flying up the hill. They were whispering excitedly, and Felicity was thrilled to see they had brought food and drink. The drink was fizzy. Colourless, yet as it moved, all the colours of the skyarc reflected in it. Like the refraction on a puddle, thought Felicity. Absolutely beautiful. It tasted like lemonade. They all gulped it down greedily, with no remorse that Georges was missing it. As they took big handfuls of the fluffy, crunchy maceypips, the black dervish, that they discovered was Tatania, was still in full throat.

'...and after all that, big man, who I hear is now called Georges – a proper Taureau name not being good enough for you – the big, old bull ran away, didn't you? They told me you would. I trusted you, you monstrous lump.' She kicked him at this point.

Georges roared in pain, but stood, stoic, as the tirade pummelled him. 'Tatty,' he said pleadingly, 'Tatty, my princess – OW!' he shrieked as she bit him.

'Don't call me Tatty, you fiend! You dirty, ancient old liar.'

'Ssshhh. Tatania, my friends are listening,' he said, trying to skip out of the way as she aimed another kick at him. She was panting now, and Georges knew by experience she would shortly run out of bellows.

'Friends. Who could be friends with such a dreadful pig?' she shouted hoarsely. But she stopped when she realised what he had said. She saw the audience. Her sides were heaving, and she was clearly very upset.

Little Green brushed off some maceypips and tentatively approached.

'I am Taurellethreethousandththirty-three,' said Tatania

formally, as Little Green faced her, 'but if you are friends of my Georges, then you may call me by his chosen name for me: Tatania. I welcome you, on behalf of this year's leading competitor, Nathaniel,' said Tatania politely. 'I apologise for my rudeness. It is surely not the welcome Nathaniel would have wanted,' she said and made a charming Taureau bow, deep and low. Her tummy prevented the full swoop, but it was still finely executed, thought Reuben.

'Nathaniel?' asked Little Green, interested. It was not a common name.

'Yes, he leads the contests. Today is the final day. The day of the unseen trials. He is there. But he asked me to welcome you,' Tatania said. She tossed her head as she spoke. It reminded Felicity so much of Georges. *They suit each other,* she thought, smiling.

Reuben stepped forward. 'We thank you for making us welcome, Tatania,' he said. 'We would love to share an hour or so of the contest, but we must be allowed to enter the sacred cave entrance by dusk.' As he spoke, he looked down the hill. Where was the best place to enter the caves? He guessed it was right behind the largest and ugliest of the guardian Taureau. The sentry's half-snapped horn suggested it unwise to upset him. Reuben sighed. They must honour the end of the contests. Tatania led them down the hill.

'Your reputation goes before you,' she said, picking out her path carefully on the hill. 'It is said the Toxics are restless and are led by one who seeks the knowledge. Can you defeat him?'

'Tatania!' Georges grumbled, worried her audacity might offend.

'It's okay, Georges,' said Reuben. 'If you could lead us to our seats for the finish of the contest, I will try to answer you, Tatania.'

'A fine gentleman,' she said in a loud voice, looking over her shoulder at Georges as she led her guests, with a dainty trot, down to the bowl and the grand finale of the Taureau contest.

The bowl was a large area of sunken land nestled amongst the surrounding green hills. The guardians took their challenges in its flat, wide space, with spectators lining each side. The hills and the Sacred Caves faced each other at either end. Georges stood close to Felicity and Reuben as they took their soft seats. The Colour Changers came with more refreshment, and they waited.

Everyone chatted as the last and hidden tests took place. I would rather have seen some sparring, thought Felicity. But the lacerations and wounds on the less successful contestants warned her it may not have been so pleasant to watch. One poor beast lay on its side, unable to move due to its broken hind leg. She looked about her. The hills gave way to rocky mountains, and beyond, as she knew, was a harsh land. Georges, who was trying to avoid speaking to Tatania, described its history.

'This part of the world was not home to any beast or creature,' he said. 'It was a forgotten place, lost between the lands of the Greens, the Sibilin, and the Lupata. The barren mountains were not a place to settle; only a curious traveller could stumble upon them. Here were laid the Roots of knowledge by the Stipple Greens. Deep within the heart of these caves is the chamber where the first Root is laid. Layer upon layer, Root upon Root, thousands of years of history, healing, harmony. Kept safe by the guardians of the caves. The bravest and the strongest of the Taureau.'

Georges looked across the great green field, and Felicity heard the wistful tone in his voice. He continued, 'The contests are hard. First, a Taureau must be strong. Only a mature Taureau may enter. There has been only one exception to this rule. Once upon a time, a young immature Taureau, seeking fame, entered the contests. His size and skill were so immense that he won all but the last. However, he returned, mature, the next year, and earnt his honoured place as a guardian to the caves. He held this position longer than any before or since. To remain a guardian, one must refight each year. The Stipples must be protected by the best.'

'Do they charge at each other to prove strength?' asked Felicity, thinking of a bison fight she had seen at the wildlife park.

'Yes, and they have tests for speed and agility. For stamina and endurance. The grassy field is four hundredd wide. They must run it twenty times and not be tired. They must ford the roaring river on the mountain. They must go without drink for all of this first day. Then the battles on day two. Tests of sheer strength and courage. They must hold their lines. The power causes pile-ups. Legs and necks may be broken,' he said.

Felicity had seen. Horrible. She stretched her legs out as he continued, 'Today, the last day, those few remaining are allowed to drink and are taken inside.'

'Why?' said Felicity.

Georges looked at her. He was fond of this young stranger. She was odd, but he admired her tenacity. 'Well, that is something only the guardians can tell you,' he said, his old eyes shining at some private joke.

'Felicity, look,' said Reuben. On the far side of the green bowl was a small copse. From behind this green screen stepped four huge Taureau. They walked slowly. Their heads were up, but Felicity could see by how carefully they trod that they were struggling not to collapse.

'The winner and his trio!' squealed Tatania.

As the mighty four walked to the centre of the bowl, the crowd roared. The spectators had been patient, and they were rewarded. Nathaniel had indeed won. Little Green stood straight as she peered across the distance. She tried to mind-share, but his mind was too tired. She absolutely knew it was him. It had to be. *Will he help me mature after the feast?* He was an incredible beast, and she felt honoured that the Old World had given her such an enharmonic. He was pale caramel. A golden Taureau. They were rare. She felt the keen interest of the Taurelles as they watched him receive his glory.

'Now he will wash and feast. My, what a fine creature!' said Tatania.

'No, first he will thank all his contestants for their worthy competition,' said Georges, 'and actually he is a little young, I think, for such a responsibility.'

'He is mature,' said Tatania. 'He cannot be too young.'

'Actually, I don't think he is,' interjected Little Green, 'mature, I mean.'

'What!' bellowed Georges. 'Never has this been seen. Only the one, many years ago. Even he did not pass the final, secret tests of reasoning and wisdom–' He cut short the sentence, and Felicity understood. *Of course. To complement courage and strength – wisdom and tolerance.* Gus approached as the spectators began to move about.

'Georges, be pleased, my old friend,' he said. 'You were the first to succeed in entering the contests as an immature Taureau. You held your position longer than ever recorded by the Roots. You are a legend, unsurpassed. But today, Nathaniel has proved his worth, as once did you.'

'I know,' Georges said quietly. Tatania came and licked his neck. He nudged her, and they walked away to sort out their misunderstandings.

'Wait, everyone,' Reuben called as they dispersed. 'After the feast, we meet at the cave entrance, where the largest beast stands,' he commanded. 'I will see you all there at dusk.'

Felicity stood and stretched. Little Green was gliding over to Nathaniel. Felicity saw the crowds part for her.

'I am glad her enharmonic is so splendid,' said Felicity to Reuben. They were alone. Wolfgang and Pippi had watched the finale from the other side of the bowl.

'Do you think they will know where to meet us?' said Felicity. Grey shadows crept across the bowl as tall clouds built up overhead.

'They will,' he said, 'and before you worry – Scratt is just over there, flirting with a group of female Thorns.'

Felicity laughed. Then her face became serious. 'What will happen to us, Reuben, when all this is over?'

'We will be together, of course,' he replied, 'and mate.'

Felicity choked on a maceypip. 'Reuben!'

'Yes?'

'It's not that simple.'

'Well, Felicity, you are part Old World now, and that is how the Orion talk here,' he said, with a smile. He couldn't resist teasing her. She was so pretty when her cheeks were pink.

'You forget I am not an Orion female,' she said. Her thoughts raced. *How can we be together? I have to go home. I want to go home. I want to stay. What will happen?*

Reuben's thoughts interrupted her own. *I think we can make it simple, Felicity. We are not so different.*

'Reuben, your—' but she didn't finish, as there was a blinding flash of light that turned the sky red and pink and orange. Its radiance lit up the bowl and shone on Reuben's face, turning his eyes a fiery crimson.

'What was that?' she asked.

Scratt came running over. 'Did you see it?'

'What was it?' Felicity repeated.

'Little Green and Nathaniel,' said Scratt. 'They have matured.'

*

The feast had begun, so they waited patiently to speak to Little Green. Gus, Felicity and Reuben ate together. Scratt went to find Wolfgang and Pippi. Reuben felt it was time for the troupe to be reunited.

'You asked them to meet at dusk,' said Felicity. 'They will come. Georges will be there early, I should think. He will want to be first in.'

'Yes, but I feel darkness, Felicity. I think the Toxics approach faster than we anticipated. I would like to leave.'

'What about the rest of the feast?' she said.

'The maceypips and trillins are very nutritious. We will be fine.'

'They weren't very filling,' muttered Felicity, thumping her tummy to stop it rumbling so loudly.

'The food here is organised by the guardians. Physical fitness is important to them. The food will nourish and energise you for twenty-four hours, but it won't fill you. It is ideal, actually, for what lies ahead,' he said.

'Oh,' said Felicity. The trillins were shaped like bananas, with grey, stringy flesh. They were not her favourite, but she was hungry.

'Perhaps it is the travelling.' Reuben smiled. It was only a small smile; his mouth felt stiff. Felicity watched him. She wouldn't think about the Toxics.

At last, Little Green returned. Her phosphorescence was so bright, they could hardly see her face. She laughed at their stunned expressions and lifted her elegant, trailing arms, making the blue light ebb and flow with the movement. As they admired her new brilliance, a sound niggled at the back of Reuben's awareness. It started as a dim rumbling behind the horizon. He looked around; the feast was over, and only stragglers and guardians remained. The sound was loud now, and spectators were looking into the skies, searching for its meaning. Felicity looked at Reuben. Where were Scratt, Wolfgang and Pippi? Georges was galloping flat and hard across the grass toward them. Felicity was relieved.

'Have you seen the others?' asked Reuben.

'No, I was busy with Tatania,' said Georges. His voice was deep and urgent. A tone Felicity had not heard before. 'They will come. Where shall I stand?'

'Can you hold the centre for us?' said Reuben, and Georges sprinted to his position without reply.

'What is that noise?' Felicity asked him.

'Arrass,' said Gus, spines lifting as the rumbling came closer.

30

The Battle

The Toxics teemed over the ridge of the hill. On each side rose the steep mountains. They looked impassable, but to Felicity's horror, more Toxics swarmed through the forests. They could see the trees moving and shaking as the diseased creatures descended.

A large torrent of water flowed down the left-hand mountain and dropped in successive falls, until it becalmed and slid silently along the left bank of the bowl before disappearing into the mouth of the largest cave entrance. Wolfgang and Pippi had been resting by the river, but as the Toxics came into view, they stood, alert. Georges and Tatania, nuzzling in the copse at the foot of the waterfall, had heard the rumbling. Georges shouted at Tatania to escape, and charged into the centre of the bowl to find Reuben.

As the black, poisonous army approached, the sight of the proud old Taureau, standing firm and strong in the centre of the arena which had once been his, tightened Felicity's throat. Her eyes clouded with tears, and she blinked them away, angry with herself.

Then Reuben was kissing her, saying, 'Head for the main entrance to the caves – stay with Little Green,' and he was gone.

She scanned the wide space. The guardians were herding the last spectators over the cave hilltops to safety. 'Go home!' they growled. 'Go home. We will deal with these renegades.'

Felicity saw the terrified expressions as those left registered the nature of the approaching mob. But even as the last stragglers were urged away, from around the bowl came Orion of all sizes and skin colours. Some were black, some pale white, some golden, and some tawny like Reuben. Their hair streamed out behind them as they pounded into the bowl. They were running on all fours, like cats, their huge black-and-white tails perpendicular to their lithe bodies. They defied the Taureau and leapt over the huge beasts. Georges called orders from the centre as chaos ensued.

'If you must stay,' he said to the Orion army, 'then do as the guardians instruct you. They are trained for combat.' His powerful voice boomed out across the arena. Reuben saw his childhood rival leading the Orion.

'Welcome Jezaniahfourthousandth. Now turn around and return home,' he said. 'This is not a game, Jez,' he added as his dark friend came close. 'These Toxics are dangerous. Look!' He spoke as the first line of Toxics reached the bottom of the hill. Their misshapen mouths drooled bile that stained the ground ochre, and their rasps and croaks could be heard above the shouts of the guardians. Those who had attempted descent in the forests were falling down the last steep slopes. They rolled and tumbled, bouncing off the tall trees.

Gus stood watching with despair. He saw the Toxic limbs snap in the frenzy. What had Arrass and Demet done to them?

Pippi now stood on the left forward flank of the grassy bowl. Her time had come, but she begged for the new life squirming inside her, to wait just a moment longer. Wolfgang beseeched her to stay close to the river and to the protection it might provide. But she would not. Her cubs would not be born for a few hours. *May I have time to see these Toxics to their conclusion*, she prayed and then curled her lip as her first threatening snarls rent the air.

Wolfgang crossed to the right flank. Reuben ran to the front and stood between them. Behind stood Scratt, Jez and the other Orion. They formed a shield across the middle of the bowl, with Georges' huge form dominating at its centre.

At the very back was Gus, ready to diffuse the Toxics who broke through.

'Remember all I taught you,' he muttered as the battle commenced. Since Sib's death, he had instructed them in the art of spine warfare, and they all carried the healing balm in their pockets. It would save their lives, but nothing could spare them the excruciating pain of the venom.

*

Little Green ran to the cave entrance.

'Can we stay here until Reuben and the others get away?' Felicity asked as she caught up with Little Green.

'Felicity, I am sorry. Arrass is not with them, have you noticed? I suspect he is heading directly for the Old Root. He sacrifices Demet and the army to achieve his aim. Arrass will destroy the Root. We must try to reach it before him.'

'But Phoebe's instructions were clear, Little Green,' said Felicity, frowning. 'We must all three go to the Root together.'

Little Green took a deep breath. The noise of the initial clashes of spine and hoof and claw were loud. The anger and violence unsettled her aura. She knew this fight must take place. The time for talking was over. The Toxics would not listen. They had to be controlled before they destroyed all that held their Old World together. She let out her breath slowly, and with it came calm thoughts. She looked down at Felicity, and Felicity noticed her eyes were of the palest blue.

'Felicity,' she said quietly, 'have confidence. Reuben will catch up. The Root is in imminent danger. Sometimes, you must simply jump.'

Looking at her dear, kind friend, Felicity knew she was right. Arrass was wicked, and she agreed with Little Green that he had probably resorted to utterly devious tactics to achieve his aim. She took a last look at the bowl. There was no hope of seeing Reuben. There were Taureau charging and tossing Toxics, Toxics fighting each other in their mindless confusion, Orion soaring over the heads of everyone with their jointed limbs, and somewhere in there, she thought, were Wolfgang, Pippi, Scratt and Reuben. Gus ran from side to side at the back, like a tennis player taking a long shot, and as a Toxic broke the ranks, Gus would grab him and corral him in an enclosure the guardians had set up. If they hadn't been so monstrous, Felicity would have found it funny. The captured Toxics stood immobile and confused as they peered through the high, woven fences.

So she followed Little Green, and together they stepped up to the guardian. He stood, nostrils flaring at the Toxic attack on the horizon.

'Stay back!' he warned, glancing down, and his eyes narrowed with anger as they did not.

'Let me pass, Taureauofunknowngenerationaldescent,' commanded Little Green in her firmest voice.

'I will not. You are unauthorised.' He looked at Felicity out of his small, shrewd eyes.

She stepped past Little Green and said, 'I am Felicity Isabel Penfold, and I have travelled from another world. Behind us is an army of demented vegetation whose aim is to enter this cave. If they succeed, the Old World will be destroyed as you know it. Your only hope,' she was now flushed with rage, 'is to let this Stipple Greenesse and I pass. Or beg mercy from the Ancients, the Strata, and the Aquatics – who all risked so much to help bring her here today.'

The mighty beast tipped his head sideways. He was a highly skilled guardian, but his training had not allowed for this. He looked at the tiny, fuming creature, and the shining cloud of aura that surrounded the fine Stipple Greenesse. Then contrary to all rules, he let them pass.

'There, that was easy,' said Felicity. As she spoke, the rocky ledge underneath her crumbled, and she plunged into the roaring riverfall as it cascaded down a hole into unseen depths.

*

Reuben faltered as he wrestled with a Toxic. The trick, according to Gus, was to grasp their two longest forward-facing spines. Once you had those firmly controlled, the others couldn't pierce you. They could scratch you, though, he thought; his arms were numb with the venom that had entered. He was also in constant mind-contact with Georges, Scratt, Wolfgang, Pippi and Nathaniel.

The aim was to subdue the Toxics and steer them into the corral. Gus would heal them later. Looking at their demonic, spitting faces, Reuben knew his task was great. Avoiding the spitting acid was particularly difficult, especially since their mouths were so irregular. His hesitation just then cost him a large gob of acid spittle on his neck.

'Aah!' he exclaimed as he grabbed the Toxic. He ducked and swerved its oral missiles as he pulled it out of the field. Along the side, guardians were erecting more corrals. He threw it inside. What had happened to Felicity? He had heard her call in his head. He tried to mind-share, but another Toxic launched at him.

Where was Demet? If he could subdue Demet, the worst would be over. These Toxics had forgotten how to think for themselves. Starved of normal reasoning and Old World energy, they were automatons. It broke his heart. The nearest creatures began to gibber in their revolting language.

'You will have to remember the language of the Old World if you want to commun—' but his words were cut off as Demet landed on him. As he pulled the evil leader off, the agony in his shoulder rendered him speechless.

'Stupid, stupid Orion,' screamed Demet. 'To think you can stop Arrass and me.'

'Where is Arrass?' said Reuben as he used his good arm to fend off the monster.

Demet closed in for the fatal puncture, his two long spines dripping their black toxins. 'In the caves!' he screamed with delight. 'In the caves, and you will die knowing you have failed.' Demet was quivering with insane excitement.

Reuben held out his hands. 'End me, then, Demet. End the quest and the Root and the Old World.'

Demet launched, and in that instant, Nathaniel charged him from the side. Demet had missed the Taureau approaching, so intent had he been on his prey. Nathaniel groaned in torment as he continued to hold the vicious Toxic down with his feet. Reuben could see them discolouring as the dark liquids entered his veins. With great caution, Reuben grabbed Demet's spikes, and together they pushed him into the corral. Demet's fury howled across the bowl.

Gradually the other Toxics stopped moving. The chant of anger that ran through their minds from Arrass and Demet had gone. They allowed themselves to be rounded up, and their crumpled faces seemed no longer wicked – just old, thought Scratt, as he helped with the shepherding.

*

Reuben found Pippi and Wolfgang near the river. Pippi was dying.

'She has fought with the courage of a queen,' said Wolfgang as he licked her wounded body. By her side lay a litter of tiny cubs. They climbed over each other in a furry tangle to reach her milk. But their mother lay on her side, eyes clouded and panting.

'No!' thundered Reuben. 'This will not happen. It cannot. It does not balance. She has fought for the world.' He was sobbing without shame.

'And her cubs will thank her for it one day,' said Wolfgang. 'I will ensure it.'

The others came running up. Georges had given instructions to the guardians, and he, Scratt and Gus had come to see what had so upset Reuben. They all gathered round. No one was unscathed, but only Nathaniel was seriously hurt, his legs barely functioning now.

'There is someone who can help,' said Georges as he gently snorted on the muzzle of the beautiful Lupata to assess her condition. He breathed in her scents. There was life, yet, and with life came hope.

'She is too weak,' said Wolfgang. He had watched her give birth, barely conscious. His grief shrouded him like a thick fog. He could not see their faces. To discover the joy of this amazing female, at an age past which such hope should have been possible. His love for her was private and untouchable. His pain, at this moment, was beyond anything he had experienced in all his years as a prime warrior. He could barely breathe, but someone was licking his face.

'Wolfgang,' said Nathaniel, 'let her ride on my back. I know of whom Georges speaks. I will take her there.'

'It will finish you, Nathaniel,' said Georges.

'I am the strongest Taureau ever to exist,' said Nathaniel, with traces of his old arrogance. 'I will succeed.'

Georges looked at this brave young Taureau, and his heart swelled with pride.

'Yes, Nathaniel, my son,' he said, 'I believe you will.'

31

Underground

Pippi was lifted on to Nathaniel, and with Georges as guide, the wounded party slowly set off into the forest. Wolfgang carried their cubs. Scratt was to remain at the bowl. The guardians, together with the band of Orion warriors, were more than capable of containing the Toxics. In spite of Demet's intermittent rails of bitterness, they were calming down faster than Gus had hoped.

Jez approached. He held something out to Reuben. It was Orion balm, mixed and gelled by the Fragrants using pollens from their forest canopies. Its healing was potent for the Orion, their enharmonics. 'Your mother sent this,' he said.

Reuben was relieved that within minutes his semi-paralysed shoulder was regaining feeling. The blue river water Jez shared with Scratt and Gus.

'Its antiseptic and cleansing properties will help purify our tainted bloodstreams,' said Reuben as he encouraged them both to have plenty.

'Did you know Nathaniel was the son of Georges?' asked Scratt, as they drank.

'I wondered when we first saw him,' said Reuben. 'Something in the stance, I think.'

'No, the head,' said Gus. They all thought of Georges' huge head.

Reuben smiled. 'A fine son,' he said and sighed. 'It's time I leave. My shoulder is functioning. I dare not rest any longer.'

Scratt was sent to help Jez, and Reuben packed up his things. He would carry only a small flask of river water and a pot of bark balm. Gus waited quietly to see him off.

But at the very last moment Reuben said, 'Come with me, Gus.'

'Why?' said Gus. 'My job is here, with the lost Toxics.'

'Because I need you when I meet Arrass,' replied Reuben. 'Jez and Scratt will help the guardians contain the Toxics until we return.'

Gus remembered Coeus' instructions. *'Remain open to all possibilities.'*

*

It was almost mid-night when they finally entered the caves. The guardian had been reluctant to let them through – the last mishap had been unfortunate – but Reuben dealt sternly with him, and they passed inside.

'Let's keep to the main path for now,' he said to Gus. He was worried about Felicity. *Why can't I hear her?*

'Don't worry, Reuben,' said Gus. 'Little Green will protect them.'

They walked faster. There was some vision, but it was poor. A little moonlight pierced the small roof holes. Reuben could feel flutterings above his head and knew they were not alone. The tiny battats that nested here were busy with their near-dawn activities. The roar of the cave fall lessened as they travelled deeper within. They were silent for a while.

Gus wondered how he might heal Demet. The challenge was great, but he had hope.

Reuben thought of Pippi. He had never witnessed such valour, though he had heard of the fortitude of the Lupata. He prayed for such courage in the final stage of the quest. He was not afraid of Arrass. He was afraid of failing the Old World.

*

Felicity gasped as the waterfall took her down. The icy water filled her nose and mouth. Holding her breath, she prayed for release. She was discharged into a large lake. As she bobbed up to the surface, spluttering and choking, she looked around. Away from the frothing flow, the lake became still and silent. The cavern she had landed in felt large. It was hard to see exactly how big, for the darkness clung to its sides. Miles above Felicity could see a roofhole. It let in a singular beam of light that struck the water's surface, a tiny spot in the gloom. She swam smoothly over to it. It barely penetrated the water with its glow. Fear trickled up her back; what lay beneath?

Speeding to the side, she climbed out and lay down, breathless. She searched in a pocket for drink. There was none. The lake lapped enticingly, but the survival instinct flickered in her tired brain. She sighed. *What now?* Lying flat on her back she contemplated. The ground that held her was warm, to her surprise. If she squinted up at the tiny speck of light above, it seemed to grow lengthways. She lay in the near-dark, considering her options, and fell asleep.

*

Little Green, at that moment, was trundling along on her growing Stipple Root, as she descended the myriad pathways of this maze cave. The water had disappeared, and the paths looked dry. She travelled as fast as she could, but the growing Root was a hindrance.

'Not yet,' she pleaded, 'I don't want to be incarcerated here just yet.' She was honoured, but why had she been picked? She wanted to find a partner and lead a normal Green life. She tripped. Elegantly raising herself, she took some deep breaths. Her phosphorescence was invaluable in this gloom, and she did not want it to dim. She must rebalance her mind.

She thought of her family, who had given so much, and she smiled. *I am sorry.* Her glow increased and lit up a hidden path, sloping steeply down and out of sight. *I must head downwards*, she thought. Felicity had plunged to depths unknown; the waterfall looked fathomless. Little Green took the precipitous path. At intermittent levels along its walls were irregular holes. *As if someone has created it.*

The steps were slippery, and she moved with caution. Felicity needed her, and she must not fail.

As she skimmed as fast as she dared down the steep slope, she heard a noise behind. It was like the wind, but there were other notes in the sound. Continuing to descend, she listened. The rushing sound was coming closer. Then, in the moment she identified the sound, it lifted her off her feet. The wave of water knocked her over, and she was carried down the sluice, powerless to prevent her watery abduction. The walls scraped as she tried to gather her trailing branches.

Finally the nightmare was over. Dizzy and shaken, she lay, like an unwanted leaf, stranded by the waning water course. She stood and assessed herself. She was bruised, and her head had repeatedly thumped the sides of the hard passage, but her branches felt intact. Knowing the water overflow might return, she left the perilous path. She scrambled through one of the wall holes and found herself in a new meandering web of passages. Pausing, she turned left.

*

Reuben and Gus were making good progress. They had continued along the main route and not taken Little Green's treacherous path. Reuben calculated that Felicity and Little Green started about five hours ahead, but he would catch up. He must catch up. He tried repeatedly to reach Felicity's thoughts. Once he had felt a whisper of sensation, as if she spoke to him in a dream, but nothing since. He would not worry Gus, but he was beginning to sense something amiss. The fact that Little Green was also silent was of grave concern.

'He was here,' said Gus into the silence. In the dim light, Gus had found smears of Toxic acid on the floor. They both looked at each other. Felicity and Little Green were far ahead, and sandwiched in the middle was Arrass.

'Can you tell how long it is since he passed?' Reuben asked. He was panting; they were marching hard.

Gus swerved, avoiding a jut of rock, and replied, 'The

patches were dry, but there was a trace of scent.'

They came to a fork in the cave's path. 'That one has better light,' said Gus, pointing to the left. But the path seemed to wander and not descend.

'Little Green told me the Old Root is laid in an inner chamber. It makes sense it will be deep. We must descend. We will go this way,' said Reuben. In the near darkness, images swamped his mind. Felicity laughing by the river. Scratt striding from the pass. Georges bellowing on the plunce. Demet's black mouth on the beach.

'Faster!' he urged Gus, his voice cracking with the dryness of his throat. His shoulder ached. *Where are they?*

*

Felicity had woken. She heard a noise high above. The tiny spot of daylight had turned navy blue. It must be dark outside, she thought. Panic rose, and she quelled it. Standing as quietly as possible, she crept to the side of the cave, into the protective shadows. There was the noise again. Her stomach filled with acid, and her heart lurched an extra beat. She knew that sound. It was a Toxic. Arrass! Tears of terror coursed down her dehydrated cheeks. The salt stung, and as her tongue licked away the liquid from her upper lip, she knew she must act.

'Reuben,' she murmured softly. With desperation, she pushed her mind up, up, through the layers of sand and limestone until finally, in a blessed gift, she found him.

Felicity!

Reuben!

Where are you and Little Green?

He sensed her fear, and felt helpless.

I fell down the big waterfall. Little Green must be some-

where above me. The thoughts rapped between them like Morse code.

Where are you now?

At the bottom of the fall, by a large lake.

Are you hurt?

No, very thirsty and weak. Nothing broken.

Can you see anything?

Tiny spot of moonlight. Hear Arrass.

Arrass!

Scared.

No, I am coming.

Scared. Love you.

Love. Hope. Light. Hide. Hide. Hide. Love you, and then Reuben heard no more. The effort of pushing her thoughts through such heavy layers of Root and earth had been exhausting. He roared in pain and frustration.

'Reuben, what is it?' asked Gus.

'Felicity. She mind-shared at last. She is alone, far below, and Arrass has found her.'

Gus howled, and Reuben saw him, like the dark Toxics; his anger changed his mellow voice to a rasp of fury. 'He will not harm her,' Gus cried.

And in the bowels of the cave, Arrass heard him. The sick creature bubbled with joy at the infidel's distress. He looked down from his rocky ledge at the calm water below.

He saw the trail in the soft ground that the stranger had left as she lay by the lake, and his diseased mouth drooled as he planned his descent.

*

Little Green could smell water. She had been travelling for a long time. Perhaps even hours, she thought, frustrated. But she was close, now. Close to the floor of this subterranean world. She wanted to find the inner chamber, but these passages twisted and turned, opening back into large cavities. She must reunite with Felicity before they sought the heart of the Roots. She could see the Roots now. Whenever there was a chink of pale light, the gnarled intertwining layers of thousands of years' planting decorated the corners and walls like organic sculptures of glory. She could almost hear the knowledge calling out to her. Once she had Felicity she knew what she had to do. The Roots would lead her to her inner sanctum.

A movement overhead caught her attention. High above there was a vast hole of light. Although she had travelled continually down, the ground above had clearly had some sort of collapse, and the magnificent fresh air reached all the way down to where she stood. Pictured above she could see tiny swirlings against the fading stars. A small contingent broke away from the flock and swooped down. They kept coming until they reached her. In the glow of her phosphorescence, Little Green watched their performance. They danced and formed shapes. She suddenly realised they were trying to communicate. Their fat bodies nimbly illustrated their message. Once she had calmed her excitement, Little Green saw their plan. They were showing her the Old Root. They drew it with their dance, and then they continued. In a sequence of shapes, Little Green saw the map these tiny creatures were so desperate to give her. They hovered as they waited for her to understand the second visual image.

She spoke aloud. 'Close to a large pool are two paths,' she murmured.

221

They squeaked in delight and spat out the water they had been dribbling from their beaks. The dance went on.

'I take the wide path. Straight, left, left, right and up. Up?' she said, confused. She thought the Old Root was down.

The battats chattered and beat her arms gently with their soft wings. They flew up, in concord, to reiterate the direction.

'Okay, up,' she said, smiling. She waited for the next part, but then they shocked her. Their pretty faces became wicked, and they flew at her, with claws outstretched.

'Ow,' she gasped as one of them scratched her face. 'Why?'

Their answer was revealed with awful clarity as they formed a large letter in mid-air. The realisation chilled her.

'Arrass!' she said.

They squeaked and danced.

'Where?' she asked, but the battats had gone. They were soaring upwards to the pure air and the light. She watched them swirl and twist until they were minute specks against a pale blue sky. They were flying home, their mission complete.

32

Arrass

Arrass looked down. The light was poor, but he revelled in the darkness. He saw the stranger. He whined with infuriation. *Be gone!* This quest had become an irritation. He hissed. He had lost Athen, converted by the traitorous Toxic. The one they called Gus. A large globule of acid tipped out of his flaccid lips and fell to the ground. He watched it drop, landing on the floor below with a sizzle that echoed in the stony heights.

His breath rasped in his throat as he leant over to watch the creature below. What was she? What right did she have to try to help these vengeful malefactors who wanted to keep the Toxics in exclusion? He lashed out and stabbed his black spines into a soft piece of rock near his face. The deep, black holes satisfied him. He was so close to the Old Root. He could smell its earthy scent. Organic and fertile, it sickened him. He would rip the heart out of this cruel world.

At that moment the cry of the traitor, Gus, penetrated the dark recesses of his mind. He smiled and started to crawl down the steep side of the cave. Anything in his way would be squashed. If the betrayer held loyalty to that pale thing who now scuttled away to hide from him, destroying her would be even more satisfying.

*

Felicity crouched against the damp wall. The powdery stone crumbled as she brushed it with her shoulder. She could hear Arrass moving, but she daren't come out to see where he was. His voice had sounded very high up. *But how fast can he move?* Her breath was shallow, and it was making her faint. She was petrified of making a sound. She leant against the stone and tried to think clearly. Unexpectedly she heard a voice.

'Ow!' it said. It was Little Green.

Felicity's legs collapsed with relief. Little Green was here. But she was on the wrong side of the wall. Felicity looked along its length. Which was the best way to go? It was impossible to tell in this shadowy world. But she had to move. Horribly, she had to leave the comfort of her rocky shelter and find its end. She counted to ten. She counted to ten again. *I can't...I must.* She took a huge breath, counted to three, and ran. Her heart thumped and she felt sick.

'Little Green!' she shrieked. 'I am here. Little Green!' She heard Arrass babbling in his foul tongue and the sound of falling stone as he tried to reach her more quickly.

On the other side, Little Green heard her with utter disbelief. 'Felicity!' she called and flowed forwards in the light cave. At the end was a narrow path. She ran down it and crashed straight into Felicity.

'Ouch!' said Felicity as Little Green's body thumped her to the floor. She stood up, shaking, and Little Green enveloped her in her phosphorescent light.

'Little Green, Arrass is here,' Felicity said.

'Arrass. Yes, the battats told me,' said Little Green. She didn't seem concerned. She spoke calmly. 'We have to go past a lake and follow the wide path. This will lead us to the Old Root. Don't worry about Arrass, dear Felicity. It's the Root, not us that he wants.' She put her trailing arm on Felicity's shoulder. 'I am so glad you are not hurt. Now, let's find the lake, because time is pressing. Reuben must be on his way, and we need to meet up, don't we? To complete our task.'

Felicity looked at her. The sensible words sifted through her panic. It was so long since she had ridden on the Ancient. What had Phoebe said? She tried to remember her task. Something about staying with Reuben and Little Green.

Well, that hadn't gone so well, then. But she did remember that they all had something to do when they found the Old Root. She could hear Arrass through the wall.

'There is a lake, where I came from. I fell into it. But Arrass is in there – I'm not going back.'

'Felicity, we must return to your cave. The Root is beyond, then, and Arrass will reach it first,' she said, and then sweeping past Felicity, she strode into the cave.

Felicity rushed after her, mouth dry as she rounded the pitted wall.

Little Green and she stood on one side of the lake. On the other was the broad path. But as they began to circumnavigate the lake, Arrass' shrieks became enraged. Little Green said nothing. He babbled and foamed at the mouth. He had descended almost to the ground. Felicity avoided looking at him. It made her feel better if she pretended she couldn't see him. She hurried after Little Green. They reached the far side of the lake, but Arrass had switched direction on the rock as they ran. Seeing them escape, he threw himself off the last part of the cliff-face and fell, breaking one of his main branch arms with a sticky crack.

Little Green paused, with Felicity behind her and Arrass prostrate between them and the exit. Then with a huge scream he threw himself upright. Standing this close to him, the stench was suffocating. Felicity gagged. He was tall, but not as tall as Little Green. His spiteful expression focused on Felicity.

'Stranger,' he said, and she understood him. He grimaced with pain and at the use of the filthy Old language.

'Stranger, you have interfered. You will be punished.' Then he leapt, his broken arm trailing. Little Green tried to block him, but he pierced her side with his main spine and held her pinioned as he moved, with her, towards Felicity.

Felicity knew there was something she could do, but it was a dim memory. Terror numbed her mind. *No!* She would not die here. She would go home. She would love Reuben. In a flash, Phoebe's words returned. *The gift!* She flung herself into the water.

'Help us!' she cried, and all at once there was a swirling and a rustling, and she was surrounded by the whispering and keening of the Aquatics. They circled her, and she heard only the sound of their sibilant speech. Nestled in their protection, she felt their tendrils rising and falling around her. She could see Arrass but not hear him. He had withdrawn his spine from Little Green and was trying to cover his ears with his good arm. *He can't bear the sound*, she realised. Little Green held her side and slowly stood. She beckoned to Felicity, but Felicity wanted to stay here. It was so lovely. Their soft, murmuring sounds rose and fell as she rocked gently in the velvet water. She closed her eyes.

Felicity! shouted Little Green into her head. *Stop listening, and get out, now!*

With a sigh, Felicity swam to the side. Arrass was staggering about, wailing. As they ran to the exit, she saw the Aquatics subside and Arrass straighten up. His face was pure malevolence.

'Run, Felicity,' said Little Green.

33

The Old Root

Gus was angry. He was aware of Reuben's dark thoughts, and it was impeding them. They were close, though. The stony passages were beginning to be decorated with Roots, and the change in the air was distinguishable.

'Reuben, for goodness' sake, stop it,' he said, irritated.

'Pardon?' said Reuben.

'Your unhelpful thoughts are slowing us.'

'It is my fault,' muttered Reuben, like a self-destructive chant. 'It is my fault. Everyone is separated. It is my fault.'

'Reuben!' yelled Gus. 'No Orion could have done better. You have held us together through calamity and loss. We are almost there, and Felicity needs you. Little Green needs you. I need you, dear Reuben.'

'But I can't forgive myself, Gus. I have lost Little Green. I am not with Felicity as she faces that monster.'

Gus stood in front of him, spines forward. 'Forgive yourself?' he said angrily. 'There is nothing to forgive, Reuben. You have acted only in everyone's best interests at all times. If we are apart, then so it was meant to be.' The large black eyes stared straight into the almond-shaped hazel ones. After a moment, they both smiled.

'Sorry,' said Reuben.

But Gus didn't reply. He was looking up, where they had stopped, and he had spotted something. A gleam of gold.

'Look!' he said and pointed to the ceiling of the passage. They both peered through the fissure. There were colours up there. Glistening, radiant colours. They looked at each other.

'It must be the inner chamber,' said Gus.

'We were told it was deep in the bowels of the cave,' said Reuben, confused.

'Protection, I suppose,' answered Gus, but Reuben was running.

'At the very least the Stipples might tell us how to find the lake,' he shouted.

They climbed a steep, steep staircase. It wound up in a spiral, and Gus had trouble tucking in his long spines. They were climbing high.

'We must be heading right away from Felicity and Arrass,' said Reuben, worried. How far had she dropped to that lake? 'How many more steps can there be?!' he said, and as he surged upwards, the last few steps were revealed, and he fell into the inner chamber.

Gus fell in behind him. They lay on their backs in astonishment. They were in a small room, brightly lit. A large funnel let in the new day's early light, and its crisp, dewy air flooded into the tiny, ornate chamber. The walls, the ceiling, and the floor were elaborately decorated and sculpted with the most glorious colours of all hues. Reuben glanced back the way they had come; the staircase continued upwards and beyond. It must connect with the outside world, he thought.

'Magnificent, isn't it?' said a deep, rumbling voice. 'Yes, Reuben, we can access the world outside, on restdays. We are not a stuffy old bunch down here, as the Ancients like to have us portrayed.'

There was a murmur of, 'Hear, hear,' and Reuben looked around. But he had no time for this.

'Sir, we need your help. The corrupt Toxic, as we speak, is upon my quest members, and I must ask you, where is the lake. I must find the lake. Immediately!' He raised his voice in alarm. How could he be just lying here? What was the matter with him? He jumped up.

Gus sighed and heaved himself upright. He was aching from the damp in this subterranean world.

'Haste, haste,' rumbled the old Stipple, 'but there, you see, they approach.'

Reuben gasped in surprise as he heard their voices.

'Quick! He didn't take our decoy path; he is coming,' said Felicity.

'That wasn't a decoy. I was lost,' replied Little Green, and they ran into the room, panting.

The atmosphere in the room tightened with tension. Interwoven with the sculptured, painted walls and Roots were the elder Stipples. They lined up around the edge like ancient kings on their gnarled thrones. The largest Root of all was planted firmly in the centre, and the stipple who had spoken sat by it.

He was tiny, thought Felicity. As her eyes grew accustomed to the blazing light, she could see he was attached, like a knitting needle to its ball of wool, and like everything in this spectacular space, he was covered in a profusion of rich colours. 'Wow!' she said.

Little Green was absorbing all in silence. And as she looked, the old men steadily watched her. 'Yes, I am a Greenesse,' she said defiantly. They continued to stare rudely at her, and so she ignored them. When she had finished assimilating the details of her new home, she turned to Reuben.

'Forgive me, Little Green, for not bringing you here safely,' he said, head bowed.

Little Green touched his shoulder. 'You were never meant to, dear Reuben,' she replied, and as Reuben turned to hold Felicity, Arrass fell into the room.

34

Peace

His broken arm dangled from its grey sinews, leaking slime onto the shining floor. His breathing was harsh, and his black eyes dull as he finally found them. He had caught up with his prey. He had found the Root. He wheezed in excitement, unable to speak. Gus stepped forwards to block his path. Arrass sniggered and froth oozed from the openings on his face.

'You can't stop me, misguided weakling,' he spat, and to his horror, his speech was of the purest Old World. He lurched towards Gus, and as the two Toxics locked in silent combat, only the noise of the creaks and pops under Arrass' poisoned layers could be heard. Breaking free, he pierced Gus in a parting act of fury, and threw himself towards the Old Root.

'I will rip you out of this world,' he cried, as he fell upon the tiny Green.

The elder lifted his arm as if to protect himself, but the movement initiated a series of semi-circular hatches to open, high in the walls of this brilliant chamber. The streams of bright light distracted Arrass, and the elders stationed around the edges of the room all fell upon the Root. Arrass looked down and screamed with frustration and fury. His spines thrashed and slashed, but the Stipple elders linked together and formed an impenetrable case of sinewy, gnarled protection.

Felicity squeezed her eyes closed. She couldn't watch. Little Green had rushed to Gus, and Reuben was circling the scene. *How could he stop Arrass?* He felt the elders' pain, and his mind slowed with panic. He imagined Arrass carving out the Ancient Root and the heart of his beautiful Old World.

'Get off them, you diseased creature from the dark!' he roared in anger and Felicity opened her eyes just in time to see him leap high into the air. Drawing up all his Orion strength and agility, he had sprung up above the murderous Toxic. For a moment he seemed to hover in the air, but then he came crashing down upon the head of Arrass.

Felicity wasn't sure who was screaming, but powerless to prevent Reuben's suicidal act, she ran to Little Green and Gus.

'Stop him!' she shouted. But it was too late. Arrass had toppled sideways with the unexpected assault, and now Little Green and Gus hurried to help the damaged elders.

Reuben called to her as he pinioned Arrass to the floor by his two front spines. 'It's okay, Felicity. I can do this,' he said but his face twisted in pain as Arrass' spines probed his body once more. Reuben gritted his teeth. He could feel Arrass weakening.

The dark Toxic leader lay on the floor, and his spines began to sag. He would soon throw off this Orion thorn in his side, he thought – but the light. The blessed, pure light seared his tortured mind. He moaned in agony and finally lay still.

The Stipples were quick to react, in spite of their damage. They leapt upon the dying Toxic, and their sinewy, trailing arms formed a tight, impenetrable weave.

From the floor, Arrass sobbed and cackled, 'As if you could stop me.'

'Your poison has no effect here,' said the oldest of the Stipple Greens. And Felicity noticed their wounds were healing as they spoke. She spun round – it was hardly noticeable where Arrass had pierced Gus. Even Reuben, who had now left Arrass to the elders, seemed in less pain as each moment passed.

'It is the healing energy of the chamber, Felicity,' explained Little Green.

Then the tiny elder, upon whom Arrass had first fallen, spoke clearly into the room, 'Arrass, it is time for you to come hear the truth that you need.'

The kindness in the voice was worse than the chamber and the Root. Arrass gave a feeble cry, as it reached parts of him that he had suppressed for so long. His black limbs jerked as he lay on the floor, and the venom and acid sizzled as it seeped, but it dispersed, hardly affecting the stunning colours.

Unable to watch his pain, Little Green spoke out, and her musical voice filled the cavity and bounced off the walls, a chime of beautiful sound. 'I am Little Green, and I am the layer of the new Root,' she said. 'This is the end of the quest. The valiant quest led by Reubenfourthousandth.'

Reuben stepped forward as she introduced him, and took over. 'There were nine who formed the troupe. Nine who risked all to save the ways of the Old World from the misguided hatred of the new Toxics.'

Arrass screeched and spat, but he was very weak now. The elder Stipples released their hold on him, and moved gently back to their seats against the wall.

Now the room was calm and listening – Reuben continued, 'And in honour of Sibilinsixteenthousandth, who we lost, we, the three key members, and Gus the Toxic who the Old World has seen fit to keep by our side, are here today to restore it – to reopen the Old Root in order that the despair of the Toxics can be healed, the Old World correct its imbalance, and all species be heard once more.'

There was no response from the Stipples. It was as if Reuben had not spoken. He looked at Little Green, confused. Felicity came close to him. The Stipples' multi-coloured, painted faces formed a theatrical tableau as the eldest finally replied.

'The Old Root cannot be reopened. We understand the

sincerity of your quest. We have followed it with interest. We thank you for defending our Roots from the Toxic army. We thank you for your great courage. We honour the lost Sibilin. But we disagree with the Ancients, the Aquatics, and the Strata. The Old Root is sealed, its knowledge passed on to each generation of Stipples who can be consulted. It is sealed to prevent corruption.'

'Its knowledge has been corrupted precisely because of its secrecy,' said Little Green, her voice raised. 'We need to realign the harmonies. The Toxics have been excluded from the full beauty of life, and this cannot have been the intention of the Old World. I was born the first Stipple Greenesse since the beginnings of the Stipples. I am descended from the original Stipples of the Western Isle, and you will not prevent me from fulfilling my destiny and the destiny of the Old World,' she cried, and her aura flew out like a flash of lightning. It bounced and reflected from all the shining surfaces and blinded the old Stipples.

'I am to lay my Root. I am to live my life here. I will entwine new Root to old, and the history of the Toxics will be bound and repaired. The truth must be let out, and then the healing begins.' She looked with pity at Arrass squirming softly on the floor. It was too late to help him. But she wanted him to hear the truth. She could give him peace before he left them.

There was silence, and Felicity knew they were all mind-sharing. Finally they bowed their heads in acknowledgment of Little Green's impassioned speech.

'We hear your truth,' they said.

The tiny elder disconnected himself from the Old Root. 'Let it be done,' he said.

Now that she had permission, Little Green hesitated. Theia had told her she would know what to do. Felicity thought of her own instructions. Reuben sighed, hoping his best had been enough. They all waited.

Gus went up to Little Green and whispered, 'Have confidence, Little Green. Believe in yourself, and the way will be clear.'

So Little Green stood in the centre of the room and gently reached out her delicate arm to feel the Root. Nothing happened. She looked at Reuben. He came beside her and held her arm and reached out his own hand. They closed their eyes and searched for the energy deep within. Reuben felt a pulse of current pass between them. Little Green staggered. Then, like an onion shedding its peel, the outer layers of the Root slid smoothly back. Felicity and Gus smiled. But as easily as it had begun, it stopped. Reuben and Little Green waited for it to continue, but the Root was still.

'Perhaps it is my turn?' asked Felicity.

Reuben put out his hand to include her. She took it, but no more layers slid open. Felicity was thinking. She remembered Phoebe's words, 'You will know what to do,' and she did. She slipped her free hand into her jeans pocket. It touched the small, hard kernel that she had slipped into her pocket on the staircase, so long ago. She carefully pulled it out. It had come with her from the very beginning. Her secret talisman from home. She kissed it once and placed it tenderly into the almost invisible grint that was hidden in the second layer of the Root. It dropped in perfectly and filled the tiny cleft. The middle layer now rotated and peeled away as evenly as the first. The inner layer was intricately inscribed with red ochre. Little Green frowned. She and Reuben and Felicity peered at the writing, but it was meaningless to them.

'What does it say?' Little Green asked the tiny elder.

He slid across the glowing floor and peered inside. 'I am not able to read this language,' he said, and his face crumpled with embarrassment.

The other elders all shuffled over one by one. Each was confident his knowledge traces would hold the clue. But each failed. Reuben felt despair. All they had achieved, he thought, to end like this. He looked down at Arrass. The sick Toxic had stopped moving. Gus followed Reuben's eyes and squatted down next to Arrass.

'Be careful, Gus,' said Felicity. She didn't trust Arrass, even now. The terrible plant flicked his eyes open and stared straight at her. She shuddered.

'Gus,' said Reuben, 'it must be you.'

'I was not even meant to be here, Reuben,' said Gus. But he straightened up, and turning his back on Arrass, came to see. He went very still.

'What is it?' said Reuben. 'Are you okay?'

Gus took a shaky breath, and as he turned to the listening room, they saw his eyes brimming with tears.

'It's in Old Toxic,' he said, and his voice trembled. He turned to Arrass. 'Arrass! Can you hear me?'

The broken Toxic opened an eye.

'The Root speaks to us in Toxic, Arrass. The Old Toxic of our ancestors,' he said.

Arrass closed his eye.

'Read it to us, Gus,' said Reuben.

'I can do better than that,' said Gus, empowered with the knowledge that the Old World so loved his kind that it had inscribed their history into its most intimate heart with the beautiful language the early Toxics had invented for themselves.

'I will show you,' he said, and to their awe, he used his mind-sharing to project the images of the Toxics' true history.

Felicity was mesmerised with the silent movie that appeared in the centre of this glorious room.

With the last of his energy, Arrass raised his head and watched the story unfold. He saw the male Orion and female Fragrant fall in love, and he saw their shame as the first Toxic was born. He grimaced as the knife of bitterness turned inside him. But there was more. His cloudy eyes watched, expressionless. They came to realise the shame was for defying an old law. Not for their child. Arrass saw them reunited and searching. All their life they had searched for their strange, wonderful child, but to no avail. And as its own life was close to ending, the first Toxic, their child, had finally had found their resting place and on it an inscription, a message for their beloved child.

'Created in love, forever.

Lost but never forgotten.

A new life from love, to be loved by all.'

There was a sickly gurgle, and Arrass' last breath expired.

'How different it could have been–' said Gus. He allowed the scene to fade from the room. '–if those three had reunited. I believe he was meant to find that stone. But his bitterness prevented him from revealing the truth.'

'And with his passing, it was lost, as all his descendants carried forth the corrupted story,' said Reuben.

'Except someone. There are always those who seek the truth,' said Felicity.

'And they ensured it was recorded here, in Old Toxic; for one day there would be a descendant worthy to hear it and repair the wrongs of the world,' said Little Green. She smiled at Gus. He went and put his hand on the still form of Arrass.

'He heard the truth, Gus,' said Little Green. 'The Toxics were meant to be accepted. Loved. A new species that would live with no enharmonic, like the Strata. I will lay new growth. The truth and the tragedy will be entwined forever.'

Gus bowed his head, and all in the chamber followed, in accord.

*

The elders arranged for Arrass to be gently removed from the chamber. He would receive a proper burial, but within the sacred caves, so his dark energy could be dispersed over time.

They were preparing to leave. Little Green wanted to settle down in her new home. She must begin at once. It wasn't such a prison, after all, she thought, looking with pleasure at the elaborate, sunny cave. The elders explained she would have restdays. She could take a partner and live a fulfilled life at these times.

'Good-bye, Little Green,' said Felicity.

Little Green smiled, and her phosphorescence flashed around the wall of the cave.

'You really have to stop doing that, young one,' said one of the elders as he wiped his watering eyes.

Little Green laughed.

'What she needs is a steadying influence,' said another. 'My grandson might be just the thing.'

'Your grandson couldn't steady a battat,' said another. 'I think my great-grandson on my cousin's side is more her match.'

'Don't be ridiculous; he has no talent,' said another.

Reuben, Felicity, Gus and Little Green edged away quietly. They stood at the bottom of Little Green's staircase to the world. Felicity hated to leave her here.

'I am content, Felicity,' she said, stroking Felicity's arm.

Felicity realised she would not see her again.

'You will see me. I shall come above and choose myself a partner very soon,' she said, laughing, as the debate inside continued. But they both knew Felicity would not be there.

'Good-bye, Little Green,' said Reuben.

Gus gave her a huge hug, too, and the three ascended the staircase, towards the new day.

35

Friends

Georges was sulking. Lupi, Felice, Wolfie and Sibbar had been left in his care. Pippi and Wolfgang had gone for a short walk to rebuild Pippi's strength. They had been gone for five hours. Georges had never thought to see the day, when he, once chief guardian of the sacred caves for forty-five consecutive years, should find his duty keeping four rude little cubs out of the river, the cave, and the forest.

'They are determined to destroy themselves,' he bellowed to Tatania, who was behaving very strangely today, he noticed.

'They are delightful, Georges my big man,' she said, 'and you are so good with them. A natural father.' She laughed loudly.

'Tatania, you show me no respect,' said Georges, tossing his head up and trotting away from the rumbustious furry mob. They skittered after him, their stumpy legs already gaining the power to leap to his kneecaps and nip.

'Ow!' he roared. 'Vicious ill-bred sprites!' He cantered into the stream to wash the minute wounds. He wondered if Tatania was a little insane. He had decided he might keep her for a bit longer, but not if she was unstable. In his lifetime he had met a lot of Taurelles. They were strong creatures and needed to show self-control. Watching Tatania still shaking with merriment at some inner secret, he was disappointed. He looked at her fine, sturdy figure. Such curves, he thought, admiring her large rump.

His temper cooled, and he trotted out of the river's tributary. They were high on the hill overlooking the bowl. Close to the path by which the quest troupe had entered a week ago. He smiled, and a warm glow entered his old heart as he thought of the moment Reuben, Felicity and Gus walked out of the cave. Well, actually they had arrived from the back of the cave hills. That irritating guardian on entrance duty had been horrified that there was, in fact, another secret passage to the caves.

Felicity and Reuben would not tell anyone where they had exited. It was Little Green's secret, they said. Georges looked down at the bowl as his thoughts wandered. He licked Tatania's back methodically and watched Gus organising the Toxics. The old Taureau's expression held an alertness that belied his age. He was not keen to abandon Gus to this task. He knew he had the full support of the guardians to help him, but Georges felt his superior strength, wisdom and intelligence were necessary.

'Georges,' said Tatania. She swung her head around, and her large, brown eyes were shining with happiness.

'Yes, my little fairy,' he said, still watching Gus trying to encourage the Toxics to speak a few words in the Old World language, and Demet spitting in the corner.

'We will have our first calf in three months' time,' said Tatania, without preamble.

'What!' bellowed Georges, and the cubs scattered in all directions, terrified at the huge sound.

*

Gus looked up from his task and wiped his face, smiling. He felt needed. Hopeful. At peace. He watched Georges begin one of his stampede tantrums on the top of the hill, and laughed. To his surprise, he heard a tiny sound escape Demet's lips. Gus stared at Demet, fascinated. Demet's mouth was lifted in one corner as he watched the massive Taureau charge backwards and forwards like an out of control comet. But the black drool still leaked from Demet's lips. Gus was not sure how he could heal the toxins this angry, bitter generation had produced. But he had hope.

The answer would lie somewhere in this beautiful world. It always did.

*

Reuben and Felicity lay on their backs, watching the beautiful patterns in the sky. It had been a week since they had left Little Green in her tinctured inner chamber. A time of reconciliation and rest. Gus alone was working from dawn to sunset. *A Toxic on a mission*, thought Felicity sleepily.

She rolled her head to the side and looked at Reuben's profile. The bump on his nose enticed her. She loved to run her finger along it. The skin was slightly stretched and smooth, and it satisfied her to feel its hardness, followed by the contours of his lips and stubbly chin.

Reuben rolled his head over to stare deeply into her green-blue eyes. The lumpy ground made a map across the back of his head. All his sensations felt heightened: The grass prickling his legs, the warm sun shining on his eyelids, the familiar, floral smell of Felicity as she lay beside him, and the gentle sound of her breath flowing softly between her pink lips.

'Scratt doesn't tire of retelling his story, does he?' said Felicity, watching the young Thorn surrounded by listeners.

Reuben watched her eyes crinkle at the corners as she smiled. 'No, he deserves a little glory. He was a brave young Thorn and has earnt his place in the story.'

'Will he go home now?' she asked.

'Well,' said Reuben, jumping up and brushing the grass off his legs, 'it's probably time to gather everyone together and find out.' He held out his hand, and as she took it, he pulled her up, hard, into his chest.

'Ow!' she said, but no more – Reuben's kiss silenced her.

They descended to the lower slopes, where Wolfgang, Pippi, Georges and Tatania were grouped. Lupi, Felice, Sibbar and Wolfie leapt on their mother and demanded food. Pippi was weak but, thanks to Georges and Nathaniel, had been healed by the Fragrant lady of the forest.

None of them would speak of her, only
a miracle she still existed. It was th
departed from this world. Georges .
times in his battle-driven youth, and ı.
still to be alive. The healer insisted Pippi ı.
before attempting to travel home to the Lupa.
of the Eastern Wastes.

'So will you take Scratt back with you?' Reuben .
Wolfgang.

'Yes, why not,' replied Wolfgang. 'He can help us with
the cubs until we leave him in the Temperate North.'

'What can I do?' said Scratt, panting from his jog up
the hill. He was going to mature tomorrow, he knew it, and
he must be physically fit. A young Thornesse had given him
her address in the Temperate North. He was going to go
straight there once he was home. He rubbed his chest. It had
felt uncomfortable since yesterday. Wolfgang saw the action,
and an old memory stirred at the back of his mind.

'What is it, my love?' asked Pippi.

Her tired, yet still beautiful face was more than he
deserved, he thought. His heart filled with joy at his glorious
family. Even Wolfie gnawing his heel couldn't anger him
today.

'Just something an old Lupata told me once,' he said to
Pippi. 'I don't think it can be possible, but–' He didn't finish
his sentence because Scratt suddenly started leaping about.
The troupe sprang into action.

'What is it?' asked Reuben, concerned.

'Scratt, can we do anything?' said Felicity, standing by
Reuben's side.

'Stand back!' roared Georges, and Wolfgang's head
swung round to look at him. For two seconds their eyes
met, and then Wolfgang howled, 'Beware the weapon of the
ancient Thorns! Behold the fable that returns to Old World
today!' His wolf-voice echoed around the bowl, and everyone flung themselves to the ground.

241

An almighty thorn, as large and thick as Scratt's head, is ejected from the centre of his chest. It flew directly cross the land and down towards the Sacred Cave entrance. Gus, the Toxics, and all the guardians watched in disbelief as this fat, lethal arrow soared over their heads and embedded itself in the top of the central stone arch. There was silence as the blow shook the ground. Then a tiny crack appeared, then another, and all at once the stony entrance crumbled and collapsed. Some of the boulders fell into the waterfall, but the large part piled up and blocked the entrance. The officious guardian stood, like a statue, as his gate crumbled about him. His tiny eyes were filled with dust and on his ridged back a layer of rubble wobbled precariously.

A cheer, led by Nathaniel, rose from the bowl, and all on the hill joined in. Then everyone started clapping, and the sound became a chant.

'Scratt! Scratt! Scratt! Scratt!' they cried.

Scratt walked slowly down the hill, stunned by what had just happened. Head high, he paraded the bowl, with hand up, acknowledging their applause.

'Oh, for goodness' sake,' said Wolfgang, growling, 'he will be unbearable on the journey after this,' but Felicity could see he was smiling.

'What was it?' she asked him.

He looked at Georges, who replied, 'That was an ancient Thorn weapon that has not been seen even in my lifetime. But I have heard tell of it. This is a day of surprises.'

'And you have a surprise, Georges,' said Tatania.

Georges looked innocent. 'Have I?'

'Yes.'

'What is it?' he asked.

'You insufferable, stubborn old–' She began to jump and kick, but Georges laughed, and she subsided.

'My friends, Tatania and I will be continuing my fine line of breeding and heritage–'

Tatania interrupted him. 'We are going to have a calf by

the end of summer,' she said, her voice rich with excitement and pleasure.

'Then let's have a mating ceremony,' said Reuben, delighted. 'Let's celebrate their official union,' he explained to Felicity.

'I thought they were already joined?' she said.

'Not quite,' said Georges meekly.

It was decided to hold it the next day. Tatania wanted to return to the Western Isle and the land of the Taureau very soon, and Georges agreed. He would stop his adventures. He would return and retire in peace. Seeing Nathaniel had helped him. What a fine boy, he thought with pride. Perhaps it was time to focus on breeding.

'Well, I want lots more children,' said Tatania.

'And you shall have them, my little lady,' said Georges, eyes twinkling.

'His spirit will never fade, will it?' Felicity asked Reuben as they lay together that night.

'I hope not,' he replied.

*

The ceremony was beautiful. Gus left the Toxics to the guardians and took a deserved day off. There would be feasting and dancing, and the troupe were together again. *Except Little Green*, thought Felicity. Pippi and Felicity collected white flowers to decorate Tatania's jet-black mane, and a blessing floated gently to Georges as he bathed his massive head in the fast-flowing river. *Joy. Love. Peace.* He knew it was from Little Green. He bowed his head. *Thank you, my friend*, he replied. They climbed to the summit of the slope – to the place where Felicity had had her first view of the sacred caves and the bowl. The two Herculean creatures faced each other and then ceremoniously stepped up on top of the thick, white stone. Everyone cheered and congratulated them.

'But nothing has happened,' said Felicity to Reuben.

'They united on the sacred stone,' he said, smiling

wickedly. 'That's all it takes. If two wish to partner for life, then they find one of the sacred stones and mount it together, with pure love and commitment in their hearts. The Great Spirit is strong in these places; it will hear and bless their union. It is done.'

Felicity tipped her head to one side. Something was troubling her. But everyone wanted to begin the feast, so she pushed her concern aside.

The quest troupe sat till the stars came out, and ate everything the Colour Changers could provide. There were earth balls, river water, sand shoots and forest peas. Nectar, stods and arctic rolls, chilli juice and gaudin cheese. Fizzruffs, maceypips, chiclas, orsi, water green. Strape, plunts, river reeds, Western water and small forest peas. Chicanes, trillins, liffles and, to Felicity's great satisfaction, the largest sticky buds Reuben had ever seen. And there was music, rhythmic chants and melodies from the seven Strata, who circled and wheeled above. The Strata had flown in Mr and Mrs O as a wonderful gift to Reuben, a thank you from the Old World for his courage.

Mrs O had a message from Orchadea. 'She wishes you both a long and happy life,' she said, hugging her son tightly and then Felicity too. *She smells of spices, like Reuben,* thought Felicity. Tomorrow, the Strata would return Mr and Mrs O back to Orionwood. Mrs O would not leave Reuben's younger siblings for more than a night.

'Take care, my precious son,' she said to her eldest child.

Mr O came up behind her and put his arm around his wife. 'Reuben,' he said, 'you have been a challenge to raise, but I would not have had it any other way. You have grown into a magnificent Orion. Go safely on to the next chapter of your life, my son.'

Reuben swallowed with difficulty as he hugged his father and then his mother for the last time.

'You'll see them in the morning,' said Felicity, with a yawn. She said goodnight to Scratt, then Wolfgang, then

Georges, who she gave a tight hug, in spite of his smell, and finally she went to Pippi.

'Good night, Pippi. Thank you for everything,' she said. 'I think Reuben said he had a plan for us, first thing. Have a good rest tomorrow, won't you? Don't let Lupi boss you around. She already tries, doesn't she?'

'Yes, but that's good, good to be strong,' said Pippi, licking Felicity with her rough tongue.

Felicity went and lay next to Reuben and the campfire. *Just like old times,* she thought sleepily, as she snuggled up against him.

'Where are we going tomorrow?' she asked.

'You'll see,' said Reuben.

36

The Final Chapter

It was time to leave. Reuben and Felicity crept out of the camp, leaving the revellers their dreams. They walked down to the bowl, across the grassy circle webbed with dew, and past the corral containing Demet. Felicity kept her eyes down as they came level with the Toxics' tall enclosures. Then Reuben led her to a green path that meandered up over the cave hilltops and safely through the hills. They came upon a valley. The valley led to the sea. Felicity could see it glistening as the sun lifted its head and looked down. As if leaving a trance, Felicity abruptly stopped walking. Where on earth was he taking her?

'Can we go back, Reuben?' she asked. She was tired and wanted to return to the others. She missed them already.

'Not yet, my Felicity,' he said and, taking her hand, started to run, laughing, towards the sparkling sea.

'Reuben!' she said as he pulled her behind him. She felt her body stretching out. She gave up resisting and ran fast alongside him. It felt good after their lazy week.

They reached the shoreline in mid-afternoon. They shared some Orion river water from Reuben's flask and dug up a few sand shoots. Felicity was still full from last night's feast.

They lay together on the beach, and Reuben said, 'You understand we are joined now, don't you, Felicity?'

Felicity smiled and looked sideways at him. 'Yes,' she said. 'On the sacred white stone. The first day we arrived at the Taureau contests, right?'

'Yes. Sorry. I couldn't resist it. We were always going to be together.'

'I know. I love you, my darling Reuben,' she said. And as the sun moved overhead, they lay and loved, with the frothy surf tumbling about them and the white seabirds crying in the big sky.

*

The sun was setting. Reuben helped Felicity stand, and they walked quietly to the waterline. They waded out, enjoying its cool velvet softness after their hot, sandy day. They stopped at a natural sea shelf. Behind them the turquoise water glinted pale blue. In front the ocean was navy, inky dark. Felicity shivered. They mind-shared, not wanting to spoil the pure tranquillity. Felicity spoke for the first time of her father, of his absence, and her sadness. Reuben reminded her that change is natural. Not to be feared. She thought quietly of the Toxics. Anything is possible, she realised. Perhaps when she went home, she would try remaining open, like Gus. Who knew what the future might bring. She inhaled a long, deep breath of the balmy, sea breeze.

'The air smells so good, Reuben,' she said, her voice muted in the vast space.

Reuben drank in the wind of the sea and of the world, his world. Then his voice, the voice she had loved since that first day in the mists, said, *It's time, Felicity.* He was holding out his hand, just like that day. She looked down at it, then neatly tucked hers inside. It felt good. They had both grown, both matured, but his hand was still square and large and warm.

All at once, he jumped, taking her with him. They sank lower and lower into the hazy depths of the water. Felicity tried to look at Reuben, but he held her too close. She felt her lungs struggling to breathe, and fear made her start fighting. His arms were a vice, but his words entered her mind. Felicity! He was shouting in her head. *Felicity, stop fighting me. Trust all you have learnt. Relax. Feel the blue water on your skin, on your hair, in your eyes. Listen to the calls of the deep. We are safe.*

Felicity still held her breath, but it hurt, so she carefully let it go. Then Felicity heard another voice. It spoke in the water and was all around them. *Reuben*, it said, *Felicity Isabel*, the familiar voice continued, *love and joy to you both. A world is healed; another awaits.* Felicity knew that voice from her past life. It was the voice of the staircase. A rumble of amused laughter then the voice continued, *Not a staircase, and yet...*but they heard no more.

Reuben let go of Felicity. She looked across at him as they fishtailed through the water. She seemed to be breathing, but didn't dare think about it too much. They were in a cool blue world together, moving alongside all the underwater treasures of the deep. Slivers of silvery fish approached the intruders and poked their fat-lipped faces right up to Felicity whilst larger shapes lurked at a distance. The dolphin-like Dauphs kept constant vigil, producing a stream of fat bubbles that tickled Felicity's nose. They swam for hours, marvelling at the underwater corals of orange, purple, green, yellow and red. It was like a glorious garden, and tiny creatures swarmed in and out of the coral like midges on a summer's evening.

How are we breathing? said Felicity at last into Reuben's mind.

The Dauphs give us air. Don't you see it between us? Reuben's eyes were large with excitement. His trust was implicit, she realised.

She looked up at the paler water. Up there, somewhere, the day's sun shone on their dear friends. Reuben pointed at a large shoal of gleaming fish; they swept past, a blaze of incandescence that swallowed them up. Felicity felt them slip over her legs and thought of the world above, of the plants and the beasts. She smiled as she pictured Georges, Gus, Little Green and Scratt. She thought of Sib, brave Sib, and Wolfgang, and lovely Pippi. A last silent thank you to Orchadea. The mountains and the rivers...liffles and sticky buds...the images flashed fast now. *Oh, how I love this world!* she thought, and at that very moment, the Dauphs came beneath and lifted her up. Up to the expanding circle of light above. She burst out of the water and gasped for air.

'Felicity?' said a voice she definitely knew. It was Al. Felicity wiped the water out of her eyes and her nose. She looked up. Al was standing by the side of the ocean. Only it was a chipped concrete edge. Felicity felt panic.

*Felicity, listen to me. Remember all you have learnt... my darling...trust...*Reuben's voice faded from her head.

'Felicity!' cried her mother, who came running up beside Al.

'Where am I?' Felicity asked, still coughing a little.

'In my old school swimming pool, darling,' said her mother, laughing.

Felicity spun about in the water. She had surfaced in a chipped, filthy square of water full of slimy weeds. She stuffed her head under the surface. Where were the Dauphs? Where was the Old World now? Horror gripped her. Where was Reuben? Violent spasms coursed through her body. She clenched her jaw as she fought them back. 'Reuben' she shouted.

'Who, darling?' said her mother, but Felicity was underneath the water again.

She swam down into the murky depths, but it was impossible to hold her breath she was so upset. She surfaced, gasped, and then dove down again. It was no good. She could see nothing. Her lungs were burning with the effort. Her throat squeezed with the strain and the pain. She burst out of the water for the last time. The bits of algae clung to her face, and she wiped them off angrily. 'Together, forever, my little Felicity Isabel Penfold,' he had said. She looked up at her mother and Al. The tears cascaded down her sunburnt cheeks, and she choked with her grief.

'Darling! My baby! What on earth is the matter? Come here, my love. What are you doing? Why did you go off swimming in this horrid pool – it's filthy,' said her mother, looking at the spongy mat of algae surrounding Felicity.

'Jesus, Flissy, it wasn't that bad over there. I actually met the mother of Harry P! She showed me a picture of him when he was a baby. She has promised to give me his email so I can tell him he must stop touring and marry me, now.'

Felicity looked at her funny friend as her mother came to help drag her out of the water. She covered her mother's pink shirt in green stains, but Mum was squeezing her so tightly. And now they were both crying. Felicity looked down at her hands. They were all smooth again. Smooth like the skin of a fourteen-year-old. She looked up to the cloud-scudded sky.

'Reuben! Reuben! Reuben!' she screamed, and a large shape high above wheeled away as if to take her message.

'Who is Reuben?' said Al and her mother at the same time.

Symbols of Old World life

STRATA

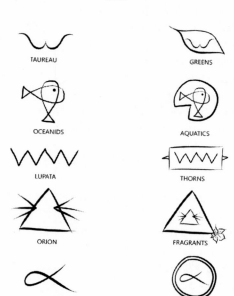

TAUREAU

GREENS

OCEANIDS

AQUATICS

LUPATA

THORNS

ORION

FRAGRANTS

SIBILIN

COLOUR CHANGERS

TOXICS

Characters

Felicity – Fourteen years old
Reuben – Reubenfourthousandth
Pippi – Lupatafourthousandthandforty-four
Wolfgang – Lupatafourthousandth
Georges – Taureautwothousandthfivehundredand
   twenty-fourth
Sib – Sibilinsixteenthousandth
Gus – Toxictoxicth
Scratt – Thornsixthousandthsixty
Little Green – Greenseventhousandthseventy
Jez – Reuben's childhood friend and rival

The Ancients

Hyperiononethousandth (m) – name represents Light
   – chosen for Gus
Theiaonethousandth (f) – name represents Sight
   – chosen for Little Green
Coeusonethousandth (m) – name represents Intellect
   – chosen for Reuben
Phoebeonethousandth (f) –name represents Prophecy
   – chosen for Felicity
Oceanusonethousandth (m) – name represents Rivers
   – chosen for Georges
Tethysonethousandth (f) –name represents Oceans
   – chosen for Wolfgang
Themisonethousandth (m) – name represents Law and
   Order – chosen for Pippi
Mnemosyneonethousandth (f) – name represents Remem-
   brance – chosen for Scratt

Toxics

Arrass
Demet
Athen
Athen II - renegade Sibilin leader named after toxic Athen
    was converted by Gus!

Glossary

Bark balm – From the South West, highly healing – suitable for all species.

Banyan – A formal ceremony staged by the Greens, and other elders. It is held to discuss and resolve problems within the community.

Battats – Small flying creatures that live in Sacred Caves. Aubergine coloured from the minerals in the caves that they drink. Not blind – they have roofholes for light and vision – but they do see better at night.

Dauph – Sea creatures similar to dolphin.

Flubbum – Ointment that provides a barrier against the cold.

Grint – A small crevice.

Hundredd – An area of land, quite large – perhaps a few fields large.

Leet – Long Viking-style narrowboat for sea crossing.

Mid-night – always hyphenated.

Orion balm – Made from flowers of forest canopies in the Fragrants' homelands. Works within minutes on Orion.

Plunce – Large airborne sled.

Roofholes – holes in the cave ceilings that let in light.

Sea-hole – Very bad place in sea! Sucks you in, of course.

Skyarc – Rainbow.

Skytrail – Departure trail of a spirit seen in the sky – similar to a cirrus cloud.

Teepee – Orion homes.

Terroire – A region of land.

Foods

Arctic rolls – Look like swiss roll – sweet, creamy filling. High energy.

Chicanes – Criss-crossed whitish rubbery shoots that wobble.

Chiclas – Giant cockroaches that actually taste like lobster when cooked.

Earth balls – Crunchy and juicy like pomegranate but more filling – found in the plains.

Fizzruffs – Multi-coloured balls, divided in two halves like tiny meringues with pale cream filling. Very fizzy. Found in the Western Isle.

Forest peas – Scaly, grey outer leaves – size of chick peas and taste like spicy, roasted chick peas –good for circulation. Found in forest.

Gaudin cheese – made by Orion women from the tiny gaudin – these are little goats that run free in the prairies. Body-building proteins to repair injuries.

Liffles – Vast curly leaves of all colours – crunchy like giant poppodums when dried on rocks in the sun. Full of energy and flavour.

Macypips – Like popcorn – very nutritious but easy to digest. Good for sparring. Found mainly in Sacred Caves territory.

Orsi – sea food – spiky outside but crack open like a coconut to give bright orange fleshy inside – taste like sweet potato but more filling.

Plunts – Thick, green leaves that taste of jacket potato.

River reeds – Like massive chives.

Sand shoots – Taste like licquorice – dug up on beaches and in dunes.

Sticky buds – Bumpy sticks like a twiglet. Caramelised nut taste. Speciality of the Lupata matings.

Stod balls – Aqua variety of stods – taste more fishy. Found by edge of water.

Stods – plain-tasting and earthy. Like a dumpling. Very filling. Found mainly in Temperate North.

Strape – Ribbon-like plant. Slightly chewy consistency. Tastes like salty, dried meat. Found in tropical forest.

Trillins – Shaped like bananas – grey and stringy – Also high energy but not over-dense.

Drinks

Green liquid – Highly refreshing and rehydrating. Found in forests.

Nectar – Amber liquid Felicity first tastes in Gus' leaf flask. Sweet yet spicy like sweet chilli – highly reviving in times of stress and trauma.

Orion river water – Turquoise coloured and aniseed flavoured. Cleansing internally and externally. Antiseptic properties.

Red liquid – Tastes fruity and sweet like Ribena – full of vitamins that protect against chill.

Western water – Pale, lemon-coloured liquid. Simply refreshing. Like a good mineral water.

If you enjoyed this book, please visit Isabel Burt's website
www.isabelburt.com